a few good murders

Forge Books by Cady Kalian

As Dead as It Gets
A Few Good Murders

A FEW GOOD MURDERS

cady kalian

A Tom Doherty Associates Book FORGE® New York

This is a work of fiction. All of the characters, organizations, and events portrayed in this novel are either products of the author's imagination or are used fictitiously.

A FEW GOOD MURDERS

Copyright © 2007 by Irma Kalish and Naomi Gurian

A Forge Book
Published by Tom Doherty Associates, LLC
175 Fifth Avenue
New York, NY 10010

www.tor-forge.com

Forge® is a registered trademark of Tom Doherty Associates, LLC.

Library of Congress Cataloging-in-Publication Data

Kalian, Cady.
    A few good murders / Cady Kalian.—1st ed.
        p.   cm.
    "A Tom Doherty Associates book."
    ISBN-13: 978-0-7653-1365-2
    ISBN-10: 0-7653-1365-0
    1. Women screenwriters—Fiction. 2. Actresses—Crimes against—Fiction. 3. Motion picture industry—Fiction.   4.   Los Angeles (Calif.)—Fiction.   I.   Title.
    PS3611.A4336F49   2007
    813'.6—dc22

                                                                        2007009594

First Edition: August 2007

Printed in the United States of America

0 9 8 7 6 5 4 3 2 1

Dedicated to
BURT AND ROCKY
for being there always
and to
LUCY,
who loved every line

acknowledgments

Thanks to
Claire Eddy
Ellen Geiger
Julie Sediq
Kristin Sevick
Deputy Shawn Brownell

And special gratitude to
Nancy Biederman
Mitch Horwits
Austin Kalish
Vicki Horwits-Stern
Dan Horwits
Bruce Kalish

a few good murders

1

Carpe diem.

Seize the Day.

Whoever first said that back in ancient Rome would certainly never have *carped* this *diem*. If one could have gotten out of bed in the morning and known what this particular Monday held in store, and the murders it would later lead to, one would never have—

Okay, enough with the impersonal "one." It's the personal me I'm talking about. Me. Maggie Mars. Transplanted New Yorker. Former investigative reporter. And current screenwriter for however long it lasts.

I would have stayed in bed, cowering under the covers, and never would have washed my face, brushed my hair, put on my lip gloss, and driven to the Malibu set where they were shooting my movie.

My movie. *Murder Becomes Her*. Written by Maggie Mars. "Written by Maggie Mars . . . " The most beautiful four words in the English language. Until murder became a reality off-screen as well as on.

As it was, all unknowing, I backed my studio-loaned car out of the garage and thought again of how nice it would be to have a limo come by and pick me up. But executive transportation isn't for writers. Directors maybe, producers probably, and, of course, stars. Stars like Allegra Cort, who had been cast in the role of my heroine, Mercedes Pell.

"Blecccch," said Mercedes Pell.

"'Blecccch'? What's that supposed to mean?"

"It's a euphemism for 'what a bitch'!"

Well, that's Mercedes for you. My alter ego. The free spirit who says all the stuff I think of but can never get past my Politically Correct lips.

"What dumbass was responsible for having her play me?" Mercedes said. "She doesn't look like me at all. She's got two whole cup sizes to go!"

Now that wasn't exactly true, but I didn't say so aloud. There's only so much talking to myself I can do in Los Angeles traffic.

Besides, whether Allegra Cort looked like Mercedes was not the issue. At least not with me. From the first day we met in Fowler Mohr's office, Allegra and I were not on the same page. Hell, we weren't even on the same planet.

"I love the script," she said to me. "I positively adore the script," she said to Fowler, who beamed. That was sweet music to any producer's ears, as well as to the writer who wrote it.

"I can hardly wait," she then said, "until I can give Maggie my ideas for rewrites."

Which she did. Starting on page one. Every day she asked for more changes in her lines, which meant more rewrites, and sometimes whole new scenes. At first I sought a Rodney King why-can't-we-all-get-along approach.

"Why not first try the lines as written," I said.

Even the director was in favor of that. "Sounds like a plan," Buzz Harding said. "We can always change them later."

"Not later, now," Allegra said. "It's just not happening for me. F'rinstance . . ."

Allegra Cort could f 'rinstance you to death. She'd riffle through the script pages, and tap a glossily enameled fingernail on one or more lines of dialogue.

Last Friday the line was in the jail scene. "'I've got this dickhead detective torn between trying to get in my pants and arresting me . . .'" she said, reading. And then, looking up, "'Dickhead detective . . .' I would never say that kind of language."

"You're not saying that," I said. "Mercedes is."

That was my failing. I was being reasonable.

"There's your trouble, right there," Allegra said. "Mercedes needs to be a little more feminine . . . a little more Scarlett O'Hara . . ."

"Well, fiddle-dee-dee," said Mercedes. "That friggin' feminine enough for you?"

"Allegra," I said. "You don't want to soften Mercedes' character. Her attitude is what makes her so special and different. It sets her apart from your usual run-of-the-screen heroines. Reese, Keira, Charlize—"

She cut me off with a dismissive wave. "Spare me the laundry list." A dramatic pause, and then, "I'll think about it," she said.

Blecccch, I thought.

And, as usual, she swept off to her trailer dressing room, trailed by her pallid mouse of an assistant, Lisa Lindsey, and didn't reappear for hours. Production ground to a halt. Cast and crew sat around, waiting, earning good Minimum Basic Agreement wages for not doing anything.

"For God's sake, Maggie," Buzz Harding said. "Help me out here."

"But the lines are okay as they are. You said so."

"They're just words. It's not neurosurgery."

"Brain surgery," I said.

"Whatever. They're not carved in cement."

And Buzz was on *my* side. At least that's what he claimed when he took me out to dinner at Doug Arango's. The first of several

13

evening meetings—I guess you could call them dates—during pre-production. Buzz and I were both members of the Creative Artists Union—the one known as CAU—and our friendship had risen several notches above the traditional writer-director antipathy. Nothing, of course, for Joe Camanetti to feel alarmed about. But then, who knows with Joe.

That's the price I pay for being in a relationship with a detective. Ever since we had picked up on the West Coast where we had left off on the East Coast, Joe had been more adept than ever at playing Good Lover, Bad Lover.

My own producer, Fowler Mohr, who had attempted to nurse me through every comma, colon, and question mark of the script, came down on Allegra's side.

"A little bit of honey goes a long way," he said.

"I may barf," said Mercedes.

Me, too, but I was the one who had to knock on Allegra's dressing room door and agree to make a few changes. The latest of many changes, with no end in sight and a writer slowly being driven mad. Little did I know I wasn't the only one being driven mad . . . There was someone who would act on it.

2

This morning, as I drove up the Pacific Coast Highway, I was amused by the curious reactions of drivers in the other lanes. Since my car was in for repair—when was it not—my studio-loaned car varies from day to day according to what's available. Last night I borrowed a Ford Crown Victoria, a black-and-white prowl car used by the studio's Transportation Department for police scenes. The insignia had been temporarily covered over, but there was no mistaking the contours and the color profile.

I tried not to notice the stares, resisted the urge to pull someone over, and wondered instead what further difficulties Allegra might be waiting to stir up.

At the front gate of the Malibu estate where we were shooting, I greeted Eric, the security guard, stopped to exchange a few brief reviews on the weather, and then, noticing, asked him what was up with the network cameras outside Lew Packard's office trailer.

Eric said Lew was being interviewed. Yet again.

I drove on in, thinking about Lew, our esteemed studio boss, who was actively running for governor even though, cagily enough, he kept announcing that he hadn't yet decided.

From the movies to politics . . . What else was new. I suppose he wanted to follow in the footsteps of Ronald Reagan and Arnold Schwarzenegger. Well, I guess movie people are the same as everyone else, only more used to having every line written for them.

As I pulled into my parking space, I thought of my mother and If Only She Could See Me Now. Me with my own Reserved parking space. I got out of the car, stood for a moment breathing in the sea air, without smog today, and geared up for Allegra. Then I headed for the beach home that had been rented for the shoot.

Before I even reached the front door, I was headed off by a not-so-welcoming phalanx of grim faces. Buzz Harding, Fowler Mohr, Rod "Ram Rod" Burnside, who was our Director of Photography, and Lisa Lindsey.

"Okay," I said. "What does she want now?"

"It's nothing much, really it isn't," Fowler said. "It's just—"

Buzz put a hand on his shoulder. "Let me," he said. "It has to do with Sheri's dialogue."

"Sheri? Now Sheri Davis is asking for rewrites?"

"Well . . . Allegra thinks—"

He stopped right there, but there was no need for him to go on. I couldn't believe it. And yet I could.

"Allegra wants a change in Sheri's lines?"

Fowler said, "Just a tweak."

"Here. Tweak this," said Mercedes.

"No," I said, already walking off.

Ram trailed after me, a fortyish man with a sallow complexion, unwashed stringy brown hair, and paled-out hazel eyes. This morning he was wearing his usual Cubbies baseball cap, jeans, and black T-shirt.

"She's raised the stakes," he said.

"No," I said again.

"If her wishes aren't your commands," Ram said, "you're to be

16

thrown off the set and another writer hired who will do the rewrites."

"Allegra said that?"

"The gospel, according to Lisa."

Buzz joined us. "I'm sorry, Maggie."

"Where is she?"

"In her trailer."

"Tell her I did a lot of soul-searching, and after much consideration, decided I liked Sheri's lines just the way they are. But thanks, awfully, for the suggestion."

"Meanwhile," Ram said, "we haven't got anything in the can today and we're losing the light."

Why do D.P.'s always say that? It was barely mid-morning and the coastal sun was shining bright.

"The answer is still no," I said. "I don't have a trailer to go hide in, so if anyone wants me I'll be in the honey wagon."

That was pretty brave of me—translation: foolhardy—considering Allegra Cort had a more impressive track record as a star than I had as a screenplay writer. But still, I had had it up to here with having to make pointless changes in the screenplay over which I had labored so hard and so long.

It was Gene Fowler, the famous journalist, who said, "Writing is easy. All you do is stare at a blank piece of paper until drops of blood form on your forehead." Well, my life's blood was on the pages of that script.

Besides, there was a little matter of integrity.

A little matter that wouldn't make my credit card payments or help with my dad's room and board at the Pacific Sunset Village. But I'd sleep better at night.

Yeah, sure.

Word of the gridlock brought the Man himself, Lew Packard, out onto the set. Obviously, the interview must have ended.

Lew, as head of Griffin Studios, was known as the-buck-stops-here guy. He was small in size, standing five feet, five inches tall, but had a weight lifter's brawn. Balding, with wisps of salt-and-pepper hair, he used to have a moustache, but, legend says, shaved it off when Elizabeth Taylor asked him why he was hiding behind it.

Lew always wore an Armani suit and a collarless black T-shirt. That was his uniform. I liked that no-tie look about him. It has always amused me to reflect that ties must have been invented by a woman who was getting even for high heels.

"Maggie, Maggie, Maggie," he said.

Uh-oh. That was bad. Maggie to the third.

Then he put his arm around me, walked me down to the beach, and the talking began. I was treated to an onslaught of overinflated promises and let's-be-adults wheedling. . . . The honey and sugar poured out in a torrent, meant to sweep indefensible me away on its current. . . . If I weren't already a diabetic, I would be after this walk on the beach.

That's how come I found myself contemplating the prospect of meeting with Allegra in her dressing room trailer that evening.

"Over a nice cup of tea," Lew said. "Just the two of you."

"Tea?"

"Yes."

"Her idea?"

"She wants to make peace. After all, Maggie, the conflict between the two of you is not conducive to good moviemaking. It's not only bad for the morale of the crew, but it's causing costly delays in production."

"What can I do about it? I'm not the one continually asking for changes."

"What you can do about it," he said, "is meet with her tonight. You and Allegra may find that you have a lot in common."

"Like what?"

"Like wanting this movie to happen. After all, Maggie, it is your baby."

"It used to be," I said, beating Mercedes to the punch.

"Come on, sweetheart. Don't be pigheaded. Just listen to what

Allegra has to say. She's promised me that she'll keep an open mind and listen to you. I'm confident this way you can build a better relationship for the future."

"Allegra doesn't have relationships," I said. "She takes hostages."

"Maggie? This one little favor? For me?"

We started back toward the set, slogging through the sand. I picked up a piece of driftwood. It was beaten and worn by the constant action of the waves. Kind of how I felt.

"And if I don't say yes to this summit meeting?" I said. "Will you hire another writer?"

"You know I don't want to do that."

"But will you?"

"I'll do whatever I have to," he said.

He would. And I knew then that I was screwed.

I flung the driftwood far into the water and watched it borne away on the tide. Glancing at Lew, I nodded reluctant agreement.

After that, Allegra emerged from her trailer. Shooting commenced and nothing more was said about any changes in anyone's lines. Even as I was enjoying the comparative smoothness and serenity of the day's accomplishments, and wondering why the whole film production experience couldn't be like this, I knew the evening's get-together was going to turn into a war, and I couldn't help but dread it.

I wasn't sure whether that was because I knew I would stand my ground, and so be replaced by another writer—or because I knew I would cave in, like the utter coward I am.

Allegra and I didn't speak the same language, so there was no way we were going to come to anything resembling a compromise. She didn't know the meaning of the word, and my scruples were against it, because she was asking for changes that enhanced her role and detracted from other roles, particularly a role being acted by a younger, prettier woman.

Whether the rest of the production personnel knew about the summit meeting I couldn't say. I thought there seemed to be more than the usual whispered conversations going on around me, which suddenly aborted when I looked over, but that proved nothing other than the fertility of my imagination.

Somehow I got through the rest of the day and girded my lines. No, that's not a mistake. The lines were in my script, and I was determined to protect them.

3

Late that evening I found myself standing at the door to Allegra's trailer. When you are describing Allegra's accommodation on the set, the word "trailer" is a definite understatement. It was more of a spacious and luxurious home away from home. Stars like Allegra could and did demand private quarters and special furnishings with all the extras their inflated egos require. Very often Allegra would stay overnight, as she was doing tonight, to avoid the long drive north to Hope Ranch, where she lived on an *estancia,* and the long drive back for an early morning call.

I knocked on Allegra's trailer door and was welcomed with a melodious "Come in, come in, whoever you are."

"It's Maggie," I said, just in case whoever I was was not really the whoever she was expecting.

"I said—come in!" This time more strained than melodious.

I went in. Allegra wasn't in view.

"Be right with you," her voice called from somewhere behind a closed door. "Make yourself at home."

I looked around. The living room was furnished with white leather couches, two freestanding swivel chairs to match, and a row of built-in display shelves and bookcases, all lacquered a shiny white. I could see a small but perfect gem of a kitchen off to the right and, to my left, two doors. One was open and I caught a glimpse of a surprisingly well-outfitted gym and a massage table. The other door was closed and led, I surmised, to the bedroom.

The thought crossed my mind that there might be someone inside there with Allegra, someone who would be waiting for her to come back to bed. I never discounted those rumors about her and her co-star, Chris Balboa.

On a prominent spot in one bookcase, there it was. Allegra's Oscar. For Best Actress three years ago. I remember her accepting the award, all teary and effusive with thanks to her agent, her producer, her director, her hairdresser. Naturally no mention of the writer of the screenplay, even though it wasn't Allegra who was there when the pages were blank.

I picked up the golden statuette and held it in my hand. Surprising hefty.

Only last Sunday there was a spread in the *Los Angeles Times West Magazine* featuring Allegra in this very setting. There was the Oscar in the background, and there was Allegra saying, "Of course it travels wherever I go. It's my good luck charm."

I carefully replaced the Oscar just as the door opened and Allegra appeared onstage. She was wearing something caftanish, a low-cut, ankle-length black chiffon splashed with a large fuchsia print.

"Maggie," she said, "how dear of you to come see me."

Uh-huh.

As though it weren't a command performance.

She crossed over to one of the white couches and proceeded to make a nest for herself there in a thicket of colorful needlepoint pillows. A small tiled coffee table was in front of her. On it there was a silver cocktail shaker, two oversized martini glasses, a few cocktail napkins, and a saucer of olives and lemon slices.

The lemon slices were the closest thing to Lew's "nice cup of tea."

"Please sit down." She patted the seat cushion next to hers. "And help yourself." She indicated the setup on the table.

"Tea would be nice," I said. "If it isn't too much trouble."

"Tea?" She laughed. "I don't have any. But wasn't that a nice homey touch on Lew's part?" Once again, she patted the divan.

I sat.

"I thought we gals would indulge in something more comfy," she said. "Nothing like vodka to raise the morale and lower the inhibitions."

She poured a frosty libation into one of the glasses and held it out to me.

"Thank you, but no."

"No? Ohh? I should have asked. A.A.?"

"Just . . . not tonight." I didn't care to let her know that no-alcohol had to do with my diabetes and not with my transgressions.

"I get it." She put down the glass. "You keep a clear head while I get so muddled and befuddled I'll agree to anything you suggest. That it?"

She didn't seem to expect an answer. She filled her own glass, took an appreciative sip, and then settled back into the pillows once more.

Once she was comfortable, I said, "Maybe a little water. With ice."

She narrowed her eyes into slits and stared at me, not quite sure if I was being deliberate or if I was timing challenged. She opted for the latter and gave a help-yourself nod in the direction of the sink. But the lines were drawn.

I found a glass, half-filled it with water, located some ice in the minirefrigerator, and returned to my perch.

"Well," I said, "now that the amenities are done with, shall we get down to the agenda of the evening?"

She pursed her lips in a performance of contemplation. "The agenda of the evening . . . I like that. You ought to put it in a script sometime."

I somehow came up with a smile, aimed it at her, drew a deep breath, and began.

"Allegra, I know you'd like a rewrite of Sheri's lines in the airport scene—"

"Oh, that." She waved her hand, as though shooing a pesky fly. "I've changed my mind."

Well, well. That was welcome news. Maybe this get-together hadn't been such a bad idea, after all. It might not be the start of a beautiful friendship, but it definitely beat being on a combat footing.

I brought my glass to my lips. "So . . . no rewrite."

"Well, just a little one. . . ."

And kept it hovering there.

"I want her out of the scene entirely," Allegra said.

I put the glass down. "You don't mean that."

She nodded. Yes, she did.

"The poor girl ends up a corpse in the next scene," I said. "Those are the only lines she has."

Allegra merely raised one famous eyebrow.

The eyebrow did it. In spite of Lew's call for an armistice, this was too much. If I were to make this revision, the future was clear. More and more edits. More and more changes. More and more demands. If I didn't draw a line in the sand right now, the script would no longer be mine. It would be Allegra's.

I jumped to my feet, thereby putting the table at peril and shaking the martini in her glass. My glass was not so fortunate. It fell over and fragmented on the tile.

"Forget it," I said, raising my voice. "I will not, negative, not take Sheri out of that scene."

"Yes, you fucking will." Allegra was speaking softly and appeared calm, but her meaning was clear.

"Or else fucking what!" Louder still.

Now she matched my decibels. "I'll call Lew! You're off the movie!"

"You mean I'll never have tea in this town again?!"

24

"Forget tea," Mercedes said. *"You may never eat in this town again."*

I hate to admit it, but she was right. If I lost this movie, who knows when I would get another writing job. How was I going to pay my bills and support my father in the style to which I had accustomed him?

My disheartened thoughts were interrupted by a thin little voice saying, "Excuse me."

I turned. Lisa Lindsey was standing just inside the trailer door. I hadn't heard her come in and I had no idea how long she had been standing there.

Allegra said, "What do you want, Lisa?"

"Miss Cort, I have tomorrow's call sheet—"

"Fine. Roll it up real thin and then guess what you can do with it."

Lisa scurried out, leaving the door ajar behind her.

Allegra went on as though there had been no interruption. "Hear me, Maggie. Hear me good. One word from me and Lew will get someone else to do so much of a rewrite that your fucking union won't even acknowledge you for credit!"

"Go ahead and hire another writer, Allegra," I said. "But it'll be over my dead body!"

I headed for the doorway, paused there.

"Or yours!" I said. "Whichever the fuck comes first!"

"You rock, girl," said Mercedes.

MEMO TO MAGGIE: Any time Mercedes appreciates something you said, you can be damn sure you shouldn't have said it.

I left. I never noticed Lisa waiting outside in the shadows. At that moment I just wanted to get out of there.

4

I drove home on autopilot, my brain numb from the absolute arrogance of the lady, the absolute sense of entitlement she radiated. I got out of the car, and when the elevator arrived I was still so angry that I punched the floor button hard, wishing it were Allegra's face.

The doors opened on our floor, and, as I might have expected, Lionel was waiting for me.

"Where have you been? I've been worried sick. Do you realize it's one thirty in the goddamn morning? I tried to call the set but never connected."

I put down my script bag. "Hi, honey. I'm home."

"You might at least have had the courtesy to let me know you were going to be late. It's not that I worry, but I worry."

I made my way to the couch. My ultimate destination was bed after a long, soaking bath, but first I wanted to get off my feet, put my head back, and simply relax. By this time, Lionel realized that A, I wasn't paying any attention, and that B, I was more than just normally out of sorts.

Troy appeared with a warm cup of tea in his hands.

"Thanks," I said, reaching for it.

From the quizzical glance he gave me, I figured the tea hadn't been for me but for himself. Nevertheless, I was grateful for it.

Lionel is my more-or-less permanent roommate, or to put it more accurately, I am his roommate, having a bedroom and bath in *his* condo. When I left New York and my investigative reporting job, I came to Los Angeles to write a screenplay, bunked in temporarily with Lionel, my childhood pal, and that temporary arrangement has lasted for four years now.

Troy is a new addition. One of Lionel's oldest and closest friends, Troy, of the platinum hair and slim boyish frame, was staying with us while his house was being tented for termites, sleeping on the couch, and sharing Lionel's bath.

If you live someplace where there is actually weather, and changing seasons and cold winters, then you probably don't know much about termites. Here in sunny, smoggy Hollywood land, the termites feast on wood constantly. The sight of a huge apartment building or a house tented in blue plastic is just as much a part of the landscape as the FOR SALE signs.

Lionel started in again, unused to silence.

"If you had one shred of decency in your bones, you would have spared me all the worry and fear. But no, you're so busy hobnobbing with the stars, you forget all about poor me."

"And poor me, too," Troy said. "I wasn't worried, but Lionel wouldn't let me go to sleep until you came home."

"Sorry," I said by way of a peace offering.

"Sorry?" Lionel said. "Is that all you have to say for yourself? Why aren't you talking? What's wrong? Did something happen? Did you take your insulin?" He fired salvos at me so quickly that, although I tried to respond, I couldn't fit an answer in between shots.

Troy saved me. "Lionel, leave her alone. She's trying to tell you."

I said, "Well, you know Allegra."

"You can't stand her guts," Lionel said, cutting to the chase.

"True," I said, "but we do have to work together on the film, and everyone keeps reminding me what an unusual event it is to have the writer on the set, working with the director and the stars. . . . Anyway, you know how close I am to Mercedes."

"*Mucha loca* if you ask me," Lionel said.

"No one is asking you, so zip it up," Troy said.

"Guys, I'm really tired, and if you keep this up I'm going to bed and you can get your news from *Variety*."

They subsided, and I gave them an abridged version of the one-on-one with Allegra.

"At Lew's insistence, I agreed to meet with Allegra in her trailer after the day's shoot was over, so that we might come to some agreement about the script. Fat chance! We had some tea, in her case lemon vodka, and I listened to her twaddle and then I just packed it in. I'd had enough. And I've had enough of you two as well. Good night. I'm taking my insulin and going to bed."

I started toward my bedroom.

"That's a great idea. Let's all go to bed," Troy said.

He proceeded to lie down on the couch, covering himself with one of Lionel's spare blankets. Groucho and Harpo, Lionel's two feline acolytes otherwise known as a pair of Persians with attitude, jumped up on top of him and settled there.

I was halfway to the door when Lionel intercepted me.

"There's more to it than what you told us, isn't there, Maggie?"

I nodded. "I'm on the verge of being kicked off the film."

"Oh, dear. Well! Don't you worry about being dropped from the picture. We'll give it a positive spin in the trade papers." He embraced me warmly and kissed my cheek.

I was so tired, I almost missed the pronoun. But it hit me just after I opened my bedroom door.

"We?" I said. "What we?"

"For a while now, ever since you told me about the troubles you were having with Allegra Cort, I've had the feeling that what you need is your own personal flack, you know, a publicity person, a press agent."

"I know what a flack is, Lionel. And I've told you before. I can't afford one."

I could have sworn he practically simpered. "You can afford me."

"Oh no you don't."

"We'll talk about it in the morning. And, by the way, your father called. It seems you invited him to visit the set one of these days, and he's coming by tomorrow."

"Don't change the subject. You are not a publicity person."

"Did I mention that Joe also called?"

That diverted me. "Joe?"

"That yummy-looking dick you're carrying on with." He sighed. "He said you should call him at home no matter what time you got in. Want me to ring him for you?"

"No! And forget about being my press agent!"

"You know I'd be good at it. I'm on a pet name basis with practically everyone who is someone in this town, and your little movie can use all the publicity it can get."

"By tomorrow it might not be my little movie anymore, and the answer is still no!"

A rumpled Troy stood up, wrapped in Lionel's prize Pendleton blanket.

"I can't sleep," he said. "You're talking too loud. Why don't I just move into Lionel's room."

He padded off.

Lionel blew. "Troy, come back here!" He hurried after him. "Don't you dare put any part of your body in my bed! Troy!"

With a sigh I trudged off to my room and secluded myself there. I lay down on my bed, wondered if I could just forget everything: shower, dirty face, unbrushed teeth, insulin . . . and then, I remembered. Joe.

Joe Camanetti was the on-again-off-again love of my life. Right now I wasn't even sure whether the switch was on or off. I was busy playing writer and he was busy playing police detective. Occasionally the twain of us would get together for a meal, several times—but who's counting—for a sexual interlude. Sustaining it all were the leftover memories of those delicious years in the deep dark past, when we shared the same New York rent control apartment.

It was very difficult to put a label on the relationship.

I picked up the phone and dialed.

"Hi," he said. "You just get home?"

I said, "It's been a long day. Don't ask."

"Okay, I won't. But I was going to ask you something else."

Warily: "Okay. Go ahead."

"It's not an over-the-telephone kind of thing."

I sat up in bed. "What am I supposed to do? Get out of bed, jump into the car, and meet you somewhere?"

"Works for me. What are you wearing?"

"I'll call you tomorrow. Hold on to your question."

"That's not what I'm holding on to right now."

"Night, Joe."

I smiled to myself and went into the bathroom to prick my finger and check my blood sugar reading. It had been one of our better conversations.

5

The following morning I awoke early, but Lionel and Troy had invaded the kitchen even earlier.

"Morning, Lionel . . . Troy."

"No comment," Lionel said.

"What's that supposed to mean?"

"I just wanted you to see how well I can handle a 'No comment.' So when the shit hits the fan and the press are all over you, I can answer their questions with a terse, 'No comment.'"

"Sounds terse to me," Troy said.

"Lionel, I don't need a press agent. You stick to selling your classical records and I'll try not to do anything embarrassing."

"Fine. Just don't come crying to me when there's no one to lead you down the red carpet."

"What red carpet? I'm not going to be nominated for any awards."

Troy said, "That's because you won't let Lionel handle your publicity."

"Thank you, darling." Lionel blew him an air kiss.

"Troy," I said, in desperation, "are you moving back to your place today?"

"Oh no, it'll be a few more days. That's poison gas they're pumping in there."

I busied myself with preparing my orange juice and half a whole wheat English muffin for breakfast, and eventually Troy left, and then Lionel.

Lionel's old Schwinn bicycle had been put out of commission in a hit-and-run accident, and he was now the proud owner of a bright green Vespa. He had taken to wearing a black beret, a black turtleneck, and tight, shiny black pants and humming "Arrivederci, Roma" en route to his music shop.

My morning's drive to Malibu, considering the traffic, was pleasant enough. I thought about Joe, wondering idly what it was he wanted to ask me, and tried not to let any speculation about Allegra ruin my mood. There was no doubt I was in for a rough session once I arrived at the set, maybe even a public showdown between the temperamental star and me.

"Well, fuck her very much," said Mercedes.

Great. Mercedes was not exactly your poster child for tact and diplomacy.

Eric gave me his usual "Good morning" smile and welcome and waved me right through the gate. So far so good. I was still persona grata.

I spied Buzz at the Crafts Service table. "Crafts," not as in "Arts and Crafts," but "Crafts" as in all the snacks and munchies that Props prepares for the care and feeding of cast and crew. Buzz was dipping his hand into a big bowl of M&M's. That early in the morning? Not a good sign.

I said, "I suppose Allegra told you about last night."

"What about last night?"

He offered a few M&M's. I shook my head. "She didn't broadcast the news?"

"Nope. You want to tell me?"

I ignored the question. "That's not like her."

"She hasn't come out of her dressing room this morning."

"Now that's like her."

"Okay, Maggie, lay it on me. What happened with you two last night?"

"We had our usual meeting of the minds. Only I came equipped and she didn't."

He shook his head. "I was hoping to have my first shot in the can by now."

Lew Packard came up to join us, with Chris Balboa hovering behind. Chris was better looking than any man deserved to be, lean and lithe, with blond hair that many a woman would just itch to run her fingers through. I had managed to immunize myself, but, if gossip was to be believed, not so our star.

"Not my fault," I said, anticipating Lew's accusations. "She wanted Sheri out of the airport scene and I told her no can do."

"Send Lisa in to get her," Lew said, all the while staring at me.

"Already did," Buzz said. "She's not answering and the door is locked."

"Who has a key?" Lew said.

"Don't look at me," said Chris, even though everyone was already looking at him.

Buzz said, "Zack!"

"Yo!" Zack Briscoe came running. He was the set gopher, an errand boy, about as far down as you can get on the Hollywood totem pole and still draw a salary.

"Find someone with a key to Ms. Cort's trailer," Buzz said, "open the door, and tell her that the honor of her presence is urgently requested on the set."

Zack looked fearful. He was a tall, skinny mope of a kid.

Short on looks, short on guts, and long on Fowler Mohr being his uncle.

"Uh . . . what if she won't . . . uh . . . come?"

"Then do whatever you have to do to get her ass moving."

Zack still seemed beset by doubts, but he hustled off.

I barely suppressed a smile, imagining Allegra's mortification when lowly gopher Zack showed up at her trailer with his peremptory summons.

We waited.

"You know, Maggie," Lew said, after a while, "you could give some thought to losing Sheri Davis from that scene. It's no big deal."

"It is to me," I said, "and it is to Sheri. It's her only scene and it's a pivotal one."

"I suggest we talk about it," said Lew.

Chris Balboa cleared his throat. "Maggie, when you have a minute, I'd like to ask you a few questions about my lines in today's scene."

I glared at him.

"Or maybe not." He subsided.

Several more minutes crawled by, while we stood around, each lost in private thoughts.

"I guess I could shoot around her for a scene or two," Buzz said. "But I'd really rather not."

Lew said, "You won't have to. I'll speak to her myself if necessary. And Maggie, I'm sure, will try to be a little more accommodating." He had the good sense not to direct that remark at me.

I opened my mouth to retort, and shut it again. What was the use? I was trying to remember when the last time was that someone used the words "Maggie" and "accommodating" in the same sentence.

It was at that moment Zack came hurrying up to us. He looked ashen. That is, a little more ashen than usual.

"Well?" said Buzz.

Zack went over to him and whispered something in his ear.

Buzz was momentarily transfixed. "What!"

Zack whispered some more, and Buzz took off in the direction of Allegra's trailer.

Lew turned to Zack. "Speak up, for God's sake," he said. "What did Ms. Cort say?"

"She didn't say anything," Zack said. "She's like . . . dead!"

6

Lew, Chris, and I made a dash for the trailer and, clogging the doorway, we peered over Buzz's shoulder and took in the scene.

Not only was Allegra Cort dead, she was extremely dead. Most likely due to a severe case of a bashed-in skull. Still wearing the black chiffon caftan, she was on the floor, her head resting against the edge of the divan, her left profile—which was her good side—turned up, and her one visible eye staring off into nothingness. From underneath her matted hair there was a red-brownish seepage of congealing blood, and a rivulet of something gross and unidentifiable was trickling from her mouth.

The coffee table was overturned alongside, with shards of glass, olives, and lemon slices scattered all around.

Buzz took charge. He closed the trailer door and ordered the set closed and security posted at the entrance. Immediately.

"No one is to leave and no one is to enter," Lew said, by way of unnecessary amendment.

Chris said, "Gee. I've never been in a picture with a dead actress before."

"Chris, why don't you go to your dressing room and stay there till you're needed," Buzz said.

The actor left, stopping to talk to several other cast and crew members as he went. We knew he was spreading the word.

"I'll call the police," Lew said, retrieving his cell phone.

"It's the Malibu/Lost Hills Sheriff's Station," Buzz said, as the other man moved off.

"Tell me something I don't know." Lew never did like to be corrected.

That left me alone with Buzz. He put his arm around me. "You okay?"

I nodded, although not sure of how okay I was going to remain.

He said, "Allegra was fine when you left her last night."

It was a flat statement, but I could hear the question mark in his voice.

"Of course. You can ask Lisa."

But, remembering Lisa coming in on us the night before, I wasn't sure I wanted her asked about anything. Only it was a given that she would be.

Zack approached. "Uh . . . Ms. Mars?"

I turned. Considering that he had been the one to discover Allegra's body, he had made a surprising recovery. I had the feeling he was priming himself for his fifteen minutes of fame.

"There's someone here to see you. He's being detained at the gate."

Buzz shot an inquiring glance at me. "The press?"

"No. They couldn't have gotten word yet," I said. "I'll go see."

I might have known. Standing there with the security guard, wearing a pair of flip-flops, khaki shorts, and a navy windbreaker open enough to reveal a T-shirt that read THIS IS MY OTHER SHIRT was U.G. Ulysses Grant Mars. My father.

"What are you doing here?" I said, still too shaken to come up with anything more original.

37

Eric said, "He told me you invited him to visit the set today."

"Yeah," said U.G. "Remember?"

Obviously, I hadn't remembered. Not under the circumstances.

"I'll have to give you a rain check, Dad," I said. "The set is closed. No visitors."

"How come? I drove up from Manhattan Beach especially."

Against my better judgment, uneasy about U.G. being able to keep a secret but not knowing what else to tell him that would satisfy him and send him away, I said, low, "We're awaiting Deputies from the Sheriff's Station. It seems that . . . well, it looks like . . . someone's dead."

"You mean another murder!" he said, loud.

"Shhh!"

But it was too late. Eric was already looking at us and had moved closer to hear better.

"I swear, Maggie," U.G. said, "wherever you go, you find bodies."

"I do not find bodies," I said to Eric. To my father I said, "Now go away, U.G., and please, please don't say anything to anybody. Promise?"

"You're worse than what's her name, Jessica Fletcher."

"Promise!"

"Okay, okay. Could you meet me for lunch—"

"U.G.! We're busy here!"

"Okay. For dinner then?"

"I'll try. I'll call you."

He gave me a kiss on the forehead and headed for the parking area.

"My father," I said to Eric, whose eyes still showed suspicion. "He's a great kidder."

He nodded. He said, "Who's Jessica Fletcher?"

I didn't answer. My gaze was fixed on U.G., who was climbing up behind the wheel of a bright yellow Hummer and starting the motor.

A Hummer? What was U.G. doing in a Hummer? He couldn't afford a bus pass, let alone a Hummer.

Putting that aside for later analysis, I returned to the set.

Looking around, I gained a new respect for Buzz. Almost without effort, he had secured the crime scene. Cast and crew hung around in little huddles. There was no sense of chaos, no confusion, no trace of panic. Allegra's trailer had a security guard posted by the only door. Everything and everyone was on hold until the Law got there.

I was standing over at the side of the living room set, nearest the terrace that overlooks the sea. Even though the ocean in this area isn't very interesting, no rocks or boulders that break the surface, the waves roaring in and pulling back out again were mesmerizing.

"If I guess your thoughts, what do I win?" It was Ram, the camera guy, or cinematographer, to give him his correct title.

"A chance to buy me a cup of decaf. Props has stopped serving."

"Any guesses on Whodunit?"

I shook my head.

Ram said, "If all the people who might have wanted to do it were laid end to end . . ."

"I wouldn't be a bit surprised," I said, filling in the rest of the old joke.

7

The first sheriff's car arrived, and two uniformed deputies walked in through the gate. A hush rippled over the crowd of people standing around, like the Wave at a baseball game.

Buzz walked up to the deputies without his usual swagger, and with his shoulders sagging. Shaking hands with both of them, he introduced himself, and then the three of them conversed, too quietly for the rest of us to hear.

Small whispers of other conversations started up. I could see Lisa talking with Zack and Chris. Crew members were standing together in small clumps, sipping Cokes, talking quietly, and trying not to look at me.

Well, what was there to look at? I was the same person as I was yesterday, when almost everyone ignored me. Today, however, I had taken on a new persona. I may have been the last person to see Allegra alive.

The scene when Lew, Buzz, Chris, and I looked into her trailer earlier was stamped on my brain in bloodred ink. I unspooled the memory tape of my meeting with Allegra and recalled how I left her. She was on the couch, draining the last of her drink. I remembered that when I arrived the thought had crossed my mind that someone may have been in the bedroom waiting for her, and now, briefly, I wondered about it again.

Or maybe she had a heart attack or a stroke? Or an accident of some kind? It could happen. And how was I going to convince anyone of this? The entire cast and crew would, no doubt, prefer to have me in the role of a murderess, and then they would become the stars in their own lives, telling and maybe selling the story of how they knew I would kill, they saw it in my eyes.

I could just see the headline in *Variety* or *The Hollywood Reporter* or, heaven forbid, the tabloids at the checkout counter:

WRITER WRITES OFF ACTRESS TO PROTECT SCRIPT

My reveries ended with a shudder as I came back to reality. I saw one of the deputies going up the steps into Allegra's trailer, and then Buzz called for our attention and the other deputy began to speak.

"My name is Jonathan Hoyle, Deputy Hoyle, and my partner is Deputy Luis Renaldo. We are here because . . ." he looked at some notes in a small notebook dwarfed by his left palm, ". . . Allegra Cort has been found dead in her trailer. We don't know the cause of death yet, as our investigation is just getting under way. Your director . . ." another glance downward at his notes, ". . . Buzz Harding, has sealed off the entire set, and has allowed no one to enter or leave. That correct?"

He looked at Buzz for confirmation and got it when Buzz nodded. Hoyle's look was so penetrating that others around Buzz were also nodding yes. I guessed that anyone he focused that laserlike stare on would agree to anything he said.

"As soon as possible we will talk to each of you," Hoyle said.

"We'll take down your names and addresses, phone numbers, and then you can go. The set will remain closed during this first phase of our investigation, but we will wind that up as quickly as possible so that you can get back to work."

"What work?" I heard someone near me say.

Deputy Luis Renaldo was approaching his partner, talking into his cell phone at the same time. He had a beautiful form for a small man, short in stature but very buff.

He finished his call and whispered something to Hoyle. Then Renaldo walked back to the trailer and stood there by the entrance, still on guard. Every eye in the place was riveted on him, but his eyes were hidden behind his Ray-Bans.

"We have sent for additional help," Hoyle said, "and it should be arriving soon." He put away his notebook and moved off to join his partner outside Allegra's trailer.

Talk started up again and people moved around, joining first one and then another conversation. Somehow I found myself alongside Buzz and Chris and Ram.

Chris said, "I imagine they'll want to know who was the last person to see her alive."

"The deputies will ask the necessary questions," Buzz said.

"Okay, but it wasn't me," Chris said. "I wasn't the last one."

"Nobody said it was."

Lisa said, "It was Maggie."

I turned to face Lisa, who was standing off to the side, her eyes red rimmed and her face tear streaked.

"You don't know that for sure," I said.

"Well, you must have been. You were with her last night. You were arguing. I saw you."

"Lisa, that's enough," Buzz said. "The deputies will want to talk to everybody. So in the meantime, let's just play it cool and keep talk to a minimum, especially rumors."

"Lisa, did Allegra have any health problems?" I said.

"Health problems? What do you mean?"

"Well, I know, the whole world knows, that she's been in rehab many times. Was she still drinking, doing drugs? Prescription drugs?"

"No! She wasn't into any of that!"

It was much too emphatic a denial.

I pressed on. "Was her heart okay? Could she have had a heart attack?"

"Word is she didn't have a heart," Ram said.

Lisa was visibly angry. "What's the matter with all of you? She's dead! You don't say rotten things about someone who's dead!"

"Nil nisi bonum," said Mercedes.

Oh my God, now she was spouting Latin! I'd be heckled in two languages!

The tears were rolling from Lisa's eyes and she dabbed at them with a seriously used Kleenex.

"Her heart was fine! There was nothing wrong with her." Lisa glared at me. Unspoken was, "Nothing wrong with her until you came along!"

She sniffed and walked away.

The ensuing silence was broken by the arrival of more deputies, lugging assorted cases of gear and paraphernalia. They were wearing jackets that said CRIME SCENE on the back.

Ringo, the assistant director, came up to Buzz and indicated the technicians. Buzz nodded and left to lead them off to join their colleagues.

As the son of one of the network heads, Ringo had a certain Beverly Hills type of entitlement about him. He didn't care what he said or to whom he said it.

What he said now was, "Allegra was a bitch and Lisa is a bitch in training. She just doesn't have Allegra's style yet."

Chris laughed. I left them to their private amusement.

Ram said, "I know where there's some decaf. I'll see if I can scrounge you up a cup."

He walked away in the direction of the wardrobe department

and I managed to call out a "thank you" after his retreating figure.

The morning's rush of events was just now catching up with me. Allegra Cort dead? It didn't seem possible, and yet the evidence was all around. More deputies had arrived and were cordoning off the set with crime scene tape. Camera and crew equipment were being removed to the side, no longer needed for shooting.

More and more it appeared that Allegra had not died an accidental death but had been murdered. I knew for a certainty now that I must have been the last person to see her alive—that is, except for the murderer.

Whoever that was, I wanted him or her revealed sooner rather than later, just to stop the stares and the speculation. Glancing over the crowd, I wondered who it was. . . . One of us, the family, so to speak? On a film, everyone puts in such long, hard hours, working so closely together, that we all become like a family—a large dysfunctional family, true, but it hurt to think that a family member would kill Allegra.

What would happen to my movie, I wondered. Would they get a new star and reshoot the scenes already in the can? Or would they just dump the production and eat the losses? I gave myself a mental kick for even entertaining those self-centered thoughts. I would write another movie, maybe lots of movies, but Allegra Cort would never act again.

"Good riddance," Mercedes said.

I made a disapproving face. It wouldn't stop Mercedes, but I wouldn't want to think of myself as totally heartless.

"Everyone! May I have your attention. . . ."

Deputy Renaldo's voice jarred me out of my reflections. He really didn't have to ask for attention. It was something he attracted without trying.

"Deputies Barnes and Flannery will be sitting at those tables being put up over there." He nodded at the back of the set. "If you will form a line in front of one or the other, they will take your information and you will be free to go."

As people began to line up, I noticed two additional people walking up to the deputies. They were in plainclothes but were definitely cops. You can't live with a cop as long as I did without learning to recognize the walk.

This time it was Hoyle who addressed us. "I would like you to meet Detective Myles Jordan, and Detective Rita Perez. They will be handling this case from here on in."

With that, the two deputies huddled with the two detectives and, after a few minutes, the deputies left.

The line was growing longer, and, as we waited, the chatter escalated in volume. Most of the talk was about Allegra and what would happen to the film now that she was gone. I imagine they were all concerned about losing their jobs.

I was behind Chris and Ringo, who were discussing when and if the set would reopen and who would be cast in Allegra's role.

"If I know Lew, this baby will be recast in a heartbeat, and we'll be back at work soon as the funeral is over," said Chris.

"Easier said than done. They'll need to know who's available on short notice and who can pick it up quickly," Ringo said. He was squinting and I could tell he was running through a mental Rolodex of actresses.

I would have added my own two cents, but just then Detective Rita Perez tapped me on my shoulder.

"Will you come with me, please," she said.

"Me?" I could have kicked myself. What an idiotic thing to say when she was standing directly alongside me.

"You are Maggie Mars, I believe?"

"Guilty," I said, and winced. Another kick.

"We have a few questions we'd like to ask you."

She moved off. Out of the corner of my eye I spotted Ram returning with my cup of decaf.

"Excuse me, I'll be right there," I said, calling after her.

I ran over to Ram, grabbed the cup, told him to line up with the others, and hurried back to keep pace with Perez. I smiled an apology.

She kept walking, and I trailed her, sipping from my cup as I went. She was wearing a black jacket, over a pale beige T-shirt and beige pants. The tee and the pants fit her like a glove, and she had that shapely figure small women often have. She reminded me of one of the Desperate Housewives. I can't remember her name, but it's the one with the provocative form and glorious black hair. Perez's hair was shiny black, and cut in a full but short bob that flattered her face, what I could see of her face. She, too, was hiding behind Ray-Bans. Must be a cop thing.

She led the way out to a terrace overlooking the sea. There were tables and chairs here, under umbrellas, and Detective Jordan was already seated, waiting for us. I slid down into one of the chairs and tried to breathe normally. Someone, Lisa no doubt, had probably already mentioned to them that I was with Allegra last night.

Perez sat, too. She now had a pencil poised over a small spiral notebook.

"Your full name is Maggie Mars, is that correct? Or is the '*Maggie*' short for '*Margaret*'?"

"It's '*Maggie*' and short for nothing," I said, and I was immediately upset because there was a quaver in my voice.

What was the matter with me? To compensate, I took the offensive.

"Since you guys are here, this looks like a homicide investigation to me so obviously Allegra didn't die a natural death. Who killed her do you know yet?" I said, barely pausing for breath.

Rita Perez immediately appeared interested. "How do you know this looks like a homicide investigation? Have you been involved in one before?"

"Yes, I have." I quickly sought to explain that. "In a past life, when I was an investigative reporter for *Vanity Fair*."

46

I left it at that and didn't mention the more recent murders I was mixed up with. I figured the police had to be fed a bite at a time and if they wanted more they could always ask for a second helping.

Deputy Jordan, who was sitting with his chair tilted all the way back on its hind legs, letting the sun warm his face, said, "I remember you now. You were involved in those Red Underwear killings." Now he settled his chair back on all its legs. "You remember, Reet."

At this, "Reet" narrowed her eyes at me. It was quite obvious she remembered.

She turned and whispered something to Jordan, and they excused themselves for a moment and moved off a little ways. I couldn't pick up any thread of their conversation, but I could see Rita punching in numbers on her cell phone. She turned her back on me.

Myles Jordan returned, sat down, and said, "Okay, why don't you tell us about last night."

So I did, emphasizing the fact that when I left Allegra in her trailer she was alive and well.

Her call finished, Perez sat down again. "We understand that you and Ms. Cort didn't get along. Can you tell us what that was all about?"

She had no expression on her face but mild interest. I was wondering whom she found it necessary to call when she learned about my background.

I said, "Allegra and I didn't get along because we had what's known in the industry as creative differences. If you ask around—"

Perez interrupted. "So you hated her."

"I didn't like her, but 'hatred' implies much too strong a feeling. I didn't care for the way she treated the people who worked with her, and her utter disregard for their feelings."

"Specifically, what were you two arguing about last night?" She seemed very well informed for being on the job only a few hours.

"As usual, we were arguing about the script changes Allegra wanted me to make."

"And you refused," Jordan said.

"Of course. You see, the character Allegra was playing, Mercedes Pell, is an outrageous, irreverent woman who is beautiful and tough and uses rather bawdy street language. Allegra wanted to round off her rough edges, sterilize her dialogue, and show that her toughness is only a shield for a soft heart. You get the picture."

"Why were you so adamant about not making the changes?" Perez said.

Hadn't they been listening! "I just told you! Change Mercedes into the character Allegra wanted and the entire story becomes unbelievable and trite. And if you think that I killed Allegra because of that—"

"I didn't say that. Did you say that?" Perez looked to Jordan.

"Creative differences, that's what it was," Jordan said.

They continued to question me about last night and about my entire relationship with Allegra. Finally, Jordan stood up and Perez joined him, putting away her notebook.

"Well, Ms. Mars," she said, "we're going to need to talk to you again, but we'll be in touch and set that up. Meanwhile, we can reach you at the address and phone numbers you gave us."

"If you're planning any out-of-town travel, you'll let us know, won't you?" Was that Jordan's nice way of telling me not to leave town?

"I'll be around," I said. "Before I go, though, can you tell me how she was killed?"

They looked at each other a moment, and then Jordan gave a slight shrug of his shoulders and said, "She was bludgeoned to death."

"With what?"

"A piece of statuary."

"Statuary?" I was visualizing the part of her trailer I had seen. "There was no statuary in there. All there was, was . . . an Oscar."

48

Another much more significant glance passed between them.

"Someone killed her with her own Oscar?"

"Let's just say that we've collected the evidence and sent it over to the lab," Detective Jordan said.

"We'll reach you when we need to," Detective Perez said again.

I reached for my empty cup, prepared to go.

"You can just leave that," Jordan said. "We'll take care of it."

I bet they would. It had my fingerprints all over it. Just like that Oscar.

8

I went back onto the set and discovered that almost everyone was gone. The detectives and the techs were still there, filing in and out of Allegra's trailer, and yellow crime scene tape was strung all along the perimeter. Fowler Mohr, my producer, had arrived, I don't know when, and was in deep conversation with Buzz.

Fowler motioned me over to him.

"How you holding up, Maggie?" he said.

"Fine," I said. "They're interested in me because I didn't get along with Allegra. Pretty soon they'll learn that no one got along with her."

"True, but you're the one who admits to being with her in her trailer last night." Fowler put no emphasis on what he said, but it hit home to me.

"I didn't kill her. You know that, Fowler, don't you?"

"Maggie, of course I know that," he said. "Obviously someone must have come in after you left."

I sensed hesitancy in his voice. Or did I? Was paranoia taking over my mind already?

Buzz said, "Listen, we'll be in deep doo-doo with this film if we don't move quickly. We need to find a replacement, and we need to do some rehearsal and reshooting, all of which will stretch the budget to the breaking point. We'll need a little help with that, Fowler. Talk to Lew about the insurance payment."

"Will do," Fowler said. "Also, I'll call Jeff and start him working on some names." Jeff Hendricks was our casting director.

Fowler and Buzz both looked at me, noticing my silence.

"Maggie?" Buzz said. "You got a problem with that?"

"Guys, not to coin an expression, but the body isn't even cold yet."

"What do you mean yet?" said Mercedes.

Just then Perez came up to us. "Let's clear this scene, people. We have work to do."

We went outside and I noticed the Coroner's van had pulled up in front and the gurney was being unloaded from the back. They were ready to remove the body. It was not, I thought bleakly, how Allegra would have preferred leaving the studio.

As we watched, Fowler said, "Who's handling the funeral? Anybody know?"

"Lew is following through on that," Buzz said. "If her family can't or won't, the studio will."

"I never knew if she had family," Fowler said. "I thought she only had a string of exes."

Buzz nodded. "Hey, Maggie, how about getting together over dinner tonight? We can talk about what needs to be reshot."

Dinner! I had told U.G. I would meet him. "Can't," I said. "I promised my father."

"Fine. Check in with me tomorrow."

I nodded. "Sure," I said dispiritedly.

Fowler put a comforting arm around my shoulder. "Don't worry," he said. "We'll get through this."

I'd like to have believed him.

9

I walked out to the Transportation Department at the far end of the studio lot, and borrowed an old red F180 pickup truck for the night. Probably only driven to gigs by an old stuntwoman from Pasadena. I called U.G. on my cell phone, and he was both hungry and curious, in that order. We arranged to meet for dinner.

I had suggested a small place on the Malibu Pier. It had become a hangout for the crew and cast during the shoot. The valet tried to ignore me and my red truck, but I parked in the middle of the driveway, got out, and threw the keys at him. A Californian–ex–New Yorker can deal with valets with attitude without breaking a sweat. I noticed the Hummer was parked in the up-front primo spot.

U.G. was seated at a small table in the back, sipping a glass of red wine. He'd already decimated the bread and the olive oil and balsamic vinegar, which was fine with me, because I find that combo hard to resist.

"Hey, Dad, sorry to be late." I sat down and ordered an iced tea.

"No apologies necessary. Just the facts, ma'am." He was doing Joe Friday.

As briefly as possible, I explained about Allegra. I didn't want to worry him by telling him that I was the last person to have left her alive.

"It's like I said," U.G. said, not smiling. "Another dead body in your orbit. I wouldn't be surprised if soon someone tries to drive a stake into your heart."

I changed the subject. "So what's with the Hummer?"

"You remember my Jag was on its last wheels, don't you? It was in the shop more often than the mechanic."

"Of course I remember. But a Hummer? That's a little high-priced for a replacement, isn't it?"

As soon as the words were out, I regretted them. Just because I help U.G. out financially, I shouldn't turn into a nag.

He must have known what I was thinking. "Don't worry, honey, it's not going to cost you anything. It's used, or pre-owned, as the car dealers like to phrase it."

"Still—"

"Remember when our Gubernator, Schwarzenegger, was elected?" he said, plowing right on. "There was a big hullabaloo over his owning five gas-guzzling Hummers? Well, he converted one or two to hybrids or something, and the others he sold quietly at auction, where I picked this one up for a song."

More likely for an operatic aria. . . .

He sloshed another piece of bread into the olive oil, which the waiter had just replenished. "I don't worry about the gas because I don't drive so much anymore. And I have to tell you—it sure works on the girls."

I was trying to process this info when I noticed, over at the bar, Chris Balboa sitting with a woman I didn't recognize. He saw me at the same time and waved. They picked up their drinks and came over to our table. U.G. stood up and was openly staring at the woman.

53

Chris introduced us. "Mitzi, I'd like you to meet the writer of our screenplay, the very talented Maggie Mars. Maggie, this is Mitzi Elgin, a friend of Allegra's."

I introduced U.G. to them. With an endearing flourish of his napkin, he said, "Please . . . won't you join us?"

Without even waiting for their reply, he pulled out a chair for Mitzi. Mitzi sat down and accepted U.G.'s offer to replenish her drink.

As he called the waiter over, she said, "You don't know me, Maggie, but I recognize you from the set. I am . . . was a great friend of Allegra's. Her death is just such a tragedy, such a terrible waste."

I studied her, and, yes, I had seen her on the set, kind of in the background, but I couldn't remember whom I had seen her with.

Chris, who hadn't sat down, said, "I'm afraid I have to leave now, while I'm still under the limit. I've got a gig tonight. Nice to see you again, Mitzi, even under these circumstances."

He shook U.G.'s hand, gave me a kiss on the cheek, and left.

U.G. said, "Then the two of you weren't together?"

"Oh no," Mitzi said. "We just happened to run into each other."

It was only too apparent that U.G. was delighted to hear this.

Mitzi said, "I came here because this was the place that Allegra and I used to get together, at the end of the day's shoot, to chat and relax and catch up on our lives. You see, this is just about halfway between Hope Ranch, where Allegra lived, and Hancock Park, where I live. Well, maybe not halfway exactly, but it's where we used to meet."

She raised her glass. "I thought I'd come here tonight and have a drink and toast my old friend, and tell her she will never be forgotten."

U.G. joined her in the toast, and I, too, lifted my glass.

"Cheers," I said.

We settled back, and as the waiter brought more iced tea and replenished the bread and olive oil, she smiled at U.G. and I saw his throat tighten with emotion. Quite an effect she was having on him. He was clearly entranced.

Mitzi had a face to die for—creamy pale skin, rosebud pearly pink mouth, and big deep blue eyes, framed by lustrous dark red-brown hair, which waved down below her shoulders. This Titian vision was, unfortunately, set on a short, heavy square body. She was at least sixty pounds overweight, but carried herself as though she were sylphlike. She was wearing a pale blue blazer over a matching shirt, dark blue slacks, and high-heeled black sandals showing petal pink toenails.

Altogether, a very altogether woman. Looking at her, I felt rumpled and tired and older than I had been five minutes ago.

"I'm so glad to meet you," Mitzi said to me. "Up close and personal, as the saying goes."

"And how did you hear about . . ."

"I heard it on the radio. I was in my car and had to pull off the road for a few minutes. It hit me really hard. It's just awful what's happened. So difficult to believe, but not actually . . ."

Her voice trailed off, as the waiter brought a bottle of Yellow-tail, which U.G. must have ordered for himself and Mitzi. I stuck with my iced tea.

"That's another reason I came here tonight," she said then. "To pick up on any vibrations."

Vibrations? What was this woman talking about?

"I suppose I'm not making any sense," she said.

I said, "It's been a shocking event. You must be feeling that shock."

She leaned over the table and put a hand on my arm. "It's not so much the shock. You see, I had a premonition."

"A premonition?" U.G. was startled out of his reverie of staring at Mitzi. "You mean, you knew she would be murdered in her trailer?"

55

"No, nothing so specific or I would have warned her. But I did tell her I saw something murky, something very dark and dangerous, in her future. I wish I had been able to see it more clearly."

Her voice was tremulous and she squeezed her eyes tightly shut. A single tear made its way down her cheek.

That did it for U.G. "That's enough now," he said. "Let's have something to eat. You'll feel better."

I wouldn't have chosen to derail Mitzi now, but she seemed grateful, so I let it be.

We ordered and then ate, the three of us making the kind of chatter you make over dinner when there's a newcomer in your midst. Kind of like conversational *tapas*. U.G. was, if anything, even more mesmerized by her. When he wasn't thoroughly absorbed in what she was saying, he was talking about himself in the most extravagant, exaggerated detail.

It was during dessert, a dish of lemon sorbet for me, a shared slice of Amaretto cheesecake for the other two, that Mitzi, almost nonchalantly, said, "I should tell you that I am a psychic."

I put down my spoon. "A psychic?"

I'd never met a psychic before. I'd only seen those signs stuck in windows of neighborhood buildings advertising in big letters: PSYCHIC* TAROT* READINGS*

Mitzi smiled at me. "Yes," she said, "but don't confuse me with those storefront people who claim to predict your future through Tarot cards."

I gulped. Ohmigod, had she read my mind?

"I have a gift. There is no other way to explain it. My mother had the gift before me. I can see things that normal people can't. Not only the future, but the present, and sometimes the past."

"You can talk to the dead?" U.G. was in further awe.

"No, I don't talk to the dead. I believe I can, but that's not how my gift is to be used. I can see another person's aura, seem to be able to see what forces swirl around them, what's good, and, sometimes, what's bad. That is why I have been so upset about Allegra."

56

"You mentioned you were friends," I said. "How long had you known her?"

"Since we were in high school together. We remained close all these years, even though we didn't get to see each other all that often. She has—had—her life and I have mine."

She blinked away tears, and, hard-hearted me, I wondered why her mascara didn't run. U.G., of course, patted her arm by way of comfort.

"After all, she . . . was a great star," Mitzi said, "and I didn't travel in her circles. Still, we talked quite often and visited when we could. I think she needed to have someone close to her who was, you know, normal."

Normal? A self-proclaimed psychic and *she's* normal?

The waiter served cappuccino to Mitzi and U.G. and nothing to me. I was floating on a sea of iced tea.

"Allegra helped me set up my cable show, you know," Mitzi said, helping herself to a dollop of whipped cream on her cappuccino.

"You have a cable show?" U.G. said, right on cue.

"It's on local cable in the South Bay area. On one or two occasions I've been of help to the local police."

That was my cue. "Help them how?" I said.

"Well, a year ago, they had a missing child, and they brought me in for consultation. I like to think I assisted them in finding her. Her father, who was separated from her mother, had picked the child up at school and taken her to visit his parents, and, cruelly in my book, neglected to tell her mother where she was."

"How were you able to help?"

"I sensed the child was well and was with a male member of her family. So I guided the police in the right direction." Mitzi smiled at me again. "I know you're skeptical, Maggie. Everyone is, when they first learn about my gift. The movies and the practicing charlatans have poisoned the water for people like me."

"I think your gift is a miracle," U.G. said.

"Thank you." She reached across the table and squeezed his

57

hand. "Anyway, I've been of some help to the police from time to time. The news of this child was in the local papers and they hyped my show."

In spite of myself, I was fascinated by Mitzi. She spoke of her psychic abilities so quietly, so surely, and with such confidence that it was hard not to believe her. But believing her and believing *in* her were two different things.

"It all sounds like hocus-pocus, doesn't it," Mitzi said. "I really don't quite know how I do it, but perhaps when we have more time, I'll try to explain my gift more fully."

I was now too tired to talk or even think. So I excused myself, said my good-byes, and left U.G. to carry on with Mitzi.

10

I made my way home, digesting that dinner in more ways than one. A long time ago, U.G. had ceased to surprise me, but his obvious attraction to Mitzi was a new wrinkle. They were an unlikely duo, if ever there was one.

What was it about her that was bothering me? Was it because she was a psychic? Why should that matter? Was I really concerned that she might have the power to read my innermost thoughts?

My cell phone rang. I snatched it up, willing whoever it was to leave me alone.

"Go away," I said. "I don't want any."

"Okay, but you'll be sorry." It was Joe.

"Oh . . . I thought you might be a crank call."

"I am. How come you haven't called me back?"

"I was going to."

"Sure you were. . . . Hey, kiddo, more agro for you, I understand."

"Bad news really beats a path to your door."

"I have my sources, you know. I'm not a detective for nothing." I could hear the smile in his voice. "What happened?"

I repeated the same story I told my dad, this time including the fact that I was in Allegra's dressing room last night and had an argument with her.

There was a long silence.

"Hey, if you think I killed her," I said, "take a number."

"Maggie, I know you didn't kill her, but this is serious stuff. You're in a very difficult position. The cops are going to grill you hard, to see if you know more than you're telling. Do you? Are you holding out on them?"

"There's nothing more to tell. I was simply in the wrong place at the wrong time."

"Just cooperate with the cops, will you?"

I nodded, which, obviously, he couldn't see, but he took my silence for assent.

"Want I should nose around and see what I can come up with?" he said.

"Thanks, but I'm fine. This will all go away soon."

"How about if it goes away right now? I want to discuss something important with you."

"Shoot. . . . That's just a figure of speech."

"Will you move in with me?"

"What!?"

"You know. Move in. With me. At my place. Not yours. I like Lionel okay, but I'd just as soon not have him counting the ways—and the times—I love thee."

I was rocked off-kilter. Move in with him? A repeat performance? I'd thought about that. A lot. And here he was, actually asking.

"Joe, I don't know what to say. . . ."

"Try yes. It's less damaging to my self-esteem."

A pizza delivery car chose that moment to cut sharply in front of me. I braked, watching it speed ahead and vowing never to order from that place again, or maybe I would, since they obviously got where they were heading in record time.

"Maggie? You there?"

"I'm here. Listen, Joe, this is a conversation we should be having in person, not on the phone."

"Too late. We're having it."

"Well, I need time to think this over. . . ."

"How much time?"

"Why? Is there an expiration date on the offer?"

"Brilliant," said Mercedes. "No wonder you never got to be Miss Congeniality."

"Got it," he said. "You've had a better proposition from Heinrich."

"No, I haven't had a better proposition from Heinrich, I haven't had any proposition from Heinrich, and his name is Henrik."

Henrik Hudson. Who had once loved me, loved me not, but who was at this very moment defending a murderer who had tried to kill me.

I softened my tone and said, "Joe, could we both sleep on this and talk about it like tomorrow? Or the next day? Right now I'm bushed."

"Sorry, babe. Of course you are. We'll talk again. And soon."

The warning sound of a horn told me I was drifting off into another lane. I gave them the horn back just to assert my freedom of expression.

"Hey, I heard that, Mag! Watch your driving!" Joe said.

I didn't say good-bye. I just disconnected.

MEMO TO MAGGIE: Later, be sure to blame it on those damned cell phones.

11

At home, all was quiet. I put on the TV set and caught Lew's performance on one of the local news channels. He had played it perfectly. The focus of the interview was on the death of a great star and not on whodunit.

"It is with profound sadness that we confirm Allegra Cort's passing," he said. "Our thoughts and prayers go out to her family at this time and to her many fans and colleagues who have admired and respected her work for so many years."

There were questions shouted from some of the reporters about how this would affect his still unannounced candidacy for governor, and Lew deflected those questions with a very gentle and kind reference to Allegra, saying this was not about him, it was about the death of a great star. Lew said all the right words. I turned off the set.

The couch was uninhabited. No sign of Troy. Good. I could use the tranquility. I sank down into the armchair, dispossessing Harpo—or was it Groucho? All those Marxes look alike.

"Maggie?"

It was Lionel. He came out of his bedroom, fully dressed to go out, looking sorrowful, or, at least, as sorrowful as he could look with a scarlet beret perched on his head.

"Maggie," he said. "I am so sorry."

"You heard about Allegra."

"Yes, yes. I'm sorry about that also."

"Thank you, Lionel. It was—" And then it hit me. "*Also?* What else has happened?"

He heaved an outsized sigh. "I can't be your press agent anymore."

"Oh." In the chaos and excitement of the day, I had forgotten all about it.

Lionel said, "We'll find someone else. I'll ask around."

"That's not necessary, Lionel. Really it isn't."

"Don't you want to know why I'm withdrawing my offer?"

"Lionel, please, not now. I've had a rotten day. An awful day, the worst day imaginable. I was there when they found the body, you know, and now we're recasting Mercedes, and I have to think of some actresses who won't want to rewrite me—and you're obviously on your way out."

I said all this in an outpouring of words, even as I noted he was inching his way toward the front door.

"Yes, well, I'm meeting someone. Promise you'll fill me in on all the delectably grisly details about Allegra tomorrow?"

"I'll do that. Good night, Lionel. Enjoy."

He paused at the door. "When Troy comes in, just ask him to tiptoe around so he won't bother you. Oh, and tell him I have a late date with you-know-who."

It was only after the door closed behind him that I began to wonder: Who was you-know-who? And how come Troy knew-who and I didn't? And why couldn't Lionel be my press agent anymore?

It was all too much to mull over right now. After stripping off my clothes and shoes, putting on sweats, and grabbing a bottle of water from the fridge, I checked messages. There was one from Joe, one from U.G., and one from Detective Rita Perez. A mixed bag. I had already spoken to Joe, so saving Perez for last, I called U.G.

"What's up, Dad? Didn't I just leave you?"

"I wanted to know what you thought of Mitzi. Isn't she great?" U.G. sounded absolutely besotted.

"I'm sure she is, Dad, but we just met, so it's too soon for me to form an opinion." I wanted to add, "Also it's too soon for you," but wisely I held back.

"You've got to admit she's intriguing. . . . That gift of psychic powers . . ."

"Come on. You know that's bull."

Well, I hadn't held back that time. I probably sounded a little sharper than I meant to, and I felt bad.

"Listen," I said, "I don't know the lady, she seems nice, but the psychic powers stuff is very off-putting to me. You're a scientist, so isn't it off-putting to you, too?"

"It was at first. . . . But, after you left, Mitzi and I talked, and she's a very bright, unusual woman. And you know, Maggie, humans only use one-eighth of their brains."

"Uh-huh, and the other seven-eighths are used to vote for *American Idol.*"

"Mag, listen, I really like her, and I want you to like her, too. So try to have a positive feeling about her, okay?"

"For you, U.G.—anything."

We said good-bye on that peacekeeping note, and I then put in a call to Perez, who wasn't in. I left a message.

12

I was finishing the water, along with a banana from the kitchen, when the phone rang. "Ms. Mars?"

"Yes."

"This is Detective Rita Perez." Like I didn't already know that! How come people always call you back when you'd just as soon they wouldn't—and never do when you wish they would?

"What can I do for you, Detective?" I said. "I've told you everything I know. I don't have any idea who killed Allegra. She was fine when I left her. You ought to be concentrating on people who might have visited her after I left. Like an intruder. Or even a deranged fan."

"Whoa," she said. "Joe Camanetti said you had a tendency to go off on wild flights of fancy. You seem to think of life as though it were a screenplay and you were writing all the lines. This is not one of your scripts, Ms. Mars. This is serious. Real serious. Didn't Joe call you and tell you to cooperate with us?"

Perez clearly didn't like me. So what! The important question was how did she know that Joe had called me? How did she know anything about Joe? And why was he discussing my idiosyncrasies with her?

The coin dropped into the slot. Perez knew Joe. Before he came back into my life, he led a life of his own, and obviously he wasn't celibate. Rita Perez must have been part of it. He had his sources, my ass! An ex-lover was more like it. Or was she an ex?

She was saying, "Are you there, Ms. Mars?"

"Yes, I'm here." I tried to clear the debris from my head. Joe and Rita. Rita and Joe.

"We would like to talk to you. The early hours of the investigation into a crime of this nature are the most critical, and we can't waste any time. We have some more questions we were hoping you could assist us with."

"I'd be happy to," I said. What a liar! "I can drop by tomorrow sometime. Will that be all right?"

"No, it wouldn't. We'd like to see you right now."

"Now? Actually, I've just gotten home and—"

"We can send a car for you, if you like."

Uh-oh. They must be seriously interested in me.

"I can drive myself," I said. "I need to get dressed. Where do I go?"

She gave me directions, and I said I'd be there in a little over an hour. Traffic was always deadly on the 101, no matter how late at night it was, and she had said they were located at the Lost Hills station, which was way out west somewhere near Malibu Canyon Road and the 101.

As I threw on some clothes, I put aside further thoughts of Joe and Rita and began thinking about myself. For the first time since Allegra's body was discovered, I realized that I was in deep trouble. I knew I didn't kill her, but that didn't mean the rest of the world would take that as gospel.

I yanked my cell phone off its charger, dashed off a quick note to Lionel, which said only that I would be home late—after all, he hadn't told me where he was going, either—and left the condo.

Once I was on the 101, I dialed Henrik Hudson at his home and spoke to his machine.

"It's Maggie, Henrik. I could be in trouble and I think I need some legal help. The detectives want to question me about—"

Just then Henrik picked up the phone. "Hold on, Maggie, while I turn this thing off." I held. "I just walked in when I heard your voice on the machine. Did I hear you say you're in trouble?"

"Well, maybe I'm not, but it feels like it. Here's the short version. Allegra Cort was found dead early this morning. She was in her trailer on the set and I'm the last person known to have seen her alive."

"If that's the short version, spare me the long one. Where are you now?"

"On the 101 heading out to the Lost Hills station," I said. "The detectives want me to answer some additional questions, and I'm not really comfortable about it. Do I need your lawyer skills as a backup?"

"Damn right you do. I'm on my way, but it'll be a while. Do I need to tell you my next line?"

"Don't say a word until you get there. I know that."

"I mean it, Maggie. When you arrive, you tell them you're waiting for your lawyer and you are not going to say anything until he comes. Understood?"

"Understood."

We hung up. I should have been feeling comforted knowing that Henrik was there for me. But it was just the opposite. The serious way he was treating this, the pit of my stomach told me I had reason to worry. . . .

Henrik and I met while I was writing the script for *Murder Becomes Her*. It was before Joe became a factor in my life again, and for a while Henrik and I had a torrid romance, going at it hot and heavy. The only thing that marred the relationship was my nagging resentment about the scumbags he represented as a criminal defense attorney. And now here I was—one of those scumbags.

I knew then that I was in real trouble.

13

I got off the 101 at Lost Hills Road and stopped in a coffee shop. I knew Henrik would be about thirty or forty minutes behind me, and I sure as hell didn't want to spend those minutes sitting on a hard chair in a small puke green interrogation room that smelled of disinfectant and urine, staring at the wall.

Over a Diet Coke, I pondered the whys of Allegra's murder. Most murders are committed for familiar reasons. At the top of the list were love, passion, greed, and money.

I considered the first. Did someone kill her because she ended one of her notorious affairs? Or started one? Did jealousy enter the picture? I guess it was possible. Allegra was a wildly fickle woman, with several exes. If her lovers were men, always a question here in lotusland, then the jealous killer could have been a woman.

I made a mental note to find out if the murder could have been done by a woman. Those Oscars, if that indeed was the murder weapon, are very heavy. Could a woman have lifted one and swung it with enough force to kill? Sure. Would it require more than one blow? What if it was a man, jealous of Allegra's current lover? The questions and the possibilities were endless.

And what about greed or money? Who was in her will? Allegra had made a boatload of money over the years and was a notorious skinflint, tighter than her face, as someone said recently. Who stood to profit by her death?

Hey, what was I doing? I wasn't investigating this murder. Enough, I told myself. I paid for the Coke and drove the rest of the way to the station.

Once there, I waited where I was told to wait and checked out the Wanted posters on the bulletin board. Cheered by the fact that my face wasn't on one, I turned to study the deputy at the desk. Was there any glimmer of sympathy in his demeanor? Before I could get a good look, Perez came in and called for me to follow her.

I trailed her down a hall and into a small room, which was labeled "Interview Room One" and was used for interrogation no doubt. It was badly in need of air freshener and a paint job. The small steel table was dented and scratched, as were the three steel chairs. One of them was tilted on its back legs, and Detective Jordan was in it. Beside him, on the table, there appeared to be a tape-recording device.

I was ushered into the single chair on the opposite side of the table, and Perez sat down next to Jordan.

Jordan got the proceedings started. "Ms. Mars, you do understand that you are not under arrest?"

"I'm not going to say anything until my lawyer arrives," I said, dutiful client that I was.

"You've lawyered up?" Perez said, her expression unchanged. "What for? Are you afraid of revealing something? Maybe something you'd much rather hide from us?"

"Nice try," I said, "but I'm waiting for my lawyer."

After that, no one spoke. Finally the two detectives excused themselves and left the room. There I was, on a hard chair, staring at the wall.

Only a few minutes had passed when the door to the room opened and in walked Joe. I was so relieved to see him that I ran over and gave him a big hug.

"Hey, Maggie, are they scaring you?" he said.

"I'm just so glad to see you! What are you doing here? How did you know where I was?" And then I remembered my phone conversation with Rita Perez, and I pulled away from his arms and sat down again. "Oh, that's right. You have your sources."

"I heard you were coming in," he said, "so I asked if I could sit in as a favor. Not as a cop, but as a friend." He drew over one of the other chairs. "Why are these guys so interested in you, Mag? What have they got on you?"

"They don't *got* anything on me, Joe. I didn't kill Allegra, for God's sake!"

"I know that, but they're the ones you have to convince."

"Look, I went to her trailer at the studio head's urging. To see if we could work out our problems—script problems, in case you're wondering! How common is that in Hollywood?" I decided to stretch the truth just a tiny bit. "She was perfectly pleasant and so was I."

"Then why was I told you threatened her?"

"Threatened her? I did not!"

"Someone told the detectives that they overheard you use the words 'over my dead body . . . or yours.'"

Lisa, of course, but I was still taken aback. "If *someone* overheard me, then that *someone* was near enough to Allegra's trailer to kill her after I left!"

"Good point," Joe said. "Be sure to push that with the police."

"Why don't *you* mention it to your old friend Rita?"

He seemed puzzled for a moment, then shook his head in reproof. "Come off it, Maggie. You've got more serious things to worry about."

I was stunned, mad, and hurt all at the same time. But dammit, he was right.

14

The door opened and the two detectives came in, carrying another chair. Apparently they had greeted Joe earlier, because they merely nodded and sat down.

Before they could say anything, I got there first. "I'm not saying anything until my lawyer arrives, and . . ." looking straight at Rita Perez, ". . . your little ploy with your friend here," tilting my head at Joe, "didn't work."

Joe just looked at me and shook his head.

Jordan smiled. "Listen, Ms. Mars, we know your rights and ours, too. We'll get your refusal to talk on the record."

With that he put a tape into the taping machine and started it up. "This is Detective Myles Jordan and it is November sixteenth . . ." checking his watch, "eleven ten P.M. Present are Detective Rita Perez and a colleague from LAPD, Detective Joe Camanetti, here in his position as a friend of the witness, Ms. Maggie Mars."

He slid the machine on the table a little closer to me. "Ms. Mars, will you please tell us your full name, address, and telephone number?"

"No, I won't. Not until my lawyer arrives."

"Ms. Mars, that's not privileged information, and it's easy to come by."

"If it's so easy, then go find out for yourselves. I'm not saying another word."

Joe spoke up. "Maggie, is Henrik on his way?"

I nodded.

"Then we might as well wait for the lawyer, guys. I know him and he's good."

"Interview suspended at eleven thirteen."

With that, the detectives left the room again and I was alone with Joe.

He said, "What was that bit about my being a ploy of Rita's?"

"Well, you and Rita are friends, aren't you?"

"Yes, we are, and to answer your next question, we were friends before you came back into my life."

Silence filled the room. I honestly didn't want to go any farther with Joe about this, because one, I didn't want to seem jealous, and two, I thought it was reasonable that he had had friends when we weren't together—I had had them, too—and three, I *was* jealous and didn't know what to say.

"After all," he went on, "when you and Heinrich hooked up, you weren't too concerned about me and whomever then."

As always, he would mispronounce Henrik's name, but he was right about him, of course. I just wish Joe didn't have this little smile on his face that I would have loved to smack off, but then they would add a charge of assault and battery to the murder charge.

Finally, no longer smiling, he broke the silence. "We're wasting valuable time, Mag. This could turn messy. People get the wrong idea and lives can be destroyed. Even when witnesses are eventually found to be innocent, nothing is ever again the same. I don't want to see that happen to you."

He leaned in closer, looking at me with an intense, searching gaze. I wanted to avert my eyes, but I couldn't. His lips were inches away from mine. Any resistance was annihilated. Before I knew it, we were locked together in a tight embrace and a long, passionate kiss, our mouths hungrily seeking each other.

Just then the detectives returned to the room. Joe and I broke apart, and knowing she had seen us, I couldn't help sending a small smile in Rita's direction. Loving well is indeed the best revenge.

"He's here," Jordan said.

I didn't have to ask who that was. The next moment Henrik came in.

"I'm Ms. Mars's attorney for the moment," he said, "and she will answer no questions, is that clear?"

He came over to me, bent down to give me a peck on the cheek, said hi to Joe, warmly, I thought half-resentfully, and placed several of his cards on the table for the detectives.

It was obvious that Henrik had dressed in a hurry. He was usually so very well put together, and tonight he had on a pair of jeans, well-worn, and a T-shirt covered with a red plaid flannel shirt that looked as if he had polished his car with it. His feet were in tennis shoes without socks.

The sight of him plunged me into gloom. If he had dressed like that, that fast and that carelessly, here was another indication that I was in serious trouble.

Joe stood up and kissed me on my other cheek, the unused-by-Henrik one.

"Too many chiefs in here," Joe said. "I'll leave you guys to it. Mag, throw yourself on their mercy. Maybe they'll put away the rubber hoses. I'll talk to you later."

He waved all around and left. No one thought he was funny. Least of all me.

Henrik, even in his bizarre outfit, took over the room. He sat in Joe's chair, leaned back—not as far as Jordan had, but impressively enough—and said, "So, what's this all about?"

I started to answer, but his hand shot out and grabbed my arm. "Not you. Them."

Detective Jordan explained the circumstances relating to Allegra's death. I opened my mouth to correct him on a few points, but a warning look from Henrik silenced me.

"So all you have is Maggie in Ms. Cort's trailer, arguing with her over the script." He stood up. "Are you guys kidding me? You need to get out more. Creative differences are like breathing in this town. Meanwhile, you drag Maggie out here to the boondocks in the dead of night, you scare her half to death, and worse than that, you drag *me* out here! Come on, Maggie, we're leaving."

With that, he took my arm, practically lifted me out of my chair, and hauled me with him out the door.

I thought we were home free, but, unfortunately, right outside the station there was a camera crew from CBS News, with the camera focused on me.

Henrik held my arm in a grip of iron and said in my ear, "Do not duck your head. Look straight at the camera. You have nothing to hide."

I did as I was told, and when the reporter stuck a microphone in my face it was Henrik who, without breaking stride, spoke into it.

"Ms. Mars has asked me to come in and help with the inquiries being made. She has no comment at this time. She has complete faith in the Sheriff's Department that they will find and apprehend the killer very soon."

We kept walking until we reached Henrik's car.

"Get in, Maggie," Henrik said. "We'll find someplace where we can talk."

We drove to the coffee shop where I had stopped off before and pulled into the back, dark corner of the parking lot. It was strange, sitting so close to Henrik again. Sort of déjà vu–ish, our previous intimacy somewhat distorted by intervening time.

Without preamble, Henrik turned to me. "What have you gotten yourself into, Maggie?"

"It's just as you told them," I said. "All I did was argue with her over the script."

"Don't be fooled by my bluster in there. They weren't."

"What are you talking about? Didn't you mean what you said?"

"Of course I meant it, but everyone in there, except maybe you, understood it for what it was—foreplay. They must have more on you than they are letting on right now."

I started to protest, but Henrik stopped me. "Not now, Maggie. I'm beat and it's late. Come down to the office tomorrow, and we'll talk it out and see what we need to do. Right now what I need to do is get some sleep. I'm taking you back to your car. The press has probably gone by now."

He was right. None of the camera crew had lingered around.

I drove home, somewhat bewildered by Henrik, but impressed with the way he handled things. During the brief run of our past affair, I had never seen him in action. Legal action, that is. He was good, all right.

So here I go again. Having both Henrik and Joe play with my head. It was oddly disconcerting, even though I knew Henrik was the past and Joe was the future. If indeed I had a future at all. . . .

15

The next morning, Lionel and Troy were gone before I awoke. I called Fowler and sketchily filled him in on my nighttime visit with the Law. He made the right sympathetic responses and told me the set was closed for the day, out of respect for Allegra. He, along with Buzz and Jeff Hendricks, was quietly busy, trying to find a replacement lead and dealing with a myriad of other problems Lew was laying on him.

"Have you set a casting session?" I said.

"Tomorrow at my home. We'd like you there. There are going to be script revisions needed, because we can't use any of Allegra's scenes. Unless, of course, we can keep them and work them into the story. . . ."

I said, "You're kidding, right?"

"Okay, okay. I was just trying it on for size. I'll see you tomorrow. Ten in the A.M."

Fowler sounded normal, harried and with his mind elsewhere, so maybe I was still fair-haired.

When I called Henrik's office, his secretary asked me to come to the office around one for lunch. I agreed and found myself with some time, a rare commodity. I pulled on my sweats and drove to the beach. Lionel had downloaded new music to my iPod, and I plugged myself in and went for a run.

It was glorious! The bike path was empty, the sea was beautiful, and the sun was shining. Five miles later, feeling sublime, I cooled down and trotted to my car.

"Nothing like a murder charge to rev up the old engine," said Mercedes.

Trying to put that out of my mind, I drove home, showered, dressed, and left for Henrik's office downtown.

The law firm had the top five floors of the building, with their own staircases and private elevators. The offices were decorated in pale colors, calm and serene furnishings, intended to soothe the fears of their many clients. Although, as most of their clients were murderers, rapists, and drug dealers, the serenity was probably for the attorneys.

Henrik's office was at the penthouse level, with a view of the whole city, stretching all the way to the ocean. The day was still gorgeous, with no fog or smog to spoil the vista. Isabel, Henrik's right arm, showed me in.

Henrik was, of course, on the phone. When at last he had hung up, he came over and sat on the arm of my chair.

"Maggie, you really need to have a lawyer representing you."

I knew better than to interrupt. Henrik was a master at never slowing down.

"And I can't do it."

"Why not?" Then I remembered. Henrik was in a trial right now. And the defendant whom he was representing was someone from my not too distant past, someone who had tried to kill me. My awareness must have shown on my face.

"You got it," he said. "I can't represent you because it would be a serious conflict of interest, and not one I would let you sign off on."

"Then what—"

He put a finger to my lips.

"I've lined up a great lawyer for you. Next to me, he's the best criminal lawyer in the country."

I nodded numbly. The course of my life had been taken over by Henrik and now by a man I didn't even know.

"Come on," said Henrik. "We're meeting him for lunch."

We walked down the carpeted hall, hung with old etchings of Rubenesque women in various stages of dishabille. Henrik opened the door to the private dining room of the law firm. They kept a full-time chef on duty, and the food was rumored to be the best in the city.

As we entered, a man turned away from looking out over the view. He was the tallest, leanest man I had ever seen away from a basketball court. His face was deeply wrinkled, very tan, and so thin as to be all bushy, black eyebrows. His eyes were a pale, washed-out blue, as if he'd stared at the sun too long, and he had long white hair flowing down to his shoulders. Unlike most attorneys, who seemed to have been born in three-piece suits and ties, he wore jeans, plain 501's, and cowboy boots.

I was still taking inventory when he stuck out his hand to shake mine. "Hi! You're the lady in all the trouble, huh?"

He had a surprising tenor voice, not the low voice I anticipated hearing, and I couldn't help wondering how this man could possibly sway a jury. Who would listen to him?

Henrik did the introductions and I said hello to Porter Caulfield, my maybe new lawyer. I could tell by looking at him that I couldn't afford him, so this lunch was probably a waste of time, but I was looking forward to the food.

The chef came out to greet Henrik, who said, "This is Angelo, the genius we hide in our kitchen. I've taken the liberty of ordering for us, because I can't take much time now and you two will want to talk between yourselves."

We exchanged pleasantries with Angelo, and before he left the room a waiter was filling our drink orders.

Henrik had ordered fillet of sole for me, in a lemon caper

sauce, and it was followed, in European tradition, by a cool and wonderful green salad. I listened to the two attorneys conversing about some case recently decided by the Supreme Court, and then Henrik excused himself and was gone.

I was alone with Porter Caulfield. Even though I knew Henrik had to palm me off on someone else because of ethical considerations, I couldn't help feeling a little bereft. Henrik and I were no longer lovers. We couldn't even have a lawyer–client relationship. It was as though we had turned into complete strangers. And now here I was with a new man, not a romantic entanglement, but a new man upon whom my life would be depending.

How did I get myself into situations like this?

16

Porter sat back in his chair and said, "Now tell me about your problem."

I explained the finding of Allegra's body in her trailer and, in brief, about my argument with her the night she died.

Porter Caulfield, however, wasn't interested in brief. He wanted the long version, asking me to go over every detail from the moment I entered the trailer until the next day when Zack discovered her body. While I talked, Porter listened, actively. It's amazing what you can remember when you actually have someone who really pays attention to your every word, putting everything else aside.

I even told him how the thought had crossed my mind that there might have been someone inside Allegra's bedroom, someone who might have been waiting for her to come back to bed. Until just now, it had again slipped my memory.

"And what was your relationship with Allegra Cort before that night?" he said.

"It was not very good," I said.

"Not very good?"

"Okay, it was lousy," I said. "But so was everyone else's relationship with her. The woman was toxic."

"Yes, I've known some of those . . . ," he said. "Tell me about her from the first moment you met."

So I did, at length.

After that he was quiet for a long time. Then he stood up and stretched. "Now you're my client, Ms. Mars," he said, "and that means you do everything I say to do and you don't do anything until I say you can do it. Is that clear?"

"I'm afraid what's clear is that I have very little money, and my guess is you don't work for very little money."

"No, I don't. But Henrik and I have a deal. We help each other out when necessary and the bills are a wash."

That didn't cheer me one bit. "Then I'll just have to talk to Henrik," I said. "I've always paid my own way, and this is no different."

"Fine. That's for you and Henrik to discuss. But I don't mind telling you that my money's on Henrik. Meanwhile, here's my card. I've written my cell phone on the back. I won't answer the call, but leave a message and I'll get back to you within thirty minutes."

Porter and I had our validations stamped, and he saw me to my car in the underneath garage.

"Maggie, right now I don't think the cops have anything on you, except that you were arguing with her that night. I imagine we can find a dozen people who were arguing with her."

"What if they ask me to come in again?"

"If so, call me. Don't say one word to them and don't sign anything. Meanwhile, I'll do some checking around."

I still wasn't sure how the financial angle was going to work out for me, but I felt definitely encouraged. Porter Caulfield instilled confidence. Maybe a jury would listen to him, after all.

Oh, God! Would this end up with a jury! I would have to appear in a courtroom and be the cynosure of all eyes, grist for the Hollywood gossip mills. My life would be torn apart and examined

81

under a microscope by the media. Just like a common criminal, my fate would lie in the hands of a jury of my peers—

"Your peers? What? Twelve screenwriters who create fantasy for a living?" said Mercedes.

She had a point. I was doomed.

17

Meanwhile, the next morning, it was business as usual.
I had a casting session to get through, and I had to go on acting as
though I was innocent. Which I was. I knew that even if the rest
of the world didn't.

Lionel wouldn't let me out of the house until he had fluffed and
sprayed my hair, touched up my makeup, and undone the veteran
paisley scarf that I had tossed around the neck of my melon green
pantsuit.

"Lionel, please give me back my scarf," I said, entreatingly. "I
have to go."

"It looks like something the cat would have dragged in. Groucho, not Harpo. Harpo takes after me. Don't you move. I'll find
you another."

With that, he dashed off to his room.

"Lionel!" I said, calling after him. "It doesn't matter how I look.
I'm not reading for the part!"

His voice came back to me. "I can't let you go out like that.
Everyone knows you're co-habiting with a gay man."

"Co-habiting?"

"Whatever. I have my reputation to uphold."

He reappeared carrying a gorgeous, brightly colored Hermès horse-patterned silk scarf that I knew was a favorite of his. It was a birthday present from a former lover. With a few deft motions Lionel draped it around my shoulders, then stood back and appraised the result.

"There. Now you look presentable."

I hugged him. "Lionel, you're the best."

"I know," he said, smiling.

Fowler Mohr lived in the hills north of Sunset. Once you left the boulevard and the low-lying streets, you traveled up a twisting road that presented a breathtaking vista of the city below with every curving turn. The problem was that I couldn't enjoy it because I was too busy clutching the wheel and keeping my eyes glued to the next hairpin bend. When I finally reached the driveway, I would have felt much more relief had the prospect of having to go downhill again not loomed ahead of me.

It was an utterly modernistic-looking house, from the outside almost a salute to cubism. The inside was very Fowlerish, minimally furnished in chrome and leather and with a lot of primitive African sculptures. The area rug was a white shag, at least a foot deep.

Victoria Mohr, Fowler's wife, carrying a trayful of bottled water and bowls of raisins and almonds, greeted me warmly, then led me into the library area. The Mohrs, it seemed, liked to have areas instead of rooms. She deposited her offerings and left.

It was a spacious room, starkly white, with a clump of freestanding ceiling-high bookshelves at one end. At the other end there was a white stone fireplace with a real fire behind a custom sculptured steel screen, and in front of it a leather, black modular oversized sofa and three deep leather armchairs. The white terrazzo floor was broken up by several silver-and-black area rugs. Altogether the "library area" didn't look like anyplace I had ever used my library card in.

Along with Fowler, Buzz was there, and, to my surprise, so was Lew, who immediately greeted me with, "I can't stay long." Our casting director, Jeff Hendricks, handed me a list of the actresses who would be reading for us, and I noted that Sheri Davis was one of them. The others were barely familiar.

"Kidman won't read," he said, "and, anyway, her asking price is in the stratosphere."

As well it should be. At the time Allegra Cort had been cast, I had been assured by all my industry friends how very lucky I was to get her. From the looks of the list, I guess my luck had run out. Not to mention Allegra's. But I was surprised about Sheri. She had never given any indication that she was up for bigger and better roles.

After supplying Jeff with the pages we had selected to be read, I took a seat on the sofa and turned my attention to the script:

INT. L.A. POLICE DEPARTMENT—INTERROGATION
ROOM

Jack is seated across the table from an un-
shaven thug, BRUCE ELLIOTT, mid-forties. Elliott nervously puts a half-crumpled
cigarette in his mouth and checks his pockets
for a lighter. Jack pulls out a lighter and
lights Elliott's cigarette.

Outside the room, looking through the ONE-WAY
MIRROR, is Mercedes. She still has the
bruises, disheveled hair, torn clothing, and
dirt picked up in the chase and arrest.

MERCEDES

Oh, really nice, Jack. Light
that little fuck's cigarette for
him. The least you could do is
kick him in the balls and start
him inhaling.

JACK
(to Elliott)
I'm sorry my partner beat up on
you. She gets a little carried
away.

MERCEDES

Carried away?

Mercedes bangs on the glass. Jack and Bruce
look over.

JACK

Pipes. It's an old building.

MERCEDES

Carried-a-fucking-way, Jack? The
guy whacked a priest, Jack. The
guy kicked your ass, Jack! And
the guy threw a gun at me after
he emptied the clip into my
car . . . which, I may add, I
was about to sell for a good
price. . . . But chances
are . . . no one's going to buy
a car with SEVENTEEN FUCKING

BULLET HOLES IN ITS SIDE,
JACK!!!

                    JACK
We think you may have some
knowledge of the murder of Father Duncan Harris.

Jack reaches out to put a comforting hand on
Elliott's shoulder.

                    JACK (CONT'D)
I'm just guessing here . . . but
this must bring up some feelings.

                    MERCEDES
Feelings? I can't believe this.
I've tried to get you to talk
about your feelings for months
now. No, I've tried to get you
even to say the word "feelings"
for months now and it's this
asshole you decide to open up
with!!!

                    ELLIOTT
I don't feel like talking right
now.

                    MERCEDES
No problem, Jack!
        (demonstrating)
Grab him by his nuts, pull them

```
       up around his scrawny neck, and
       twist them with a pair of pliers
       until he gets some feelings.


CAPTAIN ROGERS walks by Maggie as she twists
the imaginary nuts.


               CAPTAIN ROGERS
         Morning, Mercedes. Say, how is
         that sensitivity training going?


                 MERCEDES
              (sweetly)
         Just fine, Captain.
```

I had to smile to myself. This was one of the scenes that Allegra had objected to the most vociferously.

"Too many fucking 'fucks' in that," she had said. "I wouldn't talk like that in a police station."

It was no use reminding her yet once again that it was Mercedes Pell and not Allegra Cort who was talking. As far as I was concerned, the subject was dead and buried.

And so, except for the funeral service, was Allegra.

At that time I had agreed to compromise and lose three "fucks" and one "prick." Now, in memory of Allegra, two of the "fucks" were back but not the "prick." Who said I wasn't all heart?

"Chris not coming?" Jeff said.

Fowler said, "He'll be here. You know Chris. He'll be late for his own . . . wedding." It was an inept finish and we all knew it.

Lew said, "Jeff, let's not wait. You can read the part."

Chris chose that moment to make his entrance. He was wearing a yellow sports shirt and white tennis shorts. It was obvious what had delayed him.

"Hi," he said. "Picked anyone yet?"

"Yes," said Buzz, "and now we're getting ready to recast your part."

"Okay, okay, sorry. The traffic was hellish."

Jeff gave him his sides. Chris dropped into one of the leather armchairs.

"Here we go," Lew said.

He nodded to Jeff, who left the room. We all riffled pages and waited expectantly. In a minute or two, Jeff returned with a tall, curvaceous woman wearing blue jeans and a flaming red tank top. Her streaked blond hair was in a ponytail tied up in something that looked to me like a shoelace. That isn't me being judgmental; that's me wondering if shoelaces could be a new fad.

Jeff said, "Brenda McCormack, everybody."

He didn't bother to introduce us—the aforementioned "everybody"—but we dutifully returned Brenda's "Hi."

As Jeff passed around her résumé, he said, "Maggie, would you set the scene for Brenda, please?"

No one had prepped me for this, but I cleared my throat and plunged in.

"Well, Mercedes is just outside the interrogation room of the police station—"

Brenda said, "Am I like in a hallway?"

"Like," I said, by way of agreement. "You're looking through a one-way mirror—"

"Which way?"

"Which way what?"

"Which way am I looking?"

I glanced at the others. They appeared to be engrossed in their scripts.

I said, "You're looking into the interrogation room where Jack—"

"That's me," Chris said, getting up and smiling at her.

"You're Chris Balboa! I don't believe it!" Brenda said. "I adored you in your last movie."

"Um, thanks."

89

"Moving on," I said, undeterred. "Jack is grilling Bruce Elliott, whom he has just arrested. He pulls out a lighter and lights the suspect's cigarette."

Jeff said, "I'll read Elliott and Captain Rogers. Action."

"There are no cameras," said Brenda, "so I'll just pretend." Then, reading as Mercedes, *Oh, really nice, Jack. Light that little bastard's cigarette for him.*"

"The word is 'fuck,'" I said. "'That little fuck's cigarette.'" Inwardly I was gritting my teeth. Oh, dear God, spare me from another one.

"Bastard, fuck, same thing," Brenda said, and then, back again as Mercedes, *The least you could do is kick him in the balls and start him inhaling.*"

Chris, as Jack, said, *I'm sorry my partner beat up on you. She gets a little carried away.*"

"Carried away?"

Brenda crossed to the nearby picture window and banged on it hard. Fowler winced.

Buzz said, "What are you doing?"

"It says here: 'Mercedes bangs on the glass.'"

"The glass of the one-way mirror."

"There's no mirror here," Brenda said. "I was doing improv."

And so it went, as, eventually, did Brenda. Jeff said he would call, and, flashing a smile at Chris Balboa, she left.

The next two candidates, Christine Brevard and Kim Dorsey, were passable, and I jotted some notes next to their names.

They were followed by Rachael Demeter, an absolutely gorgeous redhead, a little on the plump side but nothing that couldn't be dealt with. Along with her bounty of credits, what intrigued me most about her was her sexy, whiskey voice. Oh, how I wished I had a voice like that. There are still times when I answer the phone and the person asks to speak to my mother.

Jeff said, "Maggie, our writer, will set the scene—"

"No need," Rachael said. "I've read it and it's perfectly clear."

I said, "She gets the part."

There were a few appreciative laughs, and Rachael began to read.

She and Chris got into the scene as far as her saying, *"Feelings? I can't believe this. I've tried to get you to talk about your feelings for a year now. No, I've tried to get you even to say the word feelings for a year now and it's this asshole you decide to open up with! "*

Buzz said, "Rachael, could you read that speech again, this time with just a little more passion?"

Rachael said, "I could. But I think it should be underplayed."

"*You* think it should be underplayed?"

"You're the director, of course, but let's just give my way a try."

Buzz looked at me. Sweetly I smiled back. I guess he didn't like getting a dose of the same bitter medicine Allegra had given me.

"Back to script," he said.

They finished the scene, and Rachael was likewise told that Jeff would call her.

Several more would-be Mercedes were ushered in to read, only one of whom was worth a callback, and then it was Sheri Davis's turn.

"Hi," she said. "Funny, but you all look so familiar."

Chris and I laughed, and it kind of broke the ice and dispelled any awkwardness there might have been.

Jeff said, "Go, Sheri."

She began and never once looked at the pages. By the end of the scene, when Jeff, as Captain Rogers, read: *"Morning, Mercedes. Say, how is that sensitivity training going?"* and Sheri, as Mercedes, with just the right amount of syrupy sweetness, said, *"Just fine, Captain,"* I, at least, was sure that we had found our new Mercedes.

Sheri was the very epitome of Mercedes, as I had always imagined her, and, in fact, had conceived of her. In all the right places

91

Sheri was brazen and irreverent. Yet it was obvious she could revert to vulnerability when it was called for. She was as close to perfect as I felt we had any expectation of getting.

In the powwow that followed, when there were no more candidates to read, all but Chris agreed with my choice.

He said, "I don't know. I kind of liked Brenda."

I said, "Because the feeling was mutual?"

"Please, I'm more professional than that. But I'm the one who has most of the scenes with her. And you do have this love-hate thing going between Jack and Mercedes."

"And where does the hate come in?" Fowler said.

I said, "Chris would hate it if Brenda doesn't get the part."

Chris persisted. "Then what about Rachael?"

"No," said Buzz.

The debate went on a little longer. Lew didn't take part in it, merely listened, but in the end, as we all knew we would, we looked to him for the final decision.

"Sign Sheri Davis," he said, and got up to go. "I have to be somewhere."

His exit was punctuated by the sound of my ringing cell phone. It was Henrik, and the call brought me back to unwelcome reality. While I was listening to the actresses and taking part in the give-and-take of the follow-up discussion, my mind had switched to the details of the movie business in which I was involved. I had conveniently managed to forget about the murder investigation and my being a person of interest.

Henrik said, "Porter Caulfield told me that he has agreed to take your case."

My case. Why did that jar me so?

"Henrik, are you sure I need—"

"You need," he said. "He mentioned he had given you his cell, but he wants you to have his home number, too. Isabel will give it to you. I'll check in with you later."

He got off, and Isabel came on and gave me the number.

Numbly I jotted it down on my script pages, remembering how not so long ago Henrik would have stayed on the phone and given me the number himself. But then not so long ago I wouldn't have needed a lawyer and there would have been no number to give me.

MEMO TO MAGGIE: When going around in circles, make sure the exit ramps are plainly marked.

I went home.

18

The next morning dawned in dismal shades of gray, which is just as fitting if you're going to attend a funeral. Or even if you're going to be the centerpiece of one.

As far as celebrity funerals went, it was well attended. I would have given it a three-star rating. Besides the truly famous personages, there were the usual gawkers, straining to see who else was there, and, of course, hoping to be seen by the other gawkers. There were those who came out of respect because they might have genuinely liked Allegra—it was possible—and those who showed up to make sure she was dead.

I probably fit into neither group, but since there wasn't a category for People Who Were Suspected of Having Killed the Deceased but Actually Didn't, I went anyway. I was innocent and I was damn well going to behave that way!

Besides, Lionel insisted I had to go. "It's good P.R.," he said.

"I thought you weren't interested in being my press agent anymore. *And* you still haven't told me why."

Lionel squirmed. "I'm not, and you're right. But someone's got to look out for you. You're such a babe in the woods."

Troy said, "With the emphasis on 'babe.'"

That was so uncharacteristic of him, at the time I wondered if he had gone back into the closet. But no. The chartreuse and lavender silk handkerchief in his breast pocket, and the carefully applied eyeliner, told me he was the same old Troy.

They accompanied me to the funeral, Troy chauffeuring us in his car, a cream-colored PT Cruiser, because my car *du jour,* a black beat-up Porsche with a missing right front fender, just didn't seem appropriate for the solemnity of the occasion.

Outside the funeral chapel, I saw the expected cluster of Lew, Fowler, Buzz, Chris, Ram, Lisa, and Ringo, along with a scattering of other cast and crew members. We greeted one another formally, and set about discussing the traffic en route, the weather, and the latest industry rumors, anything but Allegra. No one mentioned seeing me in the news, so I guess they didn't run the picture they took of me and Henrik. It was a relief to go inside and not have to keep up the unnaturally stilted small talk.

I chose a seat in a middle-row pew, and Lionel and Troy flanked me, swiveling in their seats to keep up a running commentary on recognizable celebrities.

"Johnny Depp, fifth row, other side," Lionel said with a leftward tilt of his head.

"I've got one Desperate Housewife and Denzel Washington right in back of her," was Troy's contribution.

"Nora Ephron, just coming in."

I said, "I didn't think writers counted."

They ignored me, of course.

"Yum, George Clooney," Lionel said.

"Yum-yum," Troy said.

"Shh!" someone said from behind us.

We shhed as the minister began intoning. His part of the service was blessedly short, with intervals of suitable organ music. Afterward, there were no family members called on to speak, possibly because none were there. I craned to look, but I couldn't tell if there were any mourners who might be relatives in the front pews.

It was then I spotted U.G. and Mitzi up front. Mitzi was clad all in purple, looking somewhat like a ripe, plump eggplant. Hadn't I read somewhere that in Victorian England deep purple was the color for mourning clothes, especially at the death of a royal personage? U.G. was in a dark suit and purple tie and kept a comforting arm around his companion's heaving shoulders.

I hadn't seen Mitzi and U.G. since I left them at that restaurant in Malibu. They were wearing coordinating colors. Was this a date? Does going to a funeral together even constitute a date? Or had they been seeing each other regularly right along? I had no clue. U.G. hadn't said anything more to me about her. But then again he was always very circumspect about his women friends. I guess he was an adherent to the "Don't ask, don't tell" philosophy.

For a moment I felt something close to sympathy for Mitzi. She had lost someone she held to be a friend. The rest of us had come here to grieve for no one. Allegra had merely been one of Hollywood's many creations projected on a screen in a darkened theater.

The moment passed.

The minister then asked if there was anyone who would like to say a few words about the departed. Troy and Lionel both put restraining hands on my arms to keep me from rising.

"I wasn't going to say anything!"

"Shh!" someone said from in front of us.

Lew rose and delivered a carefully modulated eulogy. It wasn't exactly a campaign speech—after all, he did mention Allegra several times—but it veered perilously close to extolling his own virtues as much as his late star's.

Then came the moment, always dreaded by me, when, the service concluded, we were asked to come forward, row by row, and file past the open casket. Lionel pushed me ahead of him, making sure I wasn't going to bolt. Well, he couldn't prevent me from keeping my eyes closed, I thought. But when I reached the casket, I couldn't help myself. I stole a glance.

The morticians, the makeup people, someone, had done a masterful job with her head. Except for being dead, Allegra looked to be in perfect health.

I stopped and gazed at her for so long that Lionel had to nudge me forward with a whispered, "My turn!"

Once outside, I remained at the top of the chapel steps, deliberately staying clear of the other people from the movie. My aim was to avoid the actual burial and get into our car as fast as possible. The latter part was difficult inasmuch as Troy's Cruiser was securely lodged in the midst of a long procession of parked vehicles. I noticed that U.G.'s distinctive yellow Hummer was at the front of the line.

To heighten my impatience, Lionel and Troy were once again indulging in a spate of celebrity spotting. I paid restless inattention.

"Will Ferrell . . . over there . . ."

"I see Lindsay Lohan. . . ."

"Jessica Alba. . . ."

"And look who's with Jack Nicholson. . . ."

That jolted me. *"Who!?"*

Lionel said, "I think it's Naomi Watts."

"Not *her*! *Him!*"

Lionel was aggravatingly nonchalant. "Oh, you mean Jack Nicholson."

"Yes, I mean Jack Nicholson! Where?"

"He's just going down the steps. See him?"

I did. This was my chance and I was not going to let him get away. Jack had been my idol, my hero, okay, my obsession, for ages. If I had been a teenager and had a hallway locker, he would have been my pinup inside. I had a kind of relationship with him—very tenuous and very long-distance, true, but, nevertheless, a connection of sorts. If only I could catch up with him now and come face-to-face with those signature dark glasses, it would make this whole funeral worth having gone to.

Eagerly I started after him, running down the steps and jostling my way through the crowd. I was actually gaining on him when suddenly:

"Ms. Mars. How nice to see you."

There looming in front of me were Detectives Perez and Jordan.

I said, "Hi, but you'll have to excuse me. I'm in a hurry."

"Not to leave, I hope," Rita Perez said. "You can't get out of here till the cars start moving."

"I was . . . hoping to catch up with someone."

"Then we won't detain you."

I started off.

"Ms. Mars!"

I stopped, turned back.

"Stick around where we can get in touch with you, okay?" said Detective Jordan.

Not okay. I didn't like the sound of that.

Rita said, as though reading my mind, "Just a friendly word to the wise. Oh . . . and do say hello to Joe for me."

I left them and kept going, my thoughts in turmoil inside. Joe had asked me to move in with him. Why wasn't I feeling more secure? I berated myself. Why did I let Detective Rita have this unsettling effect on me? Then I recalled that she had walked in on Joe and me embracing. Was her remark payback? Yes! I gave a small fist pump.

Suddenly I remembered. Jack Nicholson! Wildly I looked around. Gone. He was nowhere to be seen.

Lionel came up. "Troy and I are going to wait in the car."

"Did you see where he went?"

This time Lionel had the grace not to ask me who.

"He was picked up in a limo. Even longer than the hearse. Very impressive, I must say."

"Why didn't you tell me!"

"I would have, but you were engrossed with the gendarmes."

I sighed.

Lionel put a comforting arm around me. "Don't despair, darling. There'll be other funerals."

I'm sure he didn't mean to be prophetic. But, later, those words came back to haunt me.

19

After struggling through the dreadful traffic and a stop for dinner we arrived home later that night to find Joe sitting on the condo doorstep. He stood up as we approached.

"Hey," I said, which was a prosaic replacement for running into his arms and staying there.

"Aren't you going to ask me in?"

"We're not in ourselves yet," Troy said, literal minded as always.

Lionel unlocked the door. "How come you didn't let yourself in?"

Joe said, "I would have, but I left my warrant in my other pants."

He looked at me. I wondered if he knew that the mention of his pants sent a shiver through me.

I said, "We were at Allegra's funeral."

He nodded. "Figured."

"Well," Lionel said. "The door's open. You going to do something about it?"

As I moved to enter, Joe touched my arm. "We need to talk. Can we do it in there?"

I said, "It's a little full-house right now."

"Then let's go sit in my car."

Lionel said, "Troy and I can take in a movie. Is two hours enough time?"

"Stay put," I said. "I'll be back in a few minutes."

"A few minutes?" Lionel said. "My illusions are shattered!"

He and Troy went inside. I followed Joe downstairs to his car, which was parked just a little down the street. He opened the passenger side door for me, and, just to be perverse, I slid over behind the wheel. Joe shrugged, got in beside me, and cracked the window a bit.

I waited for his opening gambit, but the silence lengthened between us. As usual, it was up to me.

I said, "I guess this is about your wanting an answer."

"I don't want to rush you, but you've had a couple of days."

"And I appreciate it. Maybe I could have concentrated on it if the small matter of a murder hadn't occurred. But it did and I haven't."

"So. Concentrate."

I took a deep breath. "I can't move in with you, Joe."

"How about if I give you a few more days?"

I smiled. "Joe, you're a police officer. You know what's going on. As long as they have me labeled as a person of interest, you shouldn't get involved any more closely."

"Hell, I know you didn't whack her."

I grimaced. "Thank you. No, I didn't 'whack' her, but I need to be able to prove my innocence without any shackles you might put on me."

"I wasn't planning on putting shackles on you, but that's an interesting idea. Kinky but interesting." He reached out to touch my shoulder. "Maggie, you've always been your own kind of off-limits investigator. I can't remember you letting my being a cop get in your way."

I nodded. "I know . . . but, Joe, please believe that this is just not the right time to take our relationship a step farther."

It was one of the hardest things I ever had to do, saying this to him. But I knew I was right. I had to keep him out of this. I simply could not embroil him in my problems, because that might damage his career and I couldn't live with that guilt. It was bad enough that my career seemed to be circling the drain.

"So you're backing out," he said.

"I'm not backing out! If you and I are meant to happen, we will. We can handle some time off, right?"

He didn't say anything.

"Joe?"

More silence.

"Okay," I said. "Good night, then."

I reached for the door handle, but before I could get it open Joe reached for me and kissed me long and hard.

He said, "How about we continue this inside?"

Coming up for air, I said, "I told you, we can't."

"Fine. Then we'll do it here."

And we did. Don't ask how. We didn't even bother to get in the backseat. Fortunately, we didn't have to deal with a center console. There was a lot of unbuttoning and unzipping and removing inconvenient garments, and soon we were back in the same warm, sensual territory we had visited so many times before. . . .

I guess I was in the mood for some great sex, and it was good. Very good. That is, if you don't count the position—definitely not one recommended in the Kama Sutra—and if you don't mind being pinned against the steering wheel and the horn blowing and blowing and blowing. . . .

20

So Joe and I are like on hold," I said to the fascinated audience of Lionel and Troy the following morning.

Lionel said, "And you're cool with it?"

"Perfectly cool."

"You're so full of bull," said Mercedes.

"What about that horn tooting?" Troy said.

I ignored both of them.

"Anyhow, what I have to do now is find out who killed Allegra, so I can clear myself."

Troy said, "It woke the whole neighborhood."

"Well," said Lionel. "There's always Heinrich. Not that he's much of a consolation prize."

"Henrik," I said for the millionth time. "And Joe and I aren't through. We're just taking a break."

Lionel said, "Maggie, sweet naïve Maggie, don't you know what's going to happen now?"

"No, but you're going to tell me, aren't you?"

"That lady dick you told me about—if that isn't a contradiction in terms—Rita what's-her-name."

"Perez, and she has nothing to do with this."

"There were dogs barking up and down the street," Troy said. "I felt like barking myself."

Lionel said, "Will you stop about the horn already? You know perfectly well what she and Joe were doing."

"Oh," said Troy. "That."

"If you're implying that Joe will pick up where he left off with Rita . . ."

Lionel shrugged. "If the implication fits . . ."

The phone rang.

"They're ancient history," I said, and hoped I sounded as confident as I didn't feel. "Are you going to get that?"

The phone rang again. Lionel picked it up.

"Well, hello, how are you? . . . Just scrumptious, thank you. The weather good? . . . I'm so glad. Here, it's a tad nippy. . . . Well, we went to this marvy funeral yesterday. . . . Uh-huh. . . . Uh-huh. . . . Uh-huh. . . . It's lovely talking to you, too. . . ." He held out the phone to me. "It's for you."

Shooting him an exasperated glare, I grabbed it away from him. "Hello."

It was Griffin Grace, Senior Articles Editor at *Vanity Fair*, for whom I had worked on several major investigative pieces.

After an exchange of catching-up chatter, he said, "Maggie, I've got a job for you."

I might have known Gracie could smell a good story from three thousand miles away.

"The Allegra Cort murder, right?"

"Will you do it? I'm planning on a multi-parter, maybe over three issues."

"I'd love to, Gracie—"

"The contract will be in the mail."

"You didn't let me finish. Only I can't."

"Can't? That word has never been in your vocabulary."

"I'm a person of interest. I'm involved."

"All the better," he said. "We've never run an article written by the murderer."

I knew Gracie well enough to figure he was joking. At least I hoped he was.

"Gracie, I'll be only too willing to write the story when they find out who did it."

For several seconds there was nothing from his end, and then: "I'm not sure our readers will want to wait that long."

"Tease them. Let them know it'll be a blockbuster of an article. With a star-studded cast."

His sigh was audible. "Tell you what, Maggie. I'll handle it my way. Give me a call when you're cleared."

There was the usual closing exchange of good wishes, and I hung up.

Of course I had to explain to the guys, and of course Lionel's opinion was that I shouldn't have turned down the job.

"Lionel, you do understand that my top priority is clearing myself."

"And you will, my darling. With my help."

Inwardly I groaned, but I managed to tack a grateful smile on my face.

"Mine, too," said Troy.

Double groan.

Lionel said, "Okay, enough chitchat. We'd better get a move on, or we'll be late."

"Late for what?"

Troy said, "Mitzi's show. She invited you, too. You know, to be in the audience."

"Actually, it was Ugh who called to invite us," Lionel said. "Very uncharacteristic of him to be that thoughtful, but so be it. He must think she's going to put a curse on us if we don't come."

Troy said, "Do psychics do that?"

"No, they don't," I said. "When did U.G. call?"

"He called last night while you were outside doing Joe. Troy was supposed to tell you, only he forgot."

Troy said, "I didn't forget. *You* were supposed to tell her."

They were still arguing about it all the way to the TV studio on Cahuenga Boulevard in Hollywood, with me feeling like Lewis Carroll's Alice, tugged between the irresistible Red Queen and the immovable White Queen.

The only reason I came along was because Mitzi had been Allegra's more-or-less guru. Her spiritual advisor. Perhaps I could get some information from her, learn something to my advantage. I was still not prepared to be a believer in her so-called occult abilities, but, as always, when I was investigating, I never knew where and when I would spot the first dangling thread. The thread that if I picked at it long enough would unravel the whole mystery.

I only hoped that the thread didn't somehow work its way around my own neck. . . .

21

Once inside the TV studio we found seats down front, leaving one empty for when U.G. would join us. I surveyed the other members of the audience, curious to know what Mitzi's fans were like. The studio was fast filling up and was about evenly divided between women and men, all of whom seemed in a high degree of expectancy, like the sightseers at the Crystal Cathedral. It surprised me that Mitzi would do her "thing" in the format of a TV show rather than a call-in radio program, but now that I was there, even I felt a prickling of edgy anticipation.

Troy said, "Lionel, are you going to ask Mitzi about you-know-who?"

"I may," said Lionel.

That maddened me. "You-know-who again! What is going on, Lionel?"

"Well, if you must know, and you being a chick dick, I suppose you'll find out—"

I didn't find out, at least not at that moment, because just then U.G. joined us.

"Hey. Great. You girls made it. You, too, Maggie."

I gave my father a warning look, which, of course, registered not a bit. What could you expect from a former high school chemistry teacher who had once blown up a lab? Three thousand miles away and several years later, he was still bound to walk heavily and carry a lit fuse. I moved over to make room for him.

He remained standing in the aisle. "I'll catch up with you later," he said. "I'll be backstage helping out Mitzi."

Well, that was new information. "You're helping Mitzi? How? Clueing her in on people in the audience?"

He patted my hand. "O ye of little faith. Who knows, Mitzi may even tell Snow White here," with a nod toward Lionel, "that someday his prince will come."

Lionel looked around him in exaggerated bewilderment. "Did somebody say something? I thought I heard a familiar croak." He focused on U.G. "My mistake, it was nobody."

Troy giggled.

"Lionel, U.G., behave yourselves," I said out of futile force of habit.

U.G. hustled off. The room was abuzz now with excited murmurs of conversation, and I directed my attention to the set, which was partially blocked by two huge TV cameras. A monitor screen perched above, dangling from a skein of wires, gave everyone an unobstructed view.

The set itself was hardly a set. There was a floral-patterned upholstered armchair, and alongside that was a small table. Fairly unimaginative, I thought. No Oriental drapes, no flickering candles, no crystal ball.

As I watched, U.G. came onstage and placed a pitcher and a glass on the table.

"Well, that's certainly an important job," Lionel said. "Water boy to Harry-etta Potter."

U.G. walked off, and a tall, blond man, wearing a shiny brown business suit, emerged from the wings and held up his hand for silence. He had teeth too white to be real and a face beloved by his plastic surgeon. Presumably, he was the announcer, and except for an almost collective intake of breath, there was instant quiet. Well, that was certainly magic.

"Hi, everyone," he said. "Welcome to our show. How are you all doing today?"

Exclamations of "Fine!" . . . "Wonderful!" . . . "Not too bad!" and similar expressions could be heard.

"That's what I like to hear. Now settle back and make yourselves comfortable, because you're in for a treat. No, we are not serving ice cream and cookies. . . ."

There was a ripple of laughter.

". . . It's something even better, and it's not as fattening."

Laughter again. I looked over at Lionel and Troy. Along with everyone else, they were paying rapt attention. It was as though I were seated in the audience at a taping of *Deal or No Deal.*

For several seconds I lost track of what the announcer was saying, and I tuned in again as he said, "You are about to be enlightened, entranced, and enthralled . . . you are about to be mystified, mesmerized, and magnetized by . . ."

Here he paused for dramatic effect, and the audience pitched right in.

"Mitzi! Mitzi! Mitzi!" the shout arose and swelled.

"The *A*-mazing Mitzi!" he said.

Mitzi appeared to the accompaniment of an eruption of enthusiastic applause. She wore a flowing black chiffon gown, long sleeved and high necked, set off by a gold necklace with a star-shaped pendant. The look of it briefly teased my mind and then it struck me. Except that it didn't have a splashy fuchsia print, it reminded me of what Allegra had been wearing when I last saw her. Determinedly I shook off the image.

"Thank you all for being here today," Mitzi said. "I'm delighted to see you. But, of course, I did sense you were coming, didn't I?"

This, too, elicited a burst of laughter.

The announcer began again, explaining the format of the

show. We could look forward, it seemed, to call-ins from the viewers at home, along with questions from those in the studio audience.

"And, please," said Mr. Entertainer, "positively no asking for the winner of next year's World Series, Super Bowl, Final Four, or the Kentucky Derby!"

Predictably, that drew forth mock groans and expressions of disappointment.

The announcer again held up his hand for silence. When all was quiet, a booming voice from the overhead speakers said, "Here we go . . . five, four, three, two . . ."

There was a fanfare of taped music.

"Ladies and gentlemen . . ." the announcer said, "please welcome . . . the *A*-mazing Mitzi!"

The half hour flew by smoothly and, at least for me, unamazingly.

Mitzi told one telephone caller-in, "You will soon gain something you have always desired." What? A new job? A husband? Some weight? Mitzi didn't get specific. She told another, "The one you are thinking of will visit you when you least expect it." Now that could be either a stroke of good luck or an unmitigated disaster.

A gentleman with a foreign accent asked Mitzi whether he should take the new job he had just been offered. She gave him an unequivocal no, saying the financial rewards were great but that it would lead to "unforeseen consequences." I hoped the poor guy wasn't looking to get into politics.

In the second half of the program, the announcer came out again and stated that Mitzi would now answer a few questions from the studio audience. Immediately a sea of waving hands surged up around me. U.G. reappeared and came down into the center aisle with a handheld microphone. He gave it to a middle-aged man a few rows behind me.

The man said, "Mitzi, I'm engaged to be married, but I'm not sure if I should go through with it. What do you think?"

Mitzi put up a stilling hand. "You have doubts because you have just suffered a great loss. The passing of a loved one."

The fellow was obviously flabbergasted. "Yes! My mother! Is . . . is she resting in peace where she is?"

Mitzi said, "She is peaceful, but she worries about you."

The man visibly paled. "I knew it. She doesn't want me to marry Carole, does she?"

"She would never stand in your way," Mitzi said. Not likely, I thought, buried and gone as she is. "But be certain, be very certain, of what you are about to do. I see a rock-strewn path ahead."

U.G. next gave the microphone to a woman who was obviously distraught, clutching a handkerchief to her tear-strewn face.

Before the woman could utter a word, Mitzi said, "Something is troubling you. . . ."

Big deal. The Amazing, Mystifying Maggie could have divined that.

"I see a circle . . . a gold circle. . . ."

"It's my wedding ring," the woman said. "I've lost it and I can't find it. I've looked everywhere. It's gone."

"This ring has special meaning for you, doesn't it?" Mitzi said.

Duh, it *was* a wedding ring.

"Especially because of something that is going to take place tomorrow. . . ."

"Yes! My husband is in the hospital. He's going to have surgery tomorrow."

"You fear that the loss of your marital ring is an omen of ill luck. That you will be a widow soon."

The tears streamed anew. "Yes! Yes!"

Mitzi placed her hand over her forehead, closed her eyes, and for a moment was utterly silent. "I see your ring," she said. "It is a plain gold band set with a half circlet of diamonds—"

"Yes! Yes! That's it!"

More silence, and then: "I see it lying on the floor covered by a small, fuzzy rug or mat—"

"A mat?" the woman said. "Of course! I must have dropped it in the bathroom and somehow it got under the mat. Oh, thank you, Mitzi, thank you!"

"Your husband will soon recover. Good health and happiness await you both."

That was greeted with cheers and applause from the audience.

"She's good," Troy said.

"Probably got her start writing fortune cookies," I said, refusing to be awed.

I suddenly became aware that U.G. was alongside me, thrusting that cursed microphone right in my face.

"Go away!" I said in as inconspicuous a whisper as I could manage.

U.G. said, low, "Come on, Maggie. Don't make me look bad."

Lionel poked me. "Don't take it. What if the cops see you when it's aired?"

U.G. said, "So what if the cops see her? She's innocent."

Now the people seated near us were straining to hear more, and Mitzi was showing her impatience onstage.

Again, U.G. waggled the microphone under my nose. I was still incensed, but I took it.

Mitzi said, "Your name . . . An inner voice is telling me that it begins with an M. . . . Am I right?"

Big deal. She already knew who I was. But the audience was gaping at me, waiting for confirmation, and I could see myself looking pathetic on the overhead monitor. I nodded.

"I sense you are deeply troubled," Mitzi said. "I see dark clouds swirling around you. . . . Do you have a question for me?"

I couldn't believe this. What the hell kind of position was she trying to put me into?

Lionel poked me again and shook his head violently.

I glared at him.

"Yes," I heard myself say. "I have a question." I drew a deep breath. "I am involved in a very serious matter. One that could change the whole course of my life. Will it be cleared up?"

Again, Mitzi's hand went to her forehead, but instead of closing her eyes, she stared off somewhere into the middle distance.

"You are in great danger," she said. "I see death all around you." And now she looked straight at me and shuddered. "There will be another one."

There was a loud gasp from someone in the audience.

I managed to stay through the rest of the show, but only because my head was still reeling from Mitzi's pronouncement. When it was over, I shook off Lionel's clutch and headed for the exit. Lionel and Troy scurried to keep up with me.

In the parking lot, as we closed in on our car, Lionel said, "Calm down. You don't believe in that poppycock—you said so yourself."

"She didn't answer my question," I said, knowing full well how unreasonable that was.

I climbed in behind the wheel, just as U.G. came running up.

"Hurry. Get in," I told the others.

But U.G. was at my window before I could start up.

"Maggie! Don't go away mad!"

"Did you hear what she said!?" I flung it at him.

"It doesn't mean anything," U.G. said. "That was just for effect."

"Effect?"

"It's what they call showbiz."

If U.G. meant that to soothe me, it had just the opposite result.

"You mean she used me as a . . . a . . . a teaser? It'll look good in the reruns, is that it?"

U.G. reached in to pat my shoulder. "It's all part of the show. Allegra didn't get upset when Mitzi told her . . ." He stopped. "Well, you'd better get going if you want to beat the traffic."

I wasn't going anywhere. "When Mitzi told her what?"

"Nothing."

"You mean Allegra was on her program?"

"Of course not. You heard that Allegra consulted her many times in her professional capacity. As a spiritual advisor."

"What did Mitzi tell—" Suddenly I realized. "Mitzi told Allegra she was going to die, is that it?"

He nodded weakly. "Well, not in so many words."

"How come you didn't mention that to me before?"

"I'm mentioning it now. What the hell difference does it make?"

"For one thing," I said, "Allegra did die."

I drove off and left him standing there.

"You sure told him," Lionel said.

Small consolation indeed.

We headed home with all sorts of disjointed thoughts tumbling around in my mind. Did Mitzi, mystifying or not, figure in Allegra's murder? I had a feeling Mitzi was genuine in her regard for her actress friend, but I knew I would have to check her out.

There would be another death, she had said. . . . Another death. The question was, whose?

22

The following day was Sunday, and the set was closed. Buzz and Chris were going to work with Sheri, rehearsing her upcoming scenes, which were crucial to the movie. They were using an empty sound stage at the studio, and wanted me around for script changes, if any were needed. Fine with me. I didn't want to be alone with my thoughts anyway. I threw my laptop into the trunk of the beat-up Porsche and headed for the studio.

Pulling in through the gate, I had to park a long way away from Sound Stage Two, which was where we were rehearsing. All the close spaces were reserved for really important people like Sheri's hairdresser and Chris's two—count 'em, two—assistants. Peasants like me had to forage for ourselves.

Going around to the rear of the car, I opened the trunk and found that my laptop was wedged in the back of the trunk, caught on a torn corner of the floor mat. Damn! Either my arms were too short or this trunk was really deep. I climbed up on my knees on the edge of the trunk, leaned in, and managed to free my laptop by giving it a big jerk.

Suddenly, before I knew what was happening, I fell forward into the trunk and the trunk lid slammed shut.

My first reaction was disbelief. This couldn't be happening to me! I put no stock in the idea that Allegra's spirit was haunting me, but maybe when I got out of here it wouldn't hurt to ask Mitzi.

"You would ask Mitzi?" Mercedes said. "Girl, you must really have hit your head."

I felt all around for some kind of inside device that would open the trunk, but either there wasn't one or it eluded my probing fingers. I had only one recourse and that was to scream for help. I did. I screamed and screamed and screamed. But the sounds just reverberated around the inside of the trunk and I knew I couldn't be heard outside. German engineering! It would have to be so damn good!

My laptop was digging into my waist, and I couldn't move it because of my contorted position. My thought was that maybe I could send an SOS e-mail to the set, but I couldn't budge my laptop open. Meanwhile, the trunk lid, only inches above my head, seemed to be coming down lower and lower. Can you spell claustrophobia!

Panic set in and my body began to shake uncontrollably. I started another round of screaming. Nothing.

I wondered what it was going to be like to die. What would people think, what would they say, when they found my body in the trunk of the car clutching my laptop? Would Jack Nicholson come to my funeral? Probably not.

What about Rita Perez? Would she attend?

"Damn right," said Mercedes.

I had to get out of there and pronto.

Now something was digging into my other side. Painfully scraping my fingers in the process, I managed to get my right hand around it and found myself holding on to a tire iron! Thank you, God, for small favors and a Transportation Department that didn't neatly put away tools.

I began pounding on the inside of the trunk lid with the tire iron. There wasn't enough room to swing the iron and really bang, so I had to be satisfied with the small tapping, scraping sounds I made.

As if I were trying to dig myself out of prison. Or out of a grave in which I had been buried alive.

Exhaustion swept over me. I rested a few minutes and my thoughts, such as I could gather, went back to that instant before I fell into the trunk. I didn't fall in, I suddenly realized; someone pushed me! Dimly I seemed to remember hands pushing on my rear end. Or was it my fevered imagination? No! Someone had definitely pushed me!

Just then, I heard loud, very loud, noises outside. There was a band playing a Sousa march; people were shouting and screaming. I heard the sounds of marching feet, drums banging, and a calliope! A calliope? What was going on? Had this car, with me in it, been flown on a magic carpet to a fantasyland circus, or was I hallucinating? That was it, of course. My blood sugar was low and I was hallucinating.

I was even hallucinating now that I heard a car door open and close. My car? I caught my breath, the shaking had stopped, and I started yelling again at the top of my poor lungs, which were getting more and more desperate for air.

"Help! Help! Help!" Anger was mixed with fear and my voice had renewed strength.

I shouted and shouted, but I couldn't compete with the marching band, or the band marching in my head.

The engine turned on, and the car started forward. Someone was driving me somewhere. I couldn't be making that up. The car drove for about five minutes over a smooth road. The band noise was receding. Summoning all my vocal power, I started yelling again and making my wimpy, mewling scratches with the tire iron.

The car stopped and I heard a voice. "Is someone in there?"

"Yes! I'm locked in this damn trunk! Get me out of here!"

"Oh my God! Is that you, Ms. Mars?" It was Eric's voice! The security guard.

"Eric, please get me out of here!"

There was another voice saying, "I'll get the key!"

Soon, miraculously, a shaft of light and a gust of air. The trunk had been opened and I was never so grateful to see anyone in a rent-a-cop suit.

23

Eric reached in and helped me out. Dimly, I realized that we were alongside the studio gate. I couldn't stand erect for the moment, so, all hunched over, I said, "Where's the driver? Who was driving this car?"

The property manager was standing in front of me, with an embarrassed look on his face.

"I was, Ms. Mars. I saw the car parked with no one in it, and I thought I'd better move it out of the way 'cause there was a carnival scene rehearsing back there. I didn't know you were in the trunk. What were you doing in the trunk?"

Good question.

"Was this another Jessica Fletcher thing?" Eric said.

Bad question.

I managed to straighten up, to the accompaniment of a few groans, just as Chris Balboa came up to us.

"Maggie, what is going on?" Chris said. "We've been looking for you. Why aren't you at the rehearsal?"

"Can I take the car now?" the property manager said. "I need to garage it and get it ready for its next scene."

"You can't take it anywhere," I said. "That car is a crime scene, and the police need to see it, and test it, and do some forensic work."

"Crime scene? What crime?" Eric said.

"Someone shoved me in that trunk and tried to kill me," I said.

"Huh?"

"Someone pushed me in when I was reaching to get my laptop."

"Oh, come on, Maggie, you're imagining things," Chris said. "Why would someone want to push you into a trunk? It must have been an accident."

"We've used this car in a lot of chase scenes and it's gotten pretty banged up," the property manager said. "The trunk latch is probably defective."

"You could've hit your head when you fell in," Eric said, not too helpfully.

"I didn't fall in! I was pushed!"

"Well, anyway," Eric said, "we're blocking the gate. We've got to move this car."

I was still shaken from my experience, but I was firm. "Drive it over to the side and see that someone stays with it until the police come."

The prop man nodded and got into the car.

"And don't touch the trunk!"

I could see him shaking his head as he moved the car to where it would be out of the way. He'd probably had enough of crazy writers.

"Did whoever pushed you, if anyone did, get into the car at all?" Chris said.

"How in hell do I know?" I said. "But it's a crime scene. Someone tried to murder me and I'm calling the police."

Chris eyed me dubiously. "I'd better get back to the set," he said, and strode away.

It was then that I had second thoughts about calling the police. I had no proof of anything. Would they think I was making this

120

up to deflect suspicion from myself? Well, screw them, I was *not* making this up. Someone pushed me. I could have died in that trunk!

I went to an open spot where I knew my cell phone could get out, and called Porter. I waited, under Eric's still-puzzled gaze, and Porter called back in three minutes. Got to love a man like that!

"Porter! Someone just tried to kill me," I said.

As I knew he would, he asked me to tell him all about it and not leave out any details. I told him my story, rushing a bit because I'm always afraid the cell phone will conk out and the call will drop.

When I finished, there was silence on the line. Oh, God, the call was dropped and I didn't know when it happened. "Hello! Are you there?"

"Yes, I'm here," Porter said. "Are you hurt?"

"Just my pride," I said, thinking of the pain in my side and the crick in my back and neck, not to mention the bloody fingertips.

"Okay. Let me call the deputies and tell them about this. I don't want you talking to them right now. Where will you be?"

"On Sound Stage Two for the rest of the day."

I went to the sound stage, and rehearsal continued without anyone commenting on what had happened to me, although I was certain Chris had told them. I knew that he was beginning to doubt my sanity, but I wasn't. Someone had shoved me into that damn trunk and I was going to discover who did it or die trying.

Bad image, so scratch that.

But I had come through. It was a close call, but I had survived. I had hopes that this dispelled Mitzi's prediction, never dreaming that my hopes would soon be dashed by stark reality.

24

The rehearsal went along as well as could be expected. Buzz seemed to have everything under control, and Sheri, bless her, read her lines as written. Once or twice, when something didn't work for her or for the continuity, I made the changes and we moved on without a hitch.

If only the traumatic experience I had just undergone and Mitzi's forecast about another death didn't prey on my mind, I would have been that rarest of the breed—a happy writer.

When there was nothing specific for me to do, I took advantage of the respite and talked to some of the other cast and crew members. I didn't exactly put on my old investigative hat, but I did try to glean some information about Allegra. I was sure her murder and the attempt on my life were connected.

It was from Lily Barrett, our wardrobe mistress, that I learned that Allegra had left three ex-husbands in her wake.

Lily was one of the old-timers in the business, a woman of indeterminate middle age, fleshy in all the wrong places, with flyaway gray hair and a harried look. She was there refitting outfits for Sheri's more buxom figure, and in between stints at her sewing machine she was only too happy to gossip away.

"She had no trouble getting men to marry her. Three times!" Lily said. "It doesn't seem fair, does it? I mean when decent women like me can't get any?"

"That's the way it is sometimes," I said. "Are they still around?"

"Who? The exes? Not likely."

"I don't mean around here. I mean—did she still see them?"

"She told me two of them were dead. I guess she wore them out."

"Know anything about them?"

"Only that they were older men and left her lots of money."

"And the third? You said there were three."

She shrugged. "I think he was the last one. You could always look it up."

"Right. I will. Thanks."

She bit off a piece of thread from the seam she was taking in. "I guess you're nosing around, huh, because the cops think you did it?"

"Well, I didn't," I said.

"Wouldn't blame you in the least," Lily said. "You deserve a medal."

That got me to wondering whether Lily might have struck the fatal blow. Jealous because Allegra had more than her share of men? It was hardly a reason for murder to consider seriously, and I doubted if Lily had pushed me in the trunk, but desperate situations called for desperate solutions.

I wandered around some more and gleaned a few other snippets of information but nothing mind-blowing. What I found was a surplus of motives to do away with Allegra Cort but a lack of suspects who might have actually killed her.

Maybe it was a gang murder, I thought. Maybe the whole crew concocted a plot to do her in. Maybe they drew straws and the one who got the shortest was sent in to finish her off and none of the others knew who that was. . . .

MEMO TO MAGGIE: Don't believe everything you think.

I shook my head to clear it.

"You've certainly been a busy little snoop," someone said.

I looked around to see Ram coming up behind me. He was holding out an open bag of potato chips.

"Thanks, Ram." I helped myself to a handful.

"Learn anything?"

I shook my head. "How about you? Can you tell me anything new and noteworthy about Allegra?"

"Only that I didn't kill her."

"Did you want to?"

"Sure. But I was very good at restraining myself."

We found a couple of apple boxes and sat down on them, munching companionably on the potato chips.

"Do you know anything about her ex-husband? The most recent one?"

"Manu."

"What?"

"That's his name. Manu de la Rua. An Argentinean. Ever hear of him?"

"Should I have?"

"Only if you follow the ponies."

"He's a jockey?"

Ram smiled. "I was referring to the polo ponies. He's a player."

"Nice," I said. "Sounds very romantic."

"I think the romance was in her money."

"You mean she supported him?"

He crumpled up the empty potato chip bag and pitched it into a nearby trash container. "Polo's a very expensive sport, and from what I hear, he lives in genteel poverty in Bad Venice."

Venice, California, like most other areas of California, is schizophrenic. There is a section of Venice, mostly on the canals, and on the shopping streets, that is lovely, well tended, and comparatively safe. That's Good Venice. There is another section that is run-down, ill kept, and more crime ridden. That's Bad Venice.

"So, yes, the likelihood is she supported him."

I thought about that. I knew I'd have to find Manu de la Rua and talk to him. Right now, though, there was something else Ram might be able to help me with.

"What do you know about Mitzi Elgin?" I said.

"Ahhh. Mystifying Mitzi. Sees all. Knows all. Have divining rod, will travel."

"Is she the real goods?"

"Allegra thought so. She didn't make a move without her." He got to his feet. "Hey, here's a thought. Maybe Mitzi can solve the crime for you."

I stood as well. "Only if she did it herself."

"Well, that's another thought," Ram said. "By the way, for what it's worth, I don't think you locked yourself in the trunk. It's just not your style."

25

The deputies arrived later in the day. Two fresh ones. Thomas and Westrup. Very politely, they asked to speak to me, and equally politely, I said I couldn't speak to them without my lawyer being present.

"We've talked to Detectives Jordan and Perez, and we've also talked to Chris Balboa, and our crime techs are examining the car now. Can you just tell us what happened?"

Oh, what the hell. How could that hurt?

So I did. At length. When I was done, they thanked me even more politely and said they would report this to the detectives and one or more of them would be contacting me soon.

They didn't believe me. I could tell.

I walked back onto the stage as rehearsal was ending, and cornered Chris.

"What exactly did you tell the deputies?" I said.

He had the smarts not to lie. "I told them that you were under a lot of pressure and maybe you were pushed and maybe you weren't. They knew about Allegra and I said that you were stressed out by being Suspect Number One. I also said you couldn't have killed her. What's wrong with that? For God's sake, it's all true."

I glared at him. "Who asked you for the truth? We're supposed to be friends!"

Before we wrapped that day, Buzz had an announcement. Tomorrow, Monday, we would move to Wilmington, where we would get on a yacht for shooting the next scenes. The yacht was rented long ago and couldn't be canceled without a heavy penalty, so the shooting schedule must be maintained.

"Don't take my word for it," Buzz said. "Take Lew's."

There was a knowing laugh at that. Everyone, crew and cast, knew how tight with a buck Lew Packard was. As for me, I wasn't looking forward to being in close quarters out at sea with a possible murderer on board, but then I realized others might be entertaining the same apprehension—only with me as the possible murderer!

26

When we broke for the day, I was told that for overnight transportation I could take an old green Buick, one of those with the holes on the sides. Before driving off in it, I had the mechanic check the car over, trunk included. It was a different mechanic, and he just shrugged when I asked him to do it. In Hollywood, I guess, everyone is used to loony requests.

I arrived home to be met by the welcoming sight of Lionel and Troy and dinner. My stomach was growling. My sugar levels were screwed up and I realized I hadn't really eaten all day. Lionel and Troy were all ears, anxious to know about the rehearsal and how Sheri was doing as Allegra's replacement.

With a wave of my hand, I said, "Later," and went into my room. I showered, changed, checked my blood sugar, and gave myself an insulin shot. Then I sat down to eat and finished my first helpings before I told my harrowing story about being locked in the trunk.

Troy was aghast. "Oh no! Mitzi was right! How could she have known?"

"Don't be a fool," Lionel said. "Mitzi didn't know anything.

She just talks in great big vague generalities that could apply to anything and anyone. Then the naïve believer, like you, does all the work, applying those generalities to the specifics that fit him—or her."

"Lionel, I heard her." Troy was persistent. "She told Maggie she was in danger. She saw death. Remember? She said so."

"Of course she said so. She knew Allegra. She was aware of what happened in that trailer. The whole world is aware." Lionel paused. "Do you think they'll have a sale of Allegra's personal items? She had some lovely caftans." He had a dreamy look on his face.

I interrupted this little exchange. "Well! Thanks for being so concerned about me. For all you care, I could have been severely injured, if not dead."

"No one who eats like you do is injured," said Lionel, who clearly wanted to return to the discussion of Allegra's caftans.

I left the table. They didn't notice I was gone.

In the living room, I sprawled out on the couch and called Porter. I wanted to call Joe, but I didn't have the energy for the conversation we needed to have. So, short-on-guts that I am, I avoided it.

Porter lit right into me. "You talked to the deputies," he said.

I was taken aback by the severity of his tone. "Okay, but I just told them what happened. I don't think they believed me."

"I told you not ever to speak to the police without me being there."

"I'm sorry. It didn't seem like a big deal."

"It could be a very big deal for you, Maggie. If it happens again, get another lawyer."

The couch got crowded. Both felines were in my lap. Lionel was perched on the couch arm, and Troy was on the floor in front of me. I had finally gotten their attention.

Porter continued. "Are we clear about this?"

"Yes."

"They are invested in finding Allegra's killer. No one saw you being pushed into the car—"

"But, Porter—"

"Don't interrupt, Maggie. No one claims to have been in the area at the time the 'event' happened. They just have your word for it. They don't believe you. I do. It's as simple as that."

"Okay, sorry, I've got it. And by the way, Porter, if you need to reach me in the next three days, I'll be at sea filming with the cast and crew."

"I'll notify the detectives," Porter said. "I don't anticipate any problem."

On that we hung up.

"I didn't hear the other end of the conversation," Lionel said. "But something tells me you could use a comfort drink. I'll get you some tea."

Off he went to the kitchen.

"Do you think . . . this could have been a prank?" Troy said tentatively. "Only it got out of hand?"

"Not a chance, Troy. Someone tried to kill me. Nobody seems to believe me except Porter—and it's his job to believe me."

"Lionel and I believe you," Troy said. "We know you wouldn't lie about this."

How sweet of him. "Thank you, Troy."

"About a lot of other things, yes."

I decided to ignore the modification. I said, "I need to clear myself. If I only had some idea how to do that."

"Why not call Mitzi," he said. "Maybe she could see who pushed you."

"Troy, please, for the last time. Her powers are bogus. She can't see any farther than you can." I got up to go to bed.

"I'm nearsighted," he said.

130

27

The next day dawned clear and sunny, without a cloud in the skies. Just as well. I had my own black cloud hanging over my head, like that guy in *Lil Abner* whose name was spelled in all consonants.

We met, that is, the crowd of us, in Wilmington, where the ships were docked. There was one sleek yacht that was for the actual shoot. It slept twelve people and had a crew of five, including a captain. I was one of the blessed, because I had a stateroom reserved for me on the yacht, so that I could attend sessions where the script was being adapted for the new star. The stateroom that was reserved for me was, unfortunately, not for me alone. I would be sharing it with someone else.

Then we had three smaller craft that were lugging film crew and equipment after us. We were cleared to sail from Wilmington to Catalina Island and back, but not directly. The sail time would depend on the footage we got, and the shooting schedule called for us to be at sea for three days, spending two nights aboard the ships.

We were all standing there on the pier, with various pieces of luggage scattered around us, when I was surprised to see Lisa Lindsey join us.

"What's she doing here?" I asked Buzz.

"Lew asked her to assist Sheri in her new starring role. I think he was just being kind, feeling sorry for her now that her former meal ticket is dead."

As for me, I had no sympathy for her. She was imbued with the poison spewed by Allegra, and was showing great promise filling her mentor's Gucci footwear, so that the world wouldn't be short one bitch.

Zack proceeded to pass out different-colored tags identifying each piece by owner, ship, and stateroom. I assumed it would all get to where it was supposed to be. That wasn't my job and I didn't spend any time worrying about it. My overnight case was small and easily replaced. Years of experience had taught me to keep my insulin and syringes in my handbag.

I wandered over to where a small catering wagon had been set up and was helping myself to a cup of decaf when Buzz came over.

"So, how're you doing, Maggie?" he said, with a hand on my shoulder.

"You mean, how am I doing considering I'm Public Enemy Number One?" I could have bitten back the words, but too late. My paranoia was showing yet again.

"No. That's not what I meant and you know it. Come on, lighten up. No one really thinks you offed Allegra."

"No one but the cops," I said.

He gave an uncertain laugh and moved over to where Lew was standing with Sheri.

I hadn't realized that Lew would be coming along for the shoot, but I guess it made sense. These shipboard scenes were the toughest ones to be shot for the film and they were critical to the story. Lew's new star had to walk a fine line, retaining plausibility and keeping the audience's empathy, without slopping over into the

132

extremes of farce or melodrama. Allegra could have pulled it off without a hitch, being a real pro. Unfortunately a dead pro.

It all translated into dollars and cents, and that was definitely Lew's bailiwick.

My thoughts were interrupted by the activity on the pier. Cameras and sound equipment were being loaded onto the three smaller ships, and the crew were going aboard with them. Luggage was also being carried onto the yacht, and it was then I noticed, for the first time, that she was called the *Prophecy*.

Shades of Mitzi! I felt a chill as I remembered *her* prophecy. All of a sudden I wished I could miss this trip. I turned, as though to tell someone thanks a lot but no thanks, I wouldn't be going after all, when Chris and Buzz came along, joined now by Fowler. They scooped me up along with them, over to the gangplank and aboard the *Prophecy*.

Even to my untrained eye, she was a beautiful ship. She looked like something Aristotle Onassis would have sailed to Antibes. She was all dark polished teakwood and shiny brass railings, with teakwood deck chairs covered in white terry cloth with sailor blue pillows. The rear portion of the main deck was open-air and roofed by a large sailor blue canvas. The crew, who came with the ship, were wearing their whites. All beautiful, neat, and welcoming.

I decided to go to my stateroom, which was down one flight of stairs and aft, according to the crew member who directed me. I think it's the rear end they call aft, but I'm not very knowledgeable about the correct nautical terms.

Finding my stateroom, I walked in, and there was Lisa. Lisa Lindsey. The one who had run to the cops with the story of my argument with Allegra.

"Don't you knock?" she said.

"I'm not in the habit of knocking on the door of my own room."

"You mean I'm sharing with you?"

"No, you are not sharing with me, and I am definitely not sharing with you!" I said. "Go talk to Fowler and get a cabin change."

"Right! And then I look like a whining creep."

"You won't get an argument from me."

Lisa got up and walked out. Over her shoulder, she said, "You are such a loser."

I flopped down on the bed that was mine by default, and bemoaned my fate. I remembered seeing *The Wizard of Oz* and I could picture mean Miss Gulch, who was Dorothy and Toto's nemesis. She was also the Wicked Witch of the West. And here I was, rooming with my own Wicked Witch of the *Prophecy*. I didn't ask myself what I must have done to deserve this, because I'm sure there was an alphabetical list of bad deeds starting with *A* for "Allegra."

In another moment I could feel the powerful motors throbbing, and soon the ship was under way. Well, I couldn't hide out here any longer.

I went into the bathroom—why it's called a head I have no idea—and washed my face and brushed my hair. Just then the door to the stateroom opened and in marched Miss Gulch.

"I'm outahere," she said.

Grabbing her overnight case, she left. Wow! Talk about having your prayers answered. A weight lifted off of my shoulders. I didn't care who moved in with me—as long as it wasn't Lisa. What sadistic person had put us together in the first place?

Lisa was definitely worth keeping my eye on for the rest of the trip.

I left my stateroom and went topside—at least that term made sense—and found the cast on the aft deck rehearsing the next scene. The channel was choppy, and I carefully made my way over to where Buzz and Fowler were sitting.

"How are we doing?" I said.

"Not bad. Glad you surfaced. I thought maybe you had mal de mer," Fowler said.

"Mal de Lisa," I said.

Indicating a chair next to his, Buzz went on with his directing, explaining to the actors how he wanted the scene played. Meanwhile, the cameras were being positioned and the lighting guy was busy taking measurements and squinting through lenses. I sat and watched.

It seemed to me that Sheri was doing quite well. She didn't have her lines down pat, but she was pretty good. Even Chris surprised me by being quietly wonderful. The rehearsal went on for about an hour, and then Buzz was ready to shoot.

The sky was still clear and the water was getting rougher. I sat there, relaxed, caught up in the artistry of the talent on board. Soon, however, I noticed that Sheri was looking slightly green around the gills. Buzz called, "Cut," and went up to her. Sheri had her hand to her mouth, and it was clear that she was seasick.

Immediately a roll call of remedies was offered. Pills and patches, ginger powder, wristbands—though what the wrist has to do with the stomach I can't imagine—and sticking to the middle of the boat. Most of these were more in the area of prevention than of cure. All I know is that if you're going to be sick over the railing, you'd better check the wind direction first.

I looked around for Lisa, but she was nowhere to be seen. I hoped she was seasick, too. I hoped she was puking her guts out.

28

We were given a short break, to give Sheri a chance to recover, and I wandered down the stairs and into the lounge area.

The color scheme here was the same nautical sailor blue and white. There were white marble tables and blue leather swivel chairs, all bolted to the floor. The wood was polished teak inlaid in a chevron pattern on the walls and floor. Behind the mirrored bar, a bartender was mixing Mojitos.

I shook my head no in answer to his silent query and went forward into the galley, where I found the chef preparing lunch. I watched him for a while, as he chopped up what looked to be a great salad à la La Scala. His name was Raul and he cheerfully asked if he could make me anything special. He ran down the possibilities for me, talking with his hands and waving the cleaver around. I decided on the salad, and left, munching on some carrots and celery.

I wandered the ship. There were twelve staterooms on three floors—sorry, decks. Besides the large lounge, where the bar was, there was a smaller lounge nearer to the main staterooms, which were occupied by Lew, Buzz, Chris, Sheri, and Fowler. Eventually,

I found my way back to my own stateroom and discovered that I had a new roommate.

Chris Balboa was sprawled out on my bed, with his feet hanging over the end, he was so tall.

"What are you doing here? Are you my new roommate?" I said.

He said, "No such luck. I needed to escape for a while and this seemed like the perfect spot. But I could stay awhile. Have you forgiven me for sticking up for you with the deputies?"

"You didn't have to say I was under stress."

"Why in hell not? You are. We all are." Well, he was right about that.

I sat down on the other bed, and he took this as an invitation to chat some more.

"I don't know, Maggie, am I nuts? I feel all this tension on the set. It's like everyone has their teeth clenched. It's hard to make love in front of the cameras through clenched teeth."

"Give it a little time," I said. "Sheri's new to all this."

"It's not just Sheri. It's everyone else. It's Buzz asking for unnecessary retakes, and Lew is enough to drive anyone crazy, and Zack keeps flitting around. I wish he'd light somewhere. And Lisa is so mournful, as if she resents our continuing to shoot the movie when Allegra's gone." He grabbed one of the carrot sticks I held out to him. "I swear she must bring up Allegra's name twice a minute as if the rest of us have already forgotten her, or would, if she didn't remind us of her, constantly."

"Well, I think they were pretty close, and—"

"Close, my ass. I think Allegra detested her. As a matter of fact, I think they actually detested each other. If you want my guess, I think Lisa bashed Allegra's head in."

I was taken by surprise. My mind began to zoom through the possibility that Lisa was the killer. True, she had been in the trailer that night. Had she returned after I left?

"Think about it, Maggie," Chris said, pursuing the point. "Anyone with half a brain knows you didn't kill her. Sure, you argued

137

with her. Hell, we all did. But to slug her over some words in a script is ludicrous. Every writer's dream maybe—but ludicrous. So why is Lisa so damn eager to let the cops know about your visit to the trailer and the fight? My theory, for what it's worth, is that Lisa did her in. Remember the Bard: 'The lady doth protest too much, methinks.'"

With that pronouncement, he put his arms behind his head, lay back, and grinned at me.

"I don't know why," I said, "but I never even considered Lisa as a possible murderer. I guess I bought into that 'I love my boss' bit."

"You should know by now. Allegra never loved anyone but herself, and Lisa learned at the master's knee." Chris hauled himself to his feet.

I said, "Chris, I really appreciate your vote of confidence. I've been getting paranoid, believing everyone has me pegged as the killer."

"Nah. The only ones who've pegged you into that slot are the guys behind the badges." On that cheery note, echoing my own thoughts, he left.

I thought over what he had said and wondered if he was trying just a little too hard to push Lisa as the murderer. And if so, why? Did he himself have something to hide?

Once again I remembered those rumors about him and Allegra. Could he have been waiting in Allegra's bedroom that night in the trailer? Maybe the man doth protest too much, as well.

29

I went to the lounge, noting that the weather had changed for the worse and the sea was unusually rough. Fowler and Buzz were there reviewing setups. I helped myself to a portion of the salad on the buffet table, and sat down with them.

Buzz said, "Are you okay with the heavy weather, Maggie?"

"As long as the deck stays horizontal."

My job was to remain at the computer, changing dialogue and reworking the story line as needed. By keeping busy and having my mind occupied, I wouldn't have time to think about my stomach doing flip-flops.

We stopped at midnight and I went to my stateroom to find my new roommate, the set decorator, Sarah Wiegel, already asleep in one of the beds. I undressed, took my shot, and fell into the other bed. Sarah snored lightly, but nothing, not even my stomach, could have kept me awake that night.

The next day was more of the same, but the weather held, not good but not worse, and the shooting was on schedule. We had to make a lot of changes to the script and Chris's bombshell indictment of Lisa was relegated to a far corner of my distracted attention.

At sunset, we finally docked in the Catalina harbor. The crew had gone ahead to set up for the night shooting, which was to be done at the old Avalon Ballroom, still standing but closed these many years. I had read about the glory days of the ballroom, when the big bands played and people danced all night and stars like Gable, Lombard, and Dietrich hung out at the bar, on shore visits from their yachts.

Looking at it from the deck of the ship, gazing at that huge, round, multi-windowed tower looking out to sea, I could almost hear the music of Glenn Miller drifting over the water as the sun set in all its glorious pinks, reds, and purples. "Tuxedo Junction" was playing in my head.

Shooting began inside the ballroom as soon as the cameras were set, and once again there was dialogue that needed some altering to fit Sheri. For the most part, she was finding her own way in the role, but she was actually very close to Mercedes as she lived and breathed in my script and in my mind.

We broke for an hour dinner, and some of the older guys on the crew were reminiscing about the times when they came to Avalon to dance the night away. I guess they were hearing Glenn Miller, too.

Shooting continued until almost midnight, when we wrapped. Fowler and Lew could see the scenes on the video cam and they were very pleased. The plan was to get back on board the ship, load up the crew and all the equipment, make sure everything and everyone was accounted for, and set off, but not for home. We needed to reshoot two of the scenes shot last night on board.

Buzz felt that we could sail north to give us more time, shoot the scenes, and when he and Lew were satisfied we would head south for home. Arriving in the morning would give us a full day on the set at our Malibu location. Not that I had any real say in the matter, but I was eager to agree and to get back home.

I was nervous as well about what awaited me, in the person of the detectives and, of course, Joe.

30

Buzz, Chris, and I stood on the dock watching the equipment being loaded. It seemed to be a form of chaos, albeit controlled chaos.

"Good work, Maggie," Buzz said. "It's not everyone who can work on the fly, and do it so well."

I said, "I find Sheri easy to work with. She's got her own natural style, which fits the character well, and she's not so insanely jealous of every other person who has a line to say."

"Meaning the way Allegra was, of course."

I chose not to say anything, remembering Mercedes' *nil nisi bonum* admonition. Still, if I couldn't speak ill of Allegra, then I would never ever again be able to mention her. As everyone in Hollywood knows, better to be spoken ill of than never to be spoken of at all.

Chris said, "Imagine how dreadful this trip would have been with La Diva here. I shudder to think of it."

None of us had noticed Lisa standing just behind us overhearing every word. At this statement by Chris she exploded.

"You are the worst dog shit Hollywood ever put into a movie!

Poor Allegra dies, and dies horribly, and all you can do is make fun of her, and talk about her as if she was the most horrible creature!"

Lisa was practically screaming, and the work on the dock all but slowed to a halt so the loaders could hear.

"And she was. She was," Chris said.

With that he strolled away, not even looking back, unafraid of curses from beyond. I admired his aplomb.

"You'll excuse me," Buzz said, and he, too, walked off.

Now Lisa turned her full wrath on me.

"And you, I don't even have words to describe how disgusting you are. All Allegra tried to do was to make your pathetic script better and you fought her on every little thing. And then, you killed her! I heard you threaten her!"

By now she had the attention of everyone within earshot, which included the crew of the ferryboat docked next to our ship.

I tried, but since I couldn't get a word in sideways, I just let her run on and on.

"Allegra was a great lady, and she was grooming me for bigger and better things. I was going places with her as my mentor."

Buzz had just excused himself and gone off. Maybe that could work for me.

"Excuse—" I said, and never got any further, because Lisa had grabbed my arm.

Her words were now a whisper, too low to be heard by our growing audience.

"You don't deserve to share the same planet with the rest of us," Lisa said. "It's too damn bad you didn't suffocate in that car trunk. Next time—"

She stopped, realizing that she might have said too much.

"Next time, what?" I said. "You'll try harder?"

"Go to hell!"

She ran away and I ran after her.

I caught up with her in the lower passageway of our ship. She

142

had tripped over the small step leading to the passageway, and was crouched over trying to catch her breath while she rubbed her ankle.

I loomed over her, not that I'm of a towering height, but anger made me stand taller and more threatening.

"Lisa, now is the time for you to come clean, or I'll see to it you're left on this island to rot." An empty threat. The ferries ran all day, every day.

She was too winded to fight me any longer. "What's the difference. There's nothing you can do about it."

"Do about what? Are you telling me you pushed me into that car trunk?"

"What if I did?" she said. "Nothing happened to you. Too bad."

"Something could have happened to me. I could have suffocated. I could have died in there. You tried to kill me."

"It's what you deserve. It's payback for Allegra. And you can't prove it."

"We'll see about that," I said. "You're a psychopath, an absolute nutcase, and I'm going to have you off this movie just as soon as I find Lew. Pack up and take another boat home. You're gone."

I looked and asked around and finally found Lew sitting in a chair in the big bar-lounge, sipping a dry martini and talking on his cell phone. He nodded at me, and motioned me to a seat. I sat and used the minute to try to organize my thoughts. Lisa was clearly a sicko, and I was now positively focused on her as Allegra's killer.

Lew got off the phone and I told him what had gone down between Lisa and me.

"So, Lisa was the one who pushed me into the trunk of the car and left me there, and, furthermore, I think she probably killed Allegra."

Lew mulled this over, then took another sip of his drink.

"Maggie," he said, "Lisa hasn't really been herself since Allegra's death, but I'm sure she didn't kill her. She loved her and was

143

dependent on her for her career. I hardly think she would have jeopardized that. As for pushing you into the trunk . . ." He shook his head. "I had our mechanics look the car over, and the trunk lock and lid were defective. It was purely an accident."

"But she admitted it to me. She said she pushed me."

"Sometimes she says things in anger that aren't true. She's kind of like a child."

"Yes. The *Exorcist* child. I don't want her around me on this movie, Lew. She's dangerously unhinged."

"Say no more. She's off the movie. We really don't need her any longer. Sheri wants to hire her own assistant, anyway. I'll see to it that Lisa finds another job. And I'll convince her to get some help. Will that make you feel better?"

Lew was just being very kind, humoring me a little, and I knew it. He didn't really believe that Lisa had pushed me into the trunk. He didn't believe anyone had. He had convinced himself it was purely an accident.

"It's not about feeling better . . . it's about feeling safer," I said.

31

The seas were very rough, but the night sky was clear, just as it was the previous night, so we were able to get a lot of film in the can with few changes required. After about an hour, Buzz said I could go and rest, I wasn't needed for the remainder of the shooting.

In my stateroom, I found I couldn't sleep. It wasn't solely thoughts of murder or jail keeping me awake, it was also my indecision about Joe. When I returned, I would have to give him an answer to his living-together proposal.

On the one hand, it was exciting to think that we could actually live together, as once we had, sleep in the same bed, and not have to rush home the next morning. The idea of sharing your innermost thoughts with the man you loved was thrilling.

I would miss Lionel, but promised myself to see him often. Dreamily, I pictured having him and Troy over for dinner, and—wait a second, Maggie. You can't cook. Hmmm. Then I remembered that Joe was a pretty good cook. I wondered if he also cleaned, and tried to picture him naked with a broom. The picture was complete, except for the broom.

On the other hand, it meant that Henrik would be out of my life completely. He had been gone for a while, because of his work. But moving in with Joe meant a real good-bye to Henrik. As I was mulling this over, I realized that, somewhere along the way, I had already made up my mind. Henrik was a great lover, but, out of bed, we weren't so well matched. It's a suit/non-suit world and we fell on opposite sides of that slash.

Overshadowing everything else, I was still very much a person of interest. It wasn't fair to Joe. He would have to understand.

Sleep was out of the question. I threw a sweater over my shorts and T-shirt, and went up on deck. The shooting had wrapped for the night. The sea now was very turbulent, and the whitecaps looked huge. The ship was rocking side to side, and far from gently.

I was alone on deck, and everything was silent around me, except for the crashing of the waves against the side of the ship. It wasn't easy to keep my footing, as I was barefoot, and so I decided to go back to the stateroom and maybe read for a while. I went below, and was in the passageway leading to the stateroom when I heard something.

It wasn't the waves or the sea. It wasn't the creaking of the ship, either. It could have been the wind, which was howling. I stood still listening for a few seconds and heard nothing more. But then, as I started down the passageway, I heard it again. I couldn't identify the sound. Was it a whimper? A yell? A scream? A chair shifting away from its bolts? I didn't know.

"Are you or are you not an intrepid investigator?" said Mercedes.

I are, I answered her, grammar be damned. And went back and up the stairs to the deck. The sea was even rougher than before, and I remembered Fowler telling me the channel crossing could be a bitch. Well, this certainly qualified. I had to hold on to the railing in order to walk. Even so, it was precarious going, and more than once I almost lost my balance. There wasn't anyone or anything to be seen.

I was beginning to think I had imagined the sounds when

I heard it again. It was a scream, muffled and short, but definitely a scream, and it seemed to be coming from the back—oops—aft of the ship. Pulling myself along the railing, I peered over the side, but the sea was in such an upheaval I couldn't see anything.

The deck chairs had been lashed down, piled up one atop the other. They were shifting and squeaking and, it seemed to me, crying in the wind. Could that have been what I heard? No! It was a scream. A human scream.

The ship was rolling from side to side and dipping up and down into the swells. Things were clinking and clanging somewhere on the other side of the deck. I pulled myself along the railing some more to see what all the noise was on the other side.

Once I reached the aft deck, I looked over the rail, pulling my light sweater closer around me. Suddenly something or someone came up behind me, pulled my legs out from under me, and I was falling, falling into the cold, dark, thrashing sea.

32

I fell, it seemed, miles under the surface of the sea, all the while fighting to come up so I could get some air. They say that when you are drowning your whole life flashes before your eyes. Nothing flashed before my eyes. I was in a black void, concentrating on holding the last bit of my breath, and pulling wildly against the raging water to get above it so I could breathe.

Just as I thought this was the end—I would never make it—a swell thrust me into the air. Beautiful air! I paddled madly, spitting and coughing water, and breathing deeply.

I tried to yell, but the sea was a crashing wild thing, and the act of opening my mouth made me swallow huge draughts of seawater. Finally I was able to manage a "Help! Help!" but it soon became clear that yelling was useless. I spotted the ship close by, only it was moving away from me.

As I turned my head to the left, over my shoulder I saw the dinghy trailing behind her. In desperation I swam over to it as fast as I could and grabbed onto the line tying the dinghy to the ship. I held on to it for dear life, trying to catch my breath and not go underwater again. But I was being relentlessly battered and pummeled by the massive swells of the seas and I was terrified. My heart was beating so fast that I thought it would break out of my chest. I began to shiver and shake from the fear and the cold.

You have to do something, I thought. You can't hold on here until you reach port. You'll freeze to death or the rope will untie or a shark will come along. Were there sharks in the channel? If only I were back home, at my computer, I could Google the information. But now I might have to find out the hard way.

Swallowing strongly, I began, hand over hand, to pull myself along the line to the dinghy. It seemed to take forever. When I got there, I reached one hand over and grabbed the rubber handle on the inside of the dinghy. I held myself there for minutes, quaking from the cold, and trying hard to calm myself.

My hands were starting to get numb with the cold, and I was afraid I couldn't hold on much longer. Psyching myself up for a great push, I managed to heave myself over the side and into the small boat. Even though it was pitching wildly and the bottom was awash in water, I felt safe.

I would have stayed there for the rest of the voyage but for the fact that not just my hands but all of me was still freezing to death. I was colder than I could remember ever having been before. Also, the dinghy was dipping up and down, frenzied in the waves. I wasn't sure it could stay upright.

After one huge lurch, it righted itself but had taken on so much water that I thought it would surely sink in minutes. I knew I had to get out of there. I looked over at the ship and saw that the dinghy's line was tethered to a hook next to the ship's ladder, which was snugly tied to the stern. If I could make it to the ladder and get back on board, I'd be all right.

I thought I would wait and maybe the sea would quiet down. Instead, a particularly heavy swell came along and the dinghy upended, throwing me back into a trough of the waves. Fortunately, I remained afloat this time, treading water, with the ship still in close sight.

I grabbed the dinghy line, pulled with all of my might, and kept pulling until I thought my arms would come out of their sockets. With one last great heave and the help of a wave crashing against the ship, I managed to grab the bottommost rung of the ladder, to which I clung for what seemed hours but was probably only seconds.

At last, I found some energy, dragged myself up the ladder, and flung myself onto the deck.

That was it. I was out of the water and absolutely out of gas. There I would stay until someone found me, or we docked, or I died, whichever came first.

33

A peculiar calmness came over me. I was still freezing and my teeth and everything else were chattering. My T-shirt, shorts, and sweater were ripped and soaked through, and I'd torn my feet on something and they were bleeding. But I was safe. I concentrated on that for a while. The wind had abated. The sea was calmer. We must be near port, I thought.

And then came the realization. Realization of which I had not been aware because I had been too busy fighting for my life. Someone had thrown me over the railing and into the water! I tried to get my mind around the reality that someone on board had tried to kill me.

My choice was still Lisa. Pushing someone, whether into a trunk or into the water, seemed to be her M.O. She had to be Allegra's murderer and the one who had tried to kill me, now, twice, or else this movie was cursed with multiple killers like a horror flick.

Which this was turning out to be.

But why me? Wasn't I everyone's choice for the gas chamber? Why didn't whoever it was leave me alone and let the detectives and the State of California finish me off?

"Oh my God! It's Maggie. She's dead!"

I opened my eyes and saw Zack, screaming and covering his eyes with his hands.

"Zack, don't be such a wuss. Stop the hysterics and give me a hand," I said.

By then Fowler was there, helping me up, taking his crew jacket off, and draping it around my shoulders.

"Maggie, what in God's name happened? Did you fall? You're soaked, and . . . are you bleeding?"

"Fowler, I didn't fall! Someone pushed me overboard!" My teeth were clacking together so loudly that maybe I wasn't getting through. So I said it louder. "Someone on this ship pushed me over the side and left me to die."

And then I started crying, crying as I had never cried before. Big, uncontrollable sobs.

"Who's the wuss now," said Mercedes.

Chris barreled his way through the gathering crowd and took over. His big arms around me, he shoved everyone away and walked me along the deck and through the hallway to a stateroom, maybe his. There he pushed me into the tiny bathroom and said, "Here. Put these on."

He handed me a pair of too-large sweats, athletic socks, and a sweatshirt that said FUTURE TROPHY HUSBAND.

I closed the door and peeled off my wet clothes, or, rather, rags. I turned on the shower water, hot, stepped in, still crying, and stayed there until finally I noticed that A, I wasn't sobbing, B, I was warm, and C, I wasn't shaking.

I took a deep breath and came up with fresh resolve. Time to get on with my life.

My life!

I gave a silent prayer of thanks for my deliverance, dried off, dressed without undies in those gigantic sweats, and stepped out of the steamy bathroom.

Chris was waiting for me. He poured me a cup of hot tea and

added a big splash of what looked like brandy. Bless him, he wasn't trying to ask a barrage of questions. I drank the tea, just as we both heard a pounding on the door.

"We'll be out in a minute," Chris said. "Give her a chance to pull herself together."

"Open this door this instant." That was the quiet voice of Lew, He Who Must Be Obeyed.

Chris opened the door. Lew came in, along with Fowler, who closed the door behind them.

"Are you all right, Maggie?" Lew said, taking my hands in his.

I nodded. "Now I am."

Fowler said, "What on earth happened?"

My heart seemed to be beating normally now, but a steel-like anger was growing within me.

As I told my story to Lew and Fowler and to Chris, who re-filled my tea, without brandy this time, I got madder and madder. Allegra was past doing anything about what had happened to her, but I wasn't. I wasn't going to let whoever had done this to me get away with it.

"Lew," I said, when I had finished, "I want to report this to the authorities. Where's the captain? We're at sea. The captain has to be told about this!"

"Now, calm down, Maggie," Lew said. "It's not going to do you, or the film, any good to go around making wild charges. Let's be sensible about this."

Chris said, "Lew's right, Maggie. It was a rough night, and, not wearing any shoes, you probably lost your footing."

I looked at him. Gratitude for the clothes, the tea, and the brandy was gone. For all his seeming niceness, he could still be playing some kind of game, with me as the pawn.

"I didn't lose my footing. I was holding on to the rail, and someone came up behind me and threw me over. Where were you when it happened, Chris? And how do you know I wasn't wearing any shoes?"

Chris looked taken aback. "You've got to be kidding, Maggie. Now you want to claim that I pushed you over? Why in hell would I do that? And why can't you admit you just fell?"

Lew jumped in. "You see? That's what I meant about flinging wild accusations around."

"Lew, I absolutely know that someone threw me overboard."

"Maggie, get a grip," Lew said. "You fell overboard, that's all. Thank God you're safe and there's no story to tell the captain."

I said, "How can you keep on saying that? Allegra is dead. Someone has tried to kill me. Twice. The third time might not be the charm. I'm reporting this to the authorities."

Lew said, "Fine. I can see you've got your mind set. Fowler, handle this, will you." He left the stateroom.

Fowler said, "Maggie, listen to us. There's nothing to report here. Just another unfortunate—"

"Accident, yeah, I know," I said. "And by the way, where is Lisa? I think we need to keep track of Little Miss Innocent."

Fowler said, "We've been looking for her, but can't seem to find her. The crew has searched the ship without any luck. She probably got off when we were still in port at Avalon."

Chris said, "Most likely after your run-in with her she decided to avoid you and us and take a ferry back home."

"Well, I'm reporting all of this," I said. "Someone tried to kill me and I'm not sweeping this under the rug."

I stood up, grabbing the extra-large sweatpants just in time to keep them from falling and ruining my exit.

"I'm going to the captain right now, and when we land I'm informing the police. No one should be allowed to leave this ship. There's a murderer on board and I'll be damned if I stand by while you let him—or her—get away."

34

I left the stateroom, only to find a crush of people gathered near the door, who obviously had been listening to everything that had been said.

"Where is the captain?" I said. "Does anyone know where the captain is?"

Someone said, "He's on the bridge. We're coming into port."

I went up to the bridge. Fowler followed me.

"Maggie, you know Lew is right. This is your film, too. And it can't withstand any more negative stuff. The insurance will be canceled. Maggie, stop for a minute."

"Not on your life. I'm reporting this."

"What? That you fell overboard? You could have been drunk." He sniffed practically right into my neck. "It smells right now like you are."

The brandy! I turned around to face him. "You know I don't drink! Chris put some brandy in my tea because I couldn't stop shaking. Fowler, someone threw me overboard. It was sheer luck that I was able to save myself. Otherwise, you'd be needing a new writer, and go explain that to your precious insurance company!"

We entered the bridge together.

The captain turned around and greeted us pleasantly, even though he must have been surprised to see me in my oversized sweatshirt and clutching the pants that threatened to fall down at any moment. He obviously knew nothing of what had happened.

"Captain, I want to report an attempted murder," I said. That got his attention.

"An attempted murder?"

"Yes. Someone threw me overboard."

Fowler just leaned against the window and shook his head, saying nothing.

The captain looked from me to Fowler and back again. "What's going on?" he said.

I told the whole story once again.

The captain looked at Fowler. "Is this true?"

"She thinks it's true," said Fowler. "She's a screenwriter and she has quite an active imagination."

"Did you go overboard, Ms. . . . ?"

"Mars," I said. "Yes, I went overboard. Someone threw me over the rail."

"She slipped," said Fowler. "She was barefoot and she lost her footing. The sea was rough, the deck must have been pitching, and she slipped."

"I didn't slip. Someone tried to kill me."

"This is a very serious accusation, you know. If this is true—"

"It isn't true," Fowler said.

The captain fixed me with a firm gaze.

"Ms. Mars, this is your last chance to tell me if this is some sick joke you movie people have cooked up, or if this is for real."

"It's the truth," I said. "Someone tried to get rid of me."

"It was an accident, pure and simple," Fowler said.

"Nevertheless," the captain said. "Even if it was an accident, we have to report it to the authorities. I'm going to ask Ms. Mars to go to her stateroom and remain there. I'll radio the L.A. County Deputies, and they'll be waiting."

He got on the radio and called the L.A. Sheriff's Department, announcing himself as Captain McCurley of the *Prophecy*. He then briefly told the deputies my story. The more it got repeated, the more unlikely it seemed, even to my ears, and I knew it had really happened.

Fowler just shook his head. He looked like he was going to cry.

I went to my stateroom and changed into my own sweats. We were close to shore, so my cell phone would probably work. I called Porter Caulfield and left a message telling him that someone had thrown me overboard and it was going to be reported to the authorities. Then I packed up the few belongings I had brought with me and sat and waited.

I expected Lew and Fowler to come by and make another effort to shut me up, but neither appeared. It occurred to me that I should have said something to the captain about Lisa's disappearing act. Probably, though, she had disembarked in Avalon, as Fowler had said, and I would have appeared even more of a nut.

My cell rang and it was Porter, who repeated to me that I was to say nothing, nothing at all, until he arrived, and he was on his way.

I knew this was wise counsel—to let my lawyer handle this. But, God, I hated to be stifled. This was *my* life on the line and I should be the one rolling the dice.

35

It seemed as if I sat in that stateroom for hours. There was an apple I had appropriated from one of the buffets, and I finished that off, ravenously. At one point, the throbbing of the ship's engines died down and I became aware that we must be back in Wilmington.

Finally, a knock came on the door, and when I opened it Captain McCurley was standing there with a man in the now familiar beige Sheriff's Department uniform and hat. He introduced himself as Deputy Donaldson and asked if I would go with him.

We went to the small lounge outside the bigger staterooms on the top deck. Lew and Fowler were there. Lew's personal assistant, Jennifer, was also there with a notebook open.

"I'm not saying anything until my lawyer arrives," I said to no one in particular.

"That's ridiculous. You've told this preposterous story so many times. Tell it again so we can all get off this ship and get back to work." That was Lew, whose acerbic tone couldn't be missed. I guessed he was no longer a fan of mine. Well, he could join the club.

"Ms. Mars, I fail to see why you feel the need for legal representation," the deputy said. "I was told by Captain McCurley that someone tried or maybe even did succeed in throwing you overboard. Why the lawyer?"

Fowler said, "That's because of Allegra's murder."

"Whose murder?" the captain said.

"Allegra Cort's."

"Who's that? Was she aboard, too?"

The one man on the planet who had never heard of Allegra or her murder.

Lew and Fowler together explained briefly about Allegra's murder. When they were done, the deputy looked at me with new interest.

"Ms. Mars. Just tell me what you've told the others. We are holding everyone on board until this is cleared up. So, please, tell me exactly what happened to you."

At that moment Porter Caulfield walked in. Talk about your perfect timing. There were introductions and an exchange of business cards. Then Porter asked to speak to me alone, and everyone cleared out. Those are magic words, coming from an attorney.

I told Porter the entire story, while he did that wonderful listening thing he did. When I finished, he said, "Give me the names of everyone to whom you told your story, and in the order you told it." So I did.

"Now tell it to me again. Spelling everything out. And I do mean everything."

I did the best I could. It took the better part of an hour. He wasn't nervous about keeping people waiting, but I was very jumpy. Everyone was stuck on board until this thing was over, and it was obvious Fowler and Lew weren't too happy with me.

I also told Porter of my run-in with Lisa and that I was now thinking she was Allegra's killer and the person who had thrown me overboard.

By the time we were finished, I was exhausted. But I'd started this and I'd have to see it through. Porter opened the door and called everyone back in. For the umpteenth time, I told the story of how I thought I had heard a sound on deck and I went on deck and then I went aft, holding on to the railing, and then someone came along and threw me into the drink.

Porter handed me a glass of water. After clearing my dry throat, I told the rest of the story—how the dinghy came along over my shoulder and how I was able to grab it and eventually climb back on deck.

When I finished there was silence in the room.

Anyone who knows me will tell you that I can't stand the sound of silence, especially when I have more to say.

"Oh, and I think you should look for Lisa Lindsey," I said. "She confessed to me that she had pushed me into the trunk of my car, and she might also be the one who threw me overboard. It seems to be her method of choice."

Deputy Donaldson looked bewildered. This was all news to him. To cover himself, he looked at his notes.

"Uh . . . what does this alleged attempted murder and the incident with the trunk have to do with the murder of . . . Allegra Cort?"

"No comment," Porter said.

I said, "Well, I have a comment—"

"Maggie, do me a favor and shut up," Porter said.

I shut up.

After that, we all trooped topside and back to where my murder had been attempted. As we went on deck, I saw everyone in the crew staring at me. They weren't looking friendly.

Donaldson eyeballed the railing and deck, while the rest of us stood around. Fowler came up to me. I was leaning against the wall, suddenly so tired I couldn't move. Maybe it was the events of the night, and maybe it was because I had only an apple to eat.

"Fowler," I said. "I haven't had enough food, and I think I need to eat, and fast."

He knew I was a diabetic and he immediately took my arm and led me across the deck and down to the big lounge, where a buffet of sorts was set out. I stood there eating an orange while Fowler filled up a plate for me.

I sat down with Fowler and ate all I could. I asked him, too, to see if he could find Lisa. It was clear that he didn't really believe that it was she who threw me overboard and locked me in the trunk—much less that she had killed Allegra. But he patted my hand and said he would try to locate her anyway.

I didn't know which was worse—being scoffed at or being humored.

36

After eating, I just stayed in the lounge. Soon, I put my head back and rested it on the back of the chair. The next thing I knew, Porter was shaking my shoulder.

"What's happened?" I said, still a little groggy from my unplanned nap.

"We're all done here. It's time to go. Deputy Donaldson is going to turn over his notes to our old friends Jordan and Perez. He thinks both events must be linked."

I was sitting up now, and my head was clear. "Then they can't possibly think I killed Allegra! They must realize that whoever threw me overboard must be the one who killed Allegra."

"It's not that simple, Maggie," Porter said. "If it was, then I wouldn't be paid the big bucks."

"From me you're getting zilch, so what do you mean, it's not that simple?"

"Don't take what I'm going to say wrong. I get the idea you're a hothead, so just hear me out before you explode."

I nodded, unhappy with his description of me.

"Everyone has been questioned. No one heard anything like a

scream. Now I understand that the seas were very rough and the waves were making a lot of noise, but the fact remains—nothing was heard, by anyone."

I started to speak and he held up his hand for me to wait.

"The deputy, the captain, and I have looked for some shred of evidence to prove that what you said occurred actually did happen—"

That did it!

"Actually *did* happen!? What are you saying? Are you telling me that I wasn't thrown overboard? Well, you can just fuck off!"

I stood up to leave, giving him the third-finger salute for emphasis.

"Hold on a second. Calm down. That's not what I'm saying. I'm reciting the facts as they appear now. There is no evidence to support your story, so the deputy, along with everyone else on the movie, seems to think that you slipped. That it was an accident. They think you fell into the trunk of that car, also. That's what *they're* saying. Not me."

"Just what are *you* saying then?"

"I'm saying you were locked in the trunk of the Porsche. I'm saying you were thrown overboard. I'm saying that they have a murderer on this movie. You're my client, ergo, you're not mistaken about what happened to you."

Mollified, I sat down. "Okay, I accept that. You don't have to fuck off, and I take back my finger. But I have to work with these people who think that, at the least, I'm a liar and, at the most, a killer. What am I going to do?"

He said, "Right now you're going to leave the ship and continue on with your life. Do you want a bodyguard?"

"Don't be ridiculous."

"You're sure?"

I nodded.

"Okay. But be careful, very careful. Maybe you should not be alone anywhere. Keep someone with you at all times. I'm going to have a chat with the detectives handling the Cort case, and we'll talk later today, or early tomorrow. Meanwhile, hold your head up, do your job, and leave the rest to me."

I smiled my thanks.

Lew was on the dock, meeting with reporters. He was saying that my going overboard was just an accident due to rough seas and all the hours we'd been working. No one noticed my driving off with Chris and Zack.

On our way to the Malibu set, after an initial awkward silence, Chris said, "I hope you're not pissed with me, Maggie. I'm on your side. You say someone threw you overboard, then someone did throw you overboard and it's up to us to figure out who."

"That's not how everyone sees it," Zack said. "Lew is really angry. All this bad publicity . . ."

"Fuck him and the horse he rode in on," said Mercedes.

My sentiments exactly!

We went back to the beach house in Malibu to shoot the next few scenes. It seemed as if it had been a year since we left it, but it had only been two days.

As soon as we entered the house, my cell was ringing. I headed for the terrace, because the best reception was out there.

"Hey! What's this I hear about you trying to swim the channel?" It was Joe.

"Yeah. Next time I'll wear a bathing suit."

"Next time don't wear anything and I'll jump in to save you." He was trying to keep it light, but I could hear the concern in his voice. "Seriously, babe, are you okay?"

"No, I'm not okay. I'm surrounded by people who are worried about insurance. Insurance, for God's sake! Someone tried to kill me, and they're worried about insurance for their stupid movie."

"Hey, it's your stupid movie, too."

164

I had to laugh at that.

"Listen, Joe, a favor. Could you and your department try to find Lisa Lindsey for me?"

I filled him in on Lisa, and he promised to do what he could.

"You see," he said, "if you were living with me, I could be holding you close and making you feel much better right now."

"Aren't you at work?"

"Hey, a cop is entitled to fringe benefits, too."

I hung up feeling that at least I had one true friend in this world, and then I remembered Lionel. I didn't want him to hear about my near-death experience from someone else, although I don't know who would have told him. To be on the safe side, I called him at work. He answered and I heard the Beatles in the background, singing "When I'm Sixty-four."

Paul McCartney *was* sixty–four or more, and why was Lionel, the Messiah of Mozart, playing the Beatles?

"Hey, Lionel, what's with the Fab Four?"

"I'm transferring old records to CDs for a client. Are you back? How was the sea voyage?"

I gave him the shortened version, and even with that, we had to stop the conversation so he could yell at me—about going out without the proper outerwear, about not wearing shoes, about being careless, I was always being careless, et cetera, et cetera.

"Lionel, cut it out!"

I finished my story with the tag about no one believing me.

"I believe you, my darling, and I bet your top cop does, too."

I could hear that someone else was trying to reach me on my cell. Promising to fill Lionel in on all the details later, I clicked over. It was Porter.

"You've found Lisa?" I said immediately.

"No, no joy yet, but I've got some good people on it. Listen, Maggie, you may as well hear this from me. I've been informed by the detectives that your fingerprints are on the Oscar, the murder weapon."

165

"Well, of course they are. There's a perfectly good explanation for that."

"I know. While you were waiting for Allegra, you picked it up."

"If I had killed her, wouldn't I have wiped off the prints?"

"That's not going to sway a jury."

There was that word again! A jury! I just couldn't accept the fact that it would come to that.

Porter said, "Look, I promised Jordan and Perez that you and I would appear voluntarily at the station to give a full incident report on what happened on the ship last night."

"Did you tell them it wasn't an incident—it was attempted murder?"

"Maggie . . ."

"Sorry."

"I bought us one or two days' grace, that's all. Meanwhile, they're asking you not to leave the jurisdiction—and to stay out of trouble."

"They said that?"

"No, I'm saying it. Bye."

I switched off, rankled once again by the idea of someone else directing my life. Ever since I was a little girl I had prided myself on my independence, and now everyone else was calling the shots about what not to do, what not to say, and how not to behave.

I had to regain custody of me somehow.

37

I went in to the set. Several crew members stared at me, making me feel as though I had a scarlet letter on my forehead. *M* for "Murderer." Zack was lolling in the director's chair that had "Allegra" lettered across the fabric, and I asked him where I might find Lew.

"Oh yeah," he said. "He had to go. He had some sort of important meeting and he asked me to give you this."

He handed me a note that had been scribbled on the back of an old script page. It read: "Maggie. It is urgent that we talk. I will call you to set a meeting." It was signed "Lewis John Packard."

Uh-oh. He signed his full name. That meant trouble. Well, what else was new.

Zack found the keys to a Pontiac Firebird that was being used in the film, and I drove it home, my mind teeming with scheming ideas of what my next moves should be. From now on I would no longer be the aggrieved—I would be the aggressor.

From now on they would have to deal with Ms. Maggie Rose Mars!

As I was approaching the condo, I realized that the same Ford Taurus was behind me as I had noticed behind me on Sunset. Too tired to take that thought further, I used the clicker to open the garage door and drove in, only to find that the Taurus was still close behind me.

I threw the car into reverse, intending to slam it into the Taurus, when a man jumped out of the car, yelling and waving a white handkerchief.

"Hold it! I'm a friend!"

I jammed the brakes on, inches from his grille, and sat there. He came up to the driver's window, and he looked so mild and since I could see both his hands I rolled the window down an inch.

"What do you want?"

"I'm harmless. Gracie sent me."

"You're from *Vanity Fair*?"

He nodded. "I'm here to do the story you turned down."

So that's what Gracie had meant when he said he'd "handle it."

I parked my car and showed him where there was a guest spot for his car.

"Come on up with me," I said. "I've had a bad few days, and you're lucky I didn't kill—I mean, hurt you." Not even in jest was I going to say that.

He introduced himself with a card as Sheppard Scott and I recognized the name. The world of magazine investigative reporters was small, and mostly we knew one another, or knew of one another. What I knew of him was that he was young, talented, and, according to Gracie, had a promising career ahead of him.

Lionel wasn't at home, so I sat on the couch and listened to Sheppard, or Shep, as he wanted to be called. It seems that when I turned Gracie down he immediately dispatched Shep to the West Coast to cover the story of Allegra's murder. He had even been hanging unobtrusively around the Malibu set but, of course, was not on the ship.

"You know, you're kind of a legend back at the office. You're spoken of with hushed tones," Shep said. "So I was wondering if you might be willing to work with me on this story. You know all the inside stuff and all the players."

"Then you've also heard that I'm a prime suspect."

"Sure, but . . . you didn't do it, did you?"

"Would you believe me if I said I didn't?"

"Yeah, sure I would," Shep said.

"Then you're a lousy reporter," I said, "and I wouldn't ever work with you. Close the door on your way out."

"Ms. Mars, Gracie worships the ground you write on. That's good enough for me. Before I left to come here, I asked him if it was at all possible that you killed Allegra Cort. You know what he said?"

I waited.

"He said, 'Maggie is perfectly capable of killing, but it would be over something of major importance, not something as insignificant as a movie script. This murder is beneath her.'"

"I wouldn't call that a ringing endorsement," Mercedes said.

I said, "Look, Shep. You seem like a nice guy, but I have a strong point of view about this killing, and you may not be thinking the same way. You're supposed to keep an open mind and gather all the facts. You can't do that with me. All I want to do is find the person who killed Allegra and tried twice to get me."

"Then we're on the same page, Ms. Mars."

"Maggie."

"I want to find the person responsible, too. It'll make a helluva terrific story. That's why I thought we could work together."

I yawned and covered my mouth, a beat too late.

"Sorry."

"Hey, Maggie . . . you're dead on your feet right now. Why

169

don't you get some rest and we'll talk about it tomorrow. I'll put my cell phone number on the card, and you can reach me anytime." Shep took the card out of my hand and wrote a number down. "I'll also put down my hotel number."

I thought about it. He seemed like a decent guy, and his reputation spoke for itself. It might be helpful to have someone at my back, someone who believed in my innocence and who knew the investigative ropes.

"Tell you what," I said, taking back the card. "Tomorrow I've decided to go see someone I've wanted to question. Allegra's ex-husband. He's an oxymoron. A poor polo player. You want to come along?"

"You bet I do."

I told him I'd call him in the morning and set a time for him to pick me up, and saw him to the door. The only thing I managed to do before collapsing on the bed was take my shot. I fell asleep with all my clothes on.

38

Shep picked me up the next morning in a rented convertible and we headed west on Sunset Boulevard to the Will Rogers Polo Club, where I had learned Manu would be playing.

Noting the convertible, I said, "What happened to the Taurus?"

"It's a beautiful day and I have a beautiful girl beside me. I want the whole world to see us. Besides, I'll put it on the expense account and let Gracie worry about it. Did you get hold of the ex-husband?"

I told him I had been able to track down Manu de la Rua by telephone. The conversations, if you could call them that, went something like this:

"Hi. My name is Maggie Mars. I was a sort of a friend of Allegra's, and I'd like to come out and talk to you about her."

Hang up.

"Hi, we must have been cut off. Can I come out and talk to you?"

"Can't stop you from coming out, but I'm not talking, about Allegra or anything else."

Hang up.

"Great," Shep said. "That bodes well for a nice, friendly interview full of information."

Driving along, I was so relaxed I took off my CAU baseball cap. My hair was destroyed by my time spent out at the beach. It was a discolored, tangled mess and I no longer cared. I let the breeze whip it into Medusa-like tendrils, while I gave myself over to enjoying the beautiful vistas of the mountains and the Pacific.

The polo field was a vast, imposing expanse of emerald green about three football fields long and three wide. My first reaction as we settled at one of the surrounding white-umbrella tables was that the polo ponies weren't ponies at all. They were full-grown horses. My second was that the players were so damn good-looking in their tight team shirts and close-fitting white jodhpurs. They were all sublime athletes, galloping across the field at top speed in pursuit of the small plastic ball.

Shep, who appeared to be something of a research fanatic and had read up on the sport the night before, kept reciting historical nuggets to me.

Did I know that the game originated among the Iranian tribes of Persia and was then adopted by the Mongolians and carried into China and eventually into India? Did I know that Will Rogers built this field in 1926 and used to spend weekends playing polo here with his friends David Niven, Clark Gable, Spencer Tracy, and Walt Disney?

No, I didn't know any of that, but right now I was only interested in singling out the play of Manu de la Rua, whom I had identified by his jersey number, 4. There was no question about it. It was stimulating to watch the graceful beauty of a great athlete in peak form.

I suddenly became aware that Shep was speaking to me. "Do we know whether the killer was left-handed or right?"

"I don't think it's been determined yet," I said. "At least no one's told me. Why?"

"Well, just in case you're considering Manu a suspect, you can't tell from watching him. The game of polo is played with the mallet held in the right hand under every circumstance. It's for safety reasons."

"You must have been up all night reading," I said.

He grinned. "I'd have preferred being up all night doing something else, but I only just met you."

I put my CAU hat back on and looked at him. I could see why he had a reputation for being successful with women. Together with his youth and good looks he had an easy, winning charm.

Just then I was distracted by the sound of thundering hooves and I returned to my Manu watching.

According to the friendly elderly couple sitting at the next table, we were watching the end of the second chukker. A few more minutes and the riders and horses were off the field and all the onlookers were on the field. I grabbed Shep's hand and we ran out also. Everyone was tamping down the divots that had been thrown up by the horses' hooves. No special equipment was needed, just your foot. Soon we were stomping along with the rest of them.

Shep wandered off to do some stomping on his own, and I maneuvered myself alongside the elderly couple while they were very carefully tap-tapping, and asked if they knew Manu.

The man grumbled something under his breath. I didn't catch what it was. He moved away, but his wife, if that's who she was, shot a delighted look at me from under the brim of her straw hat.

"Are you one of his girls?"

"Me? Oh no. I've never met him."

"Well, if you do, be prepared. He looks beautiful, but he has the personality of a wounded bear."

I couldn't think of what to say to that, but it didn't matter. She was happy to rattle on without me.

"He used to be married to that film star that was just murdered. You know the one?"

I barely had time to nod yes.

"Well, then you know she's the reason he can afford to play. He's as poor as they come." She sniffed a little, either at his poverty or because she had a cold.

I spoke into that small break. "So he doesn't have the money to play on his own?"

"Heavens no." We were now walking off the field with all the other onlookers. "She, his late wife, what was her name?"

"Allegra Cort," I said.

"Yes, that's it. Cort. She bought his ponies for him and paid for the upkeep and all." She looked at the field where Manu was now coming back with the other players. "Of course, I wasn't always old. I can see why she paid, can't you?"

Back at the table with Shep, I watched Manu, riveted by his athletic movements. I couldn't help being attracted by his muscular physique and by his handsome tanned face, set off by darker-than-dark eyes and brilliant white teeth.

Yes, I could see why Allegra paid.

By the end of the game, I fancied myself somewhat knowledgeable about polo. Only, of course, not to anyone who was *really* knowledgeable about polo.

We cornered Manu while he was drinking a bottle of water and wiping his head with a towel.

I tried again.

"My name is Maggie Mars," I said, sticking out my hand to shake his. He looked at my hand and then at me.

"I told you I was not going to talk to you and I am not. Have a rotten day." With that, he nodded at Shep and walked away.

Shep said, "Let me take a run at him alone. Wait here."

"No! I'm not giving up that easily," I said.

I took off and ran after Manu. Catching up with him—and blessing those early morning runs for my legs being in shape—I planted myself directly in front of him. He opened his mouth to talk, but I cut him off.

"Now you listen to me, you phony gentleman in a gentleman's sport. You may look good out there, but right here, off your horse, you're just as common as the rest of us. Where do you get off being so nasty?"

"And where do you get off being such a pest? I do not owe you anything."

"No, but you owe Allegra plenty."

That stopped him. We stood there staring at each other. Shep had pulled up next to me, and I noticed that others were staring at us, also.

Manu looked around at the small crowd gathering, and nodded. "Meet me at the far end of the parking lot. There is a picnic table and benches there. I am going to shower and change, and I will be about fifteen minutes."

He walked away and Shep grinned at me. "Guess you didn't need me along after all."

We got ourselves a bottle of water each, walked over to the far side of the lot, and made small talk while we waited.

Manu de La Rua looked as good in old jeans and a white shirt open at the neck as he did in his riding clothes. He sat down, lit a cigarette, and scowled at me.

"You have that typical American pushiness that the rest of the world loathes," he said. "You come uninvited to my polo game, you accost me in front of my friends and colleagues, and you call me names. You tell everyone with two good ears that I owe Allegra plenty. Well, let me tell you something, and then you can get the hell out of my life."

He lit another cigarette off the butt end of the one he was smoking, and threw the butt onto the ground. Shep got up and squashed the butt out with his shoe. That woman was right. Manu had the personality of a wounded animal. Lots of "roar," but I didn't yet know about his bite.

Manu said, "Allegra and I had an arrangement, and we were both happy with it. We *both*, and I emphasize both, lived up to our parts in the bargain."

"She paid for everything, right," I said, "so what was your end of the deal? You escorted her around?"

"You are so naïve. In other parts of the world, it is commonplace for such arrangements. One person is rich. The other person brings to the party a certain look and style. Sometimes it is a rich man and a beautiful woman. Other times it is the reverse."

When he spoke, he had a slight tinge of an Argentine accent, and along with his physical attributes it conspired to make him one of the sexiest men I had ever met.

"He's giving me a tingle you-know-where," Mercedes said.

Ignoring Mercedes and her tingle, I said, "Well, now that Allegra is dead, who is going to support this expensive hobby of yours?"

Manu stood up and threw me a pitying glance.

"I have never had a problem finding someone who appreciates me and my horses and I will not have a problem now." He stood up. "Do not bother me here again, or I will call the police and have you thrown out of the park."

He stalked away, throwing yet another smoldering cigarette butt onto the ground.

All in all, not one of my better interviews.

Shep and I returned home, after having lunch at the Fish Shack in Malibu. The sun was shining, the ocean was a luminescent greenish blue, and the whole trip out to the Will Rogers Polo Club had been a bust.

"Well, Allegra must have had her hands full with him," Shep said. "He wasn't just a docile gigolo, I'd bet."

"In my experience, Shep, the one who controls the purse strings controls the relationship. Allegra wasn't submissive, either. That

176

twosome must have been very combustible. And, anyway . . ." I hesitated.

"Anyway, what?"

"Anyway, his remark about finding someone to support his polo was glib, don't you think? I wonder what, if anything, Allegra left him in her will, considering he was an ex."

"Are you thinking he might have killed her?"

"Well, do the math. With her dead, what exactly is Manu's money situation? He clearly has an anger management problem. If she left him nothing and if he knew she was leaving him with zilch, he could have killed her in a rage. If she actually left him a tidy sum, he could have killed her to collect on it."

"Nice little headlock you've got him in," Shep said.

I said, "Not yet I don't. We'll have to pay another visit to that odious man."

39

A love scene between Sheri and Chris was to be shot on
the beach, a little ways off from the house in Malibu. I was prepared to change into my beat-up tennies and hike down there
when Lew reached me on my cell phone.

"I'm taking a golf cart," he said. "How about I give you a lift?"

I could have used the exercise, but I knew he still wanted to talk
with me.

"Sounds good," I said. "I'll meet you on the road."

I changed into tennies anyway.

Lew wasn't one for small conversation. I had just climbed into
the cart and we were on our way when he said, "Maggie, I know
you had nothing to do with what happened to Allegra, and I'm
assuming you don't know anything about Lisa's disappearance."

"What do you mean—Lisa's disappearance?"

"I don't know what else to call it. We haven't been able to locate
her. She hasn't been home and her friends haven't seen her. In fact,
the last time anyone saw her was when you two had your little al-
tercation just before we sailed for home."

He hadn't put any inflection on that statement, but it seemed to me to be an accusation.

"Lew, I didn't even know Lisa had disappeared. Fowler said that she probably got off the ship in Catalina and took a ferry back home."

"Well, it's been established now that she didn't. The police haven't found any indication that she remained on the island, either."

"What about her confession that she locked me in the car trunk!"

"We have only your word for that. Did anyone else hear her tell you that?"

"No, but . . ." I didn't finish. What was the use?

"Maggie, I'm trying to keep an open mind." Too bad you're failing so miserably, I thought. "What happened to you could have been deliberate, and it could have been an accident. Nevertheless, you were the last person known to have seen Allegra alive, and now it appears you're the last person to have had contact with Lisa."

"You mean seen her alive?"

"That's not what I'm saying."

"Okay, Lew, what *are* you saying?"

"I think it best that until things are cleared up, as of tomorrow, you should stay away from the set. The shooting seems to be going along pretty smoothly. I don't foresee any script problems that Buzz can't take care of. So it might be a good idea—"

I jumped in before he could finish. "You're barring me from the set?"

"You can call it that if you like. I prefer to call it a brief hiatus. I'm sure you'd welcome the chance to stay home, maybe get to work on another screenplay."

"What a great idea," I said. "I've had such a fun time on this one."

He ignored the sarcasm. "You've got to know that things are a little uncomfortable right now. The press has been having a field day, bugging me about one of our cast members having been murdered, another disappeared."

"And here I am, the designated murderer, still in your employ, still hanging around where I'm not wanted."

"Maggie, I don't think, not for one single minute, that you had anything to do with what happened. . . ."

I waited for the "However," and it came.

"However, I should think you'd realize that since suspicion has fallen on you, it's not good for the picture and it's pretty goddamn not good for me."

I said, "I get it. It's nothing personal, merely politics as usual."

His countenance was stony. "You can keep the studio car for a few more days, till we need it. I'll send someone for it."

We had reached the beach location where they were setting up for the next scene. Lew slowed down and I hopped out of the cart.

"Thanks for the lift," I said.

As I trudged along to the beach, I thought about what had just gone down between Lew and me. I had been barred from the set. So Allegra had finally got her wish, after all.

"Double blecccch," said Mercedes.

On the shoreline, they had already gone through two rehearsals, one with the actors Chris and Sheri and another with their stand-ins to give Ram his camera positions. I checked with Buzz to see if any rewriting was needed. It wasn't. Then Buzz and Lew had a brief whispered conversation and they were ready to shoot the scene.

"Action!"

Sheri (as Mercedes), wearing a halter-top sundress and shades, and Chris (as Jack) in a Polo shirt and rolled-to-the-calf Dockers, his hands in his pockets, walked along the crashing surf.

Chris said, *"Great dinner, huh, Merce?"* Then, off her silence: *"Thanks for calling me back. Didn't think I'd hear from you again after I had you arrested."* More silence. *"You just can't stake out my*

180

stakeouts anymore. *That's interfering with police business. Hey, re-member the last time I arrested you and a few hours in the dirty filthy containment cell with those dirty filthy street whores and addicts made you so hot?*"

Sheri stopped and turned to him. "*Jack . . . you want to do it right here?*"

Chris didn't hesitate. "*Yeah.*"

As they hurriedly started to take each other's clothes off, strip-ping down to their underwear:

"*But I'm on top,*" Sheri said. "*I want you inside me, not some frig-gin' sand crab.*"

With Chris stretched out on the sand, Sheri climbed on top of him.

"*Talk dirty for me, baby,*" Chris said.

Sheri's eyes widened as she looked off.

"What the fuck?"

"*Yes! Yes!*" said Chris. "*Now scream for me, baby!*"

We all gasped as with the next wave a body washed up next to Chris, who was lying there with his eyes closed. Sheri proceeded to scream at the top of her lungs and kept screaming.

Chris sat up, still not seeing. "Buzz, will you please call 'Cut.' I think Sheri is a little over-the-top here—" And then he, too, spot-ted the body. "AHHHHHHHHHHHHHHH!"

I froze. U.G. was right. I *was* worse than Jessica Fletcher.

40

By now the process had become so appallingly familiar, I could have written it into a script. I sat in a director's chair under an umbrella, and when Detectives Jordan and Perez got there they pulled up chairs next to mine and together we watched as the crime scene techs worked around Lisa's body.

"So, have you called your lawyer yet?" Rita said.

"He's on the way."

Jordan said, "He must be earning one helluva fee working for you."

I didn't bother to answer. The body, wrapped, was now on a gurney, and was being wheeled up the beach to a parked Coroner's van.

Porter arrived, and after he huddled with the detectives for a while he had me go over my stories with them again—the details of the trunk incident, my run-in with Lisa on the ship, and the overboard episode. When we were finished, Porter drove me back to the house, where I gathered up my things and left.

I looked at no one and no one looked at me.

At home, I was alone with the felines. Troy had finally gone back to his place, and Lionel was out. Thank heavens for small favors. I tried to rest, but it was no use.

I needed to talk to someone who would understand. Someone who would lavish a big dose of sympathy on me. Who would rub my shoulders and tell me, "There, there. Everything's going to be all right."

I needed that "there, there."

I needed Joe.

I reached him at the station, and he came right over. For a few blissful minutes I lost myself in the warmth of his embrace. We sat close together on the couch and I poured out my unhappiness, telling him everything. I talked and talked. Why didn't the detectives accept my story as true? Why didn't they just know I couldn't be guilty of either death? Why weren't they out hunting down the real killer or killers instead of just focusing on me?

Eventually, I stopped the litany of woe and misery and waited for the "there, there."

What I got was, "Who's this Sheppard guy?"

"What?"

"Sheppard something-or-other. He's been hounding me, asking questions about you."

"He's a reporter. From New York. Gracie sent him out to cover the story."

"So you've been seeing a lot of him?"

I drew back. "Shep has nothing to do with this. We've just—"

"Oh, so it's 'Shep' now, is it?"

"Joe! I don't want to talk about Shep! Did you hear anything at all that I said about the mess I'm in? About the detectives hounding me? Especially that Rita Perez?"

"She's a cop. That's what she's paid to do."

I bristled. "Why the hell are we talking about her?"

"You brought her up," Joe said.

"Because I'm well aware you had a relationship with her."

"A *past* relationship. You know. Like you and that Henry Hudson guy. Or isn't that so past anymore, now that you're probably enjoying his legal services."

I jumped up. "I'm not enjoying his services, legal or otherwise, and I'm not so sure you and Rita aren't still getting it on, and his name isn't Henry, it's Henrik. Henrik Hudson!"

Joe stood up as well. "Why the hell did I ever come here! I had a shitload of work to get through, but I thought I was doing you a favor."

"Well, do me another," I said. "Leave!"

He did just that.

I slammed into the bedroom and lay down, trailed by one of the cats. I was furious. Not at Joe but at myself. I was behaving as immaturely and as judgment challenged as a teenager in love. The tensions of the last few days seemed to have stripped me of whatever clarity of vision I claimed to have, and I had just taken it out on Joe.

It was as though I had been itching to pick a fight and there he was, right in the line of fire. The way I had acted, I wouldn't blame him if he retracted his moving-in-with-him offer and went back to Rita Perez. I wouldn't blame him—but I would sure be miserable!

There are people who insist that making up is the best part of breaking up, but there must be easier ways of getting laid.

I couldn't believe I had actually thought that! It was so Mercedes.

My emotions had gotten the better of me and I could feel my blood sugar doing jumping jacks. I got up, trailed by Groucho (or was it Harpo?), and headed for the kitchen on a quest for some orange juice.

Only I never got to the refrigerator.

41

There in the middle of the kitchen stood a large man I had never seen before. His nose was bent, there was a notch out of his right earlobe, he had several small scars on his cheeks—and he was wielding a huge pair of scissors.

I stifled a scream, my heart pounding, and grabbed up Groucho/Harpo.

"Stop where you are," I said. "I've got a wild animal, and I'm not afraid to use it."

Harpo/Groucho purred.

The man grinned at me, which made his visage all the more grotesque because his two front teeth were missing.

"You must be Maggie," he said.

From behind me, Lionel said, "Oh, good, you've met Kurt."

Groucho/Harpo jumped out of my arms and I stared from the one guy to the other.

"Kurt?"

"He's the hockey player I'm going with. I told you all about him."

No, he hadn't. But if I said so now, that might be insulting to

Kurt, and he was still holding the scissors. Obviously he was Lionel's new love whom Troy had been hinting about.

I managed a feeble, "Hi. Where did you guys come from?"

"We overheard your little contretemps from the hallway," Lionel said, "so we decided to stay out of your way, and, of course, away from your dick."

Kurt said, "We came in the back way. I'm very discreet, 'specially when it comes to dicks."

"Oh, good," Lionel said to Kurt, "you found the scissors."

"Yeah. You need a toolbox to open plastic wrappers these days. But the sandwiches are almost finished. Smoked turkey and provolone on sliced *ciabbata*. With horseradish mustard. Just the way you like them."

"We're having a snack," Lionel said. "Want in, Maggie?"

I shook my head. "Just some orange juice."

"Stay put. I'll get it for you." Kurt laid down the scissors, went to the refrigerator, and retrieved a handful of oranges. "Fresh is better," he said. "Got a squeezer?"

"Isn't he wonderful," Lionel whispered to me, as he located the squeezer in an overhead cupboard. "I knew you wouldn't mind him staying with us for a few days now that Troy's back in his place."

I had to sit down. It was all happening too fast. "You play hockey?" I said, quite inanely.

"Yup. I'm a defenseman."

Lionel said, "He's in the closet. You're going to be our beard."

Well, that was a new one. Maggie Mars, Girl Beard.

I was so happy for Lionel, I could have cried. Maybe not just for Lionel's happiness.

I said good night to Lionel and Kurt, retreated to my room, where I checked my blood sugar level and, to my surprise, found it fine, then took a shower and, while the spray ran over me, had a good sob. I couldn't tell where the water ended and the tears began. Barred from the set. No work on the horizon. And while being a

186

"person of interest" was bad enough, being a "person of interest" without Joe in my life was more than I could bear. And it was all my fault.

By the next morning, over a breakfast of toasted whole wheat muffin and small slices of Canadian bacon and low-fat cheese, enjoying sociable conversation with Lionel and Kurt, I had stopped feeling sorry for myself and was prepared to face the uncertain future.

What I was not prepared for was the unexpected arrival of U.G.

42

He came in all bright eyed and exuberant, even shook hands with Lionel and mumbled something akin to a pleasant greeting.

"Maggie, love, wait till you hear my idea. It could solve all your—"

He stopped short as Kurt came out of the kitchen carrying a cup of coffee. He was wearing a bathrobe of Lionel's that ended somewhere around his bare, hairy thighs, and it was only too evident there was nothing under the robe.

"—problems," U.G. said. No matter what, he always had to finish what he started.

"Dad, this is Kurt," I said, since it was obvious that Lionel wasn't going to say anything. "He's a hockey player."

"Defense," Kurt said. He stuck out a meaty hand.

U.G. stared at it as though it were some kind of foreign object, then tentatively shook it. "And you're . . . ?"

"Maggie's new boyfriend," Lionel said, finally finding his voice.

U.G. shot an accusatory glance at me.

I nodded, smiling in confirmation, thinking I was going to throttle Lionel the first chance I got.

Lionel said, "Kurt, why don't you and I finish cleaning up in the kitchen."

"Stay where you are!" U.G. said in a thunderous voice. "Maggie's new boyfriend, my ass! I know what's really going on here."

Lionel and Kurt exchanged an uneasy look, and they had reason to. Knowing how U.G. mercilessly teased Lionel about his gender preferences, I was sure he would blab to the world about a star athlete being in the closet.

I said, "Dad—"

He didn't let me finish. "I wasn't born yesterday. I know exactly what Kurt is doing here."

"Now, Dad, don't get excited. It's just that—"

"He's your bodyguard, isn't he."

"What!?"

"With a mug like that, what else could he be?"

With that U.G. went over and wrung Kurt's hand. "Great cover, feller, pretending to be a hockey player. But you just watch out for my little girl, you hear."

Kurt nodded, like a man in a stupor. Lionel rushed him off into the kitchen.

U.G. said, "It's about time you got yourself some protection, Maggie. The chances you take."

Oh, boy! And he didn't even know about my most recent brushes with death.

I pulled him over to the couch and we sat.

"Dad, you said you had this great idea that would solve my problems."

"Oh yeah." He looked off toward the kitchen. "Did Joe find this guy for you?"

"Dad, the idea?"

He turned his attention back to me. "Maggie, I can't help feeling that you're in real trouble now with these murders."

"Tell me something I don't know."

"Okay, then I think you should arrange with Mitzi to have a séance."

"A séance? You're serious?"

"Maybe Mitzi can contact Allegra and find out who killed her."

"You *are* serious."

"Honey, think about it. Even if Allegra doesn't reveal the name of the murderer, she might give you some leads that would help."

"Dad, Allegra is—how can I put this—she's dead."

"So who's to say you can't communicate with her?"

"Me. You know I'm not a believer."

"Then do it for me. Please, honey. It couldn't hurt."

I gave in. If I didn't, I knew he would hound me about it for days. Besides, I felt guilty about having to lie to him about Kurt or at least not tell him the truth, even though it was to protect Lionel and his closeted lover.

"Okay," I said. "You arrange it."

We stood and I followed him to the door. He said, "I have a good feeling about this. All I ask is that you be a little more open-minded." He looked back toward the kitchen. "And you keep that bodyguard around at all times, you hear. Even if Lionel has a problem with that."

I sighed. Being a beard wasn't all that it was cracked up to be.

43

Since I didn't need to be on the set anymore, I had plenty of time on my hands. I was still on salary, so bills weren't a worry. At least not for the time being. If I were to be convicted of murder, paying bills was the very least of my concerns.

I took out a fresh notebook and tried to jot down all the events that had taken place, from the night of Allegra's death to the day of Lisa's body washing ashore. It was a first step in my going on the attack and becoming more proactive.

It took hours, and while it sorted things out in my mind, I was no clearer as to who Allegra's murderer was. Lisa was perfect for the part, until she turned up dead. It was a stretch to believe in two murderers, but I couldn't discount it. When I came to Manu's name, I stopped. He certainly had a motive, as far as I could see. Maybe not means, maybe not opportunity, but a definite motive.

I picked up the phone, called Shep, and told him I wanted to pay that return visit to Manu today, now. We agreed to meet at Bamboo on Venice Boulevard for early lunch and then to drop in on Manu.

* * *

Over grilled lime chicken and plantains, Shep and I
planned our attack.

"I can't call Manu, Shep. He'll just hang up on me."

"Ah, that's where you should be grateful for my company. What
we need to do is find out whether or not he's at home. And then,
if he is at home, how to get in to see him. Leave all that to me."

We ate, and after splitting the check we walked out to a quiet
corner of the parking lot. Shep motioned for me to be silent, and
called Manu.

"Hello? . . . Mr. de la Rua? . . . This is Hank Jeffries from the
Will Rogers Polo Club." Shep shrugged at me, a little shame-
facedly, as if to say he was sorry he had to tell lies, something he
was sure I would never do. How little he knew.

"No, I don't think we have met. I'm fairly new out here. I was
brought out for a particular program in which the polo management is interested."

While Shep was talking to Manu, I gave the valet our ticket
and, when my car came, got behind the wheel. Shep got in the
passenger side, still on the phone.

"Yes, that's right, a new program they want to set up. There
would be a position of importance for someone with your abilities, and your contacts. I wondered . . .

"Well, I would like to explain further, but it's complicated and
it would be better to talk in person."

I drove out of the parking lot and turned toward Venice, moving slowly. As soon as the horns started up, telling me I was driving way too slow for L.A. drivers' convenience, I pulled over to the
side of the road. Shep was still on the phone, in his polo management mode.

"No need to drive all that way. I'm in Venice now, and I think
I must be near your home. I have the address somewhere. May I
come over now?"

192

A finger-crossing several seconds went by.

"That's very gracious of you. Could you confirm the address for me?"

Shep winked at me.

"I see. That's off of Jefferson? . . . Wonderful. I'll be there in twenty minutes. Many thanks. You won't regret waiting for me."

Shep signed off.

"If you weren't such a crack reporter, you'd make a fine criminal," I said.

The street Shep navigated us to was lined with apartments, most of which had seen better times. Manu's building was a four-unit apartment house, with faded paint of an indeterminate hue and a small front lawn landscaped in dirt and weeds. His apartment was upstairs, in the back, and we walked up to his front door in silence.

Shep knocked and we heard Manu's voice: "Who is it?"

"Hank Jeffries."

The door opened and Manu stared at us. Before he could slam it shut, Shep had his foot in the doorway and was pulling me into the apartment after him.

The room we were in was standard, one that we've all seen in movies about someone living on the cheap. The color scheme was brown and worn-out beige. Brown saggy couch, one brown saggy chair, brown wood laminate tables, and stained beige walls. The only item not standard was a large plasma television on the wall over the laminate TV stand.

Manu sat down in the one chair, stuck out his legs, and lit a cigarette. The man was great looking, even in this environment. The apartment stank of cigarette smoke and sex. Shep wrinkled his nose at the smell, but I rather liked it. It reminded me of all those 1940s *film noir* movies. I expected to see Alan Ladd enter the room at any time.

"You can get out now, or I can call the police now. Whichever you prefer," Manu said, blowing smoke at the ceiling.

"Can we please put an end to the hostilities?" I said. "I'm in trouble and I need your help."

Manu said, "Why should I care if you are in trouble? I have no interest in helping you, unless it is to show you to the door."

"Well, you should care. The police think I killed your ex-wife, Allegra."

"And did you?"

"No. Did *you*?"

He didn't answer, just gave us a look of revulsion. In the ensuing silence, Shep and I sat down on the saggy couch, and proceeded to make it look like we were prepared to stay there forever.

Manu heaved a great sigh of disgust, and capitulated to the inevitable.

"All right. But I must say, Miss . . ."

"Mars. Maggie Mars."

"It is a perverse God who creates a creature as beautiful as you are and then gives you a pushy personality and a big mouth. Now, what is it you think I can help you with?"

"Have the police spoken to you about Allegra?" I was doing the talking and Shep knew enough to keep quiet, at least for now.

"Yes, they have spoken with me. I do not know what else I can tell you."

I knew Rita Perez was not going to share any information with me, so I proceeded to ask Manu questions about his life with Allegra. Unfortunately, even though he answered with seeming candor, there were no nuggets of gold, nothing useful. It was when my questions sputtered to an end that Shep stepped in.

He said, "Why did the two of you get divorced? Was it because of polo? Other women?"

Whoa! No small talk for Shep. He went right for the jugular. No wonder Gracie sent him out to do the story.

Manu stood up, stretched his back, and walked over to the corner where a polo mallet rested. He picked it up and contemplated it.

"No, it was neither of those things. Allegra understood my

194

passion. Polo is not just a sport. It is a way of life. And, to compete among the finest, a great deal of money is necessary."

"So Allegra supplied the money to support your way of life," I said, "and you supported hers, how?"

"I told you. We had an arrangement, a very satisfactory one. She left me to my ponies and I left her to her . . . movies."

I had the feeling that he had been going to say something else and then thought better of it. Shep pursued it. "You eventually went your separate ways. Was there any one incident?"

"No incident." Manu lit yet another cigarette. The air was gray with smoke, and Shep was beginning to cough. But I had to plow on.

"Another woman in the picture? Another man . . ."

"I believe she might have been having an affair. Perhaps many. It was not something that was of great matter. It was the nature of our arrangement."

He looked away, idly swinging the mallet. "Allegra was an alluring woman, but she allowed her emotions to override her intellect. She was up and down, like an elevator." Now his glance came back to me. "She did not always get along with people, particularly those she worked with who may have crossed her. She was unforgiving. And she relied heavily on the advice of her friend, Mitzi. Have you met Mitzi?"

"Yes. The Amazing Mitzi," I said, with a smile. "The psychic."

"She is not a psychic. She is a witch. She has powers. What they are and where they come from I am not sure, but she has powers. She is the one who told Allegra to go to Alamogordo." Manu was not smiling.

Shep said, "Alamogordo? In New Mexico? Why?"

Manu just shrugged. "I did not ask."

"But it must mean something or you wouldn't have mentioned it," I said, determined to pursue that thin strand.

"As soon as Allegra returned from that trip, our relationship ended. She filed for divorce."

I said, "When was that?"

"The divorce? Sometime in 1988 or '89. I cannot remember the date, although at one time it was engraved on my heart."

It was fake sentiment, and briefly I wondered why he had bothered to offer it to us. But Shep and I had run out of questions and Manu had run out of either cigarettes or patience or both. He ushered us out the door and slammed it shut before we could even say good-bye.

Back in the car and heading back to the restaurant to drop Shep off at his car, I said, "Alamogordo? Do you think that means anything?"

Shep said, "Probably not. Most likely Allegra was on location there, or maybe doing a promo tour for a film."

We let it go at that. The visit with Manu had gone a little better than the first time, but it still hadn't been all that productive. I wondered when, if ever, I would latch onto something meaningful. Something that would clear me incontrovertibly of all suspicion of murder.

44

U.G. didn't waste any time. The next morning he called to say that Mitzi had an opening on her busy calendar and she could accommodate us with a séance.

I told Lionel about it and he was ecstatic about visiting with "the other side." He rounded up Kurt and Troy, I called Shep, and that evening found us, along with U.G., gathered at the entrance of Mitzi's Hancock Park home.

It was an old California three-story Spanish-type home. It had wooden balconies along the front of the upper floors and red bougainvillea cascading down over the railings. The lawns were manicured, with lush flower beds leading up to the front doors. They were two heavy oak doors, studded with nail heads, and in one there was a peephole at eye level.

Mitzi opened one side of the doors. She was wearing something long and purple, sprinkled with silver crescent moons and stars. She looked like she could have been one of Merlin's handmaidens. Whatever a handmaiden was.

"Welcome," Mitzi said, and led us into a small room with a coffered ceiling and wooden beams. The walls were plain white with dark draperies gathered in the corners. In the center of the far wall was a small side table with a vase of flowers. Next to this table was a reclining chair upholstered in the same fabric as the draperies. It was an odd room, with no windows.

"Tonight there is a full moon," Mitzi said. "That bodes well."

It didn't appear as though any refreshments would be served, which did not bode well. I wasn't asking for crustless sandwiches or *petit fours*, but surely a cup of herbal tea would have been a hospitable touch.

We watched while Mitzi covered a large oval table with a white sheet and placed three unlit candles, two white and one purple, at the center. There was some new age music playing, mild and soothing, as if we were in an elevator, and an unidentifiable scent of incense permeated the air.

"Frankincense," U.G. said. "It expands consciousness and aids in meditation."

"What about myrrh and gold?" Lionel said. "My consciousness is always expanded by gold."

Kurt laughed and U.G. muttered something about "heathens."

At a wave of Mitzi's hand, we sat in the seven straight-back chairs. At first there was a little uncertainty about who should sit where. We couldn't do boy, girl, boy, girl, because Mitzi and I were the only "girls"—unless you counted Lionel and Troy and Kurt. I decided to take my place between Shep and Kurt.

U.G. said to me in a whisper, "Good move, sitting next to your B.G."

"What?"

"Your bodyguard. Be sure and take him wherever you go."

I nodded weakly.

"This evening," Mitzi said, "we will attempt to contact the spirit of Allegra Cort, who has passed over, and communicate with it. This must be the only purpose in everyone's mind. All distracting thoughts should be put aside because they will interfere with maintaining a single energy." She looked around the table, at

198

each of us in turn, seeming to search into our innermost selves. "If there are those here who do not believe, go now."

I knew U.G. was eyeing me challengingly, but I stayed put, determined that I would participate. I didn't believe for a moment that Mitzi could really communicate with the dead, but the evening might prove interesting and the séance would look good in Shep's *Vanity Fair* article.

"I will now ask the participants to charge the candles. Please hold each candle in your hands and visualize the symbolic power emanating from it."

The candles from the center of the table were passed around. The only visualization I had was of Joe, and that was because, now that we had kinda sorta maybe broken up, I visualized him everywhere. Also, it didn't hurt that I was holding a phallic symbol in my hand.

When the three candles had made the rounds, they were returned to the center and Mitzi lit them. She then nodded at U.G. He rose and and drew the drapes over all the walls, then went to a switch on the wall and hit it. The lights went off and the music stopped.

Mitzi said, "Everybody . . . we will begin by joining hands with the people on either side of us and closing our eyes."

I followed instructions, my left hand almost being crushed in Kurt's beefy one. Shep's touch on the other side was warm and reassuring.

"Now please breathe in slowly through the nose . . . and out slowly through the mouth. You should feel calm, comfortable. . . . In . . . out . . . slowly . . . slowly . . . in . . . out . . ."

I wasn't sure whether I was at a séance or at a Lamaze class.

"Keep your minds blank. Be in touch with your senses."

After a few minutes of in-and-outing, Mitzi said, "Everyone, say these words after me: *Our beloved Allegra* . . ."

Dutifully we all repeated, "*Our beloved Allegra* . . ." The "beloved" stuck in my throat.

"Whom we hold in loving remembrance . . ."
"Whom we hold in loving remembrance . . ."
"We ask that you commune with us and move among us."
"We ask that you commune with us and move among us."

Mitzi said, "Again, please. We must send a love vibration to the spirit sought and repeat the chant until there is a response. . . ."

We did, several times more. Suddenly I felt a cold breeze on my face and I shivered. There seemed to have been a decrease in the room temperature.

"Allegra," Mitzi said, "if you are with us, please rap once."

Silence. And then a rap. A rap that shook the table very slightly. I ventured to open one eye and then the other. Everything was as before. Everyone's hands were still joined.

"Do you wish to communicate with us? One rap for no, two raps for yes. . . ."

Again that moment of silence, followed by two raps.

"Do you choose to speak for yourself?" One rap. "Will you speak then through me?"

We waited, and then the answer: "I will speak through you. Ask and I shall answer."

It wasn't Allegra's voice. It wasn't Mitzi's, either, but it came from Mitzi. Her eyes were half-shuttered. She was speaking in an unnaturally high range, almost toneless, trancelike.

It was U.G. who first managed a question. "Allegra, are you . . . are you happy where you are?"

"I. Am. Happy."

"Where are you?" Troy said.

At that, the table shook violently and the candles flickered.

"Sorry, sorry," Troy said.

Shep said, "Is there anything you wish to tell us?"

"I. Have. A. Message."

"For who?" said U.G.

"Whom," said Lionel.

"It. Is. For. Maggie. Mars."

200

Kurt poked me with our clasped hands.

"What is it?" I said, and hoped I didn't sound as tremulous as I felt.

"There. Is. A. Child."

"A child? What about a child?"

No answer came.

"Whose child?"

Still no answer.

Lionel, obviously impatient, said, "Can you tell us who killed you?"

Silence, and then a series of unearthly moans shivered the air.

"Is that a no or a yes?" Lionel said.

Nothing.

I took a deep breath. "Allegra, what happened in Alamogordo?" I asked.

And now there was more shaking of the table, even more violent. A flower-filled vase flew across the room and a door handle rattled noisily.

Quickly Mitzi said in her normal voice, "Spirit, go in peace and thank you for joining us." She got up. "The séance is over."

She blew out the candles and we broke the circle of hands. U.G. turned on the lights.

"Wow," said Kurt.

Wow indeed.

U.G. came over to me. "Sorry."

I offered up a smile. "It's okay, Dad. Thanks for the effort."

"Maybe you could ask Mitzi to try it again. With Lisa."

"We'll see." But I knew I wouldn't. First, though, there was something I had to find out.

I went over to Mitzi, who was resting in the reclining chair. Her right hand was shading her eyes.

I said, "What child were you referring to?"

She raised inquiring eyebrows. "What?"

"You said, 'There is a child.' I heard you."

201

"My dear Maggie," Mitzi said, and gave me what I could only assess as a pitying look. "I didn't say that. Allegra did."

We were ushered out by U.G., who silenced my efforts at trying to talk to Mitzi any further.

"A séance is very draining," he said to me. "She needs to regain her strength." I noticed, however, that he remained behind.

It crossed my mind that U.G. could be falling in love. After all these years, with my mother gone, he must be lonely at times. He would enjoy having another woman in his world. But did he want a woman who was a psychic? What would that world be like if he couldn't keep a secret because Mitzi would read his mind? If I were in U.G.'s shoes, that's what I'd be most afraid of.

But then again, maybe I had more secrets than he did.

45

By the next morning, the séance of the night before took on a dreamlike quality. I was still musing about it as I soaked in the tub, enjoying the relaxation and bliss of the aromatic bubbles, when the phone rang.

Nobody answered. It rang again.

"Lionel!"

The next moment I heard Kurt say, "Yes, she's right here. She's having a bath."

The bathroom door opened and he peered in, holding out the portable phone. "It's for you, love."

I ducked under the bubbles as much as I could. Kurt came in all the way and reached out to put it in my soapy hand. Let it be Joe, was my first thought. Then, remembering that it was Kurt who had answered the phone, I had a second thought. Please don't let it be Joe.

Having accomplished his mission, Kurt went out again, closing the door behind him.

"Hello."

"Who was that?" I winced. It was Joe.

"Nobody."

"Nobody?"

"Well . . . Kurt. You don't know him."

"Oh yeah. Your bodyguard. U.G. told me all about him. Guess you threw another fastball right past him, didn't you?"

I'd forgotten that Joe and U.G. were buddies from way back. Even when Joe and I had gone our separate ways and crossed each other off, U.G. and Joe had maintained their friendahip.

At any rate, if Joe was calling now to effect a reconciliation, this was hardly a good start.

I said, "Joe, you called to tell me something?" Like he forgives me? Like he's been miserable? Like let's get together?

"I called to give you a heads-up on the medical examiner's report. I saw Rita last night and she clued me in."

I seethed. Last night I was rendezvousing with a spirit and Joe was having his own tryst. Not with a spirit, but with a flesh-and-blood real-life person.

"With the emphasis on the flesh," said Mercedes.

"How nice of her," I said. I would have liked to add something real vitriolic and nasty, but I didn't want to get into any more hot water than was already in the tub.

Joe said, "Some time ago Allegra had a caesarean birth."

That was a thunderbolt. I was speechless.

"You still there? In the tub, I believe?"

"Yes, I'm here. It was just such a surprise."

"Well, it's all yours. Run with it."

"I will. Thanks, Joe."

"No problem. . . . And, Maggie?"

"Yes?" I waited. Something else in the M.E.'s report? Joe forgave me for my stupid behavior and wanted to see me again?

"Tell that Kurt guy, whoever he is, to take good care of you. I know you never do it yourself."

I held on to the phone long after Joe hung up. Long after the operator's voice cut in with, "If you'd like to make a call please hang up and try again. . . ."

No, I wouldn't try again.

During breakfast I had a call from Shep, who wanted to drop over later so we could talk. I heard the sound of a Call Waiting, so I quickly told him to come ahead and shifted over. It was Buzz.

A minor problem had arisen on the set. Buzz wanted to add rain to an interior night scene. He pictured it falling outside, streaking the big picture window. It would give the scene some much-needed atmosphere. Some dialogue would have to be added, too, and that's where I came in. Could I rewrite the scene to take note of the rain and e-mail it to him on the set?

Yes, I could, and how was everything going?

"Okay," Buzz said, so noncommittal a reply that it told me nothing and everything.

I put on sweats and sat down at the computer, happy to be working at least part-time. An hour later I e-mailed the new scene to Buzz, and soon after I received his reply that the rewritten dialogue was great.

Shep arrived a little later and we made ourselves comfortable in the living room. Shep sprawled in the armchair and I sat down on the couch, my little notebook in hand.

He jumped right in. "I've been asking around," he said.

I must have looked mystified.

"You know, about the child. What Allegra said at the séance."

"Shep . . ."

"Okay, okay, it wasn't Allegra—it was Mitzi. Still, maybe it means something. So this morning I've been doing a little investigating."

"And?"

He shook his head. "Nothing. No one I spoke to knows anything about a child in connection with Allegra. I asked some contacts at the trades. They dug into the files for me. I got the names of directors and stars who worked with her and queried as many as I could reach. Even called the Screen Actors Guild. Not a whiff."

"Have you spoken to Lew Packard?"

"No. Should I have?"

"He and Allegra worked together for many years."

"Okay, I'll tackle him next."

"Let me," I said.

"Want some company?"

"I think this is something I'll do better on my own."

"Sure. Let's connect up later."

We both got up and I saw him to the door. Abruptly he put his arms around me and gave me a quick kiss on the cheek. He smelled of some wonderful aftershave.

"We're a good team, you and I," he said.

Well, that was a new development. It was evident that we had become an investigative team. But that kiss, brief as it was, made a difference. I doubt that Sherlock Holmes and Dr. Watson ever kissed. Or Nero Wolfe and Archie Goodwin. Or Nick and Nora Charles. . . .

Well, those last two were obviously not too relevant an example. But still, Shep's remark, like his kiss, probably meant nothing at all.

46

I called Lew's office and asked his assistant, Jennifer, if I could see him very briefly. She put me on hold, but not for long. That was either a good sign or not. I was very ambivalent these days.

She came back on and told me I should come over at three and Lew would be glad to see me. Well, that, too, was either a good sign or not. . . .

I arrived to find Lew ensconced behind a massive oak desk that was decked with an array of family photos. Occupying a matching pair of leather chairs in front of the desk were Buzz and Chris. I warmed up a pleasant expression of greeting to mask my surprise.

Chris got up and came over and hugged me. "Good to see you, Maggie. I was just complaining to Lew about your not being on the set."

"None of us like it, but it has to be," Lew said.

Buzz said, "Lew has signed off on the rain scene."

"Oh. Good."

"Maggie . . . sit, please," Lew said.

I settled down in a third matching chair.

Lew went on. "Maggie, I'm glad you're here. Buzz and Chris are more than a little disturbed because that *Vanity Fair* person, what's-his-name—"

"Sheppard Scott," Buzz said.

"I gave him access to the set," Lew said, "and he even got past Jennifer and buttonholed me in my office here. He's been asking personal questions about Allegra."

Chris said, "Allegra and a baby."

"Not necessarily a baby by now," said Buzz.

Chris waved him off. "What's the difference. I don't know anything. Someone overhears him talking to me about a baby, it could give people the wrong idea."

Lew said, "Do you know anything about this, Maggie?"

I was caught between Lew and a hard place. I had been prepared to ask him the very same question, and now he had me on the spot. Even more so because Buzz and Chris were listening in.

I said, cautiously, "There appears to be some suggestion that Allegra may once have had a child."

"Trash talk!" said Lew. "I've known Allegra for many years. Never was there any indication that she was ever pregnant, much less actually gave birth."

I nodded. It was entirely possible that she wouldn't have told Lew. Or anyone, for that matter.

Lew said, "Maggie, I would appreciate it if you would ask Sheppard Scott to cool it. No more questions. I'm glad to see that in your time off you are trying to prove your innocence, but please direct your search elsewhere."

"Yeah," Buzz said. "I don't want him using my set as an interrogation chamber."

"I'll make sure he's no longer welcome, Buzz," Lew said. "If this kind of rumor gets around any further, it can only sully the reputation of a fine, fine actress. Let her rest in peace."

"Amen," said Chris.

That was an exit line, if ever I heard one.

47

Once on the road, I called Shep on his cell and asked him to meet me at the Bourgeois Pig, a Hollywood cappuccino bar that was favored by the computer crowd. I could always get a cup of tea and something from the baked-goods counter—something not too traumatic for my blood sugar—and it was a good place, paradoxically enough, to be alone. Although it's usually crowded with writers at all the available table spaces, they're too busy at their own keyboards to do any eavesdropping.

After placing our beverage orders, Shep and I appropriated one of the purple couches and sat down. I relayed the dictum from Lew that there was to be no more questioning on the set and also that Lew didn't know anything about a child.

Shep said, "So where does that leave us? The only lead we have at this moment is this child, who may or may not be an invention of Mitzi's. Maybe even to throw us off the track."

My guilty conscience tugged at me. If Shep and I were going to be true partners in this investigation, then there should be no secrets between us.

I said, "Shep, it looks like there might very well have been a child." I told him what Joe had said about the M.E.'s report.

He gave a low whistle. "Okay, but what we don't know is if he or she is alive or dead."

"Then that's our next step. To find out."

Shep got up to get our beverages, a double vanilla latte for him and herbal tea for me. While he was gone I retrieved my notepad and a pen from my bag and started writing.

"What's that?" he said, coming back with a cup in each hand.

"I thought it was about time we did some brainstorming, so I made a list."

He nodded approval. "A list of possible suspects. What have you got?"

I read it off. " 'Buzz,' 'Ram,' 'Ringo,' 'Chris,' 'Sheri,' 'Mitzi,' 'Zach,' 'Fowler,' and 'Lew.' "

"And 'Manu'?"

I added his name.

"And the rest of the movie crew and cast?"

"Oh, God, no," I said. "That way lies madness."

"Let's talk motivation."

"That's easy."

"Easy?"

I said, "Sure. With Sheri Davis, it was because she wanted to replace Allegra as the lead. And she did away with Lisa as well because Lisa saw her in the trailer. And by the way, I hope you don't put any stock in that. I don't."

"What about the motives of the others?"

"Lisa saw them in the trailer, too," I said. "As to why they killed Allegra, haven't a clue."

Shep said, "Well, take Chris, for example. He might have killed Allegra say, in a fit of jealousy or anger—"

I finished the thought, "And then did away with Lisa because she saw him and was blackmailing him."

"Maybe," Shep said. "And that's why he's been so quick to disparage Allegra and to put the blame on Lisa."

I nodded. "As for Manu, he couldn't have killed Lisa. He wasn't on the ship."

"But he still could have killed Allegra. . . ."

Then I had a new and startling thought. "Maybe Lisa wasn't murdered. Maybe she just fell overboard—the way everyone tells me I did."

Shep said, "Could be. Jot that down." I did. "Well, that's about as far as I can go. So much for our brainstorming."

"It was more of a brain drizzle," I said. "Look, right now the baby angle seems to be the only lead we have, so let's get moving and pursue it. Which means?"

"Mitzi," he said.

"Right. Come to think of it," I said, "she predicted death for Allegra, so maybe she did away with her in order to make her prediction come true."

"Please tell me you're not serious."

"I'm not. But what do you say we pay her another visit?"

48

In the light of day, Mitzi's house had a less sepulchral look than it had on the evening of the séance. Mitzi herself was the picture of domesticity in a beige turtleneck and blue jeans, undoing an apron as she opened the front door.

I had called her en route, asking if we could drop over and talk to her for a very short while. She turned us down at first, offering her very busy schedule as an excuse and saying that she was unprepared for a visit and couldn't possibly fit us in. Finally, though, she acceded, agreeing to spare us a mere ten minutes.

"Oh. I thought you were the pizza delivery," she said as soon as she opened the door and saw us.

"Sorry." She was a psychic. Didn't she know ahead of time we weren't going to be sausage and cheese? Or whatever she had ordered? "We just wanted—"

"No."

I was at a loss. "No, what? I haven't asked you anything."

"Please go away. I'm busy."

"You said we could have ten minutes. I need to talk to you."

She considered that. "All right then. But not him." She indicated Shep.

"He's with me. We're working together."

"Not him," she said again.

"Why not?"

Shep said, "It's okay. I'll wait in the car. If you're not out in half an hour, I'll call the Paranormal Police."

Mitzi closed the door after him.

"I sense something evil in his aura," she said as she led me into the living room.

I didn't see any point in debating the contents of Shep's aura, much less if he even had one. Besides, I had been given a deadline, so I sat down in a corner of the sofa and didn't comment.

Once again, no refreshments were offered. Either Mitzi's psychic powers gave her no inkling of what constituted hospitality or the cupboard was bare. Watching her settle her ample form into a comfortable-looking upholstered armchair, I doubted the latter.

"I wonder . . ." I said tentatively, "if you could possibly tell me anything about Alamogordo."

"It's in New Mexico."

I knew she was being deliberately irritating. "Thank you for the geography lesson. I'm asking, of course, what Alamogordo has to do with Allegra."

She shrugged. "It's quite inconsequential."

"But maybe not to me. I was told that you were the one who suggested to Allegra that she go there."

"You have been talking to Manu," Mitzi said.

"Okay. Manu did mention it. But why did Allegra make the trip?"

"If you must know, it was for a location shoot for her movie at that time. She didn't want to go there because the temperature was in the nineties. Allegra never did like the heat."

"And you advised her to go."

"Of course. It was a big-budget picture and it would have been very damaging to her career for her to refuse to go."

214

"Did Allegra always take your advice?"

"Always. She depended on me. Totally."

"So that's why she was in Alamogordo. For a location shoot." I knew it was stupid of me to repeat that, but I couldn't think of anything else to ask.

"Yes." Pointedly, Mitzi looked at her watch.

I rose. And then an increasingly urgent feeling made me think of one more thing.

"Could I use the facilities, please?"

"The facilities?"

"You know. The little girls' room. I hate that expression, don't you, but I just drank all this tea and I have to go."

For a worrisome few seconds, I thought she would refuse me. But then she got to her feet and led the way through the hallway to a pink and ivory guest bathroom.

"Thank you."

I closed the door. Something told me she was waiting outside for me to come out, but then I heard the ring of the doorbell and very soon her footsteps departing. Thank goodness for the pizza delivery.

Finished, I came out. Mitzi wasn't there and I could hear the faint sounds of her talking to someone. I hadn't left any bread crumbs on the trail, but, of course, I knew my way back to the living room.

The problem was, at the end of the hall there was a closed door and I figured it was the location of Mitzi's bedroom. I guess I had evil in my aura, too, because my investigative curiosity got the better of me. Might Mitzi have kept a journal of her Allegra days, and, if so, might it be in her bedroom? Granted that was a poor excuse for snooping, but who needs a good one?

I tiptoed down the hall and, quietly as I could, opened the door.

It was a sensuously furnished bedroom. On one wall there was a huge mural depicting a group of frolicking—euphemistically speaking—shepherds and shepherdesses. There were several gilded

215

chairs with satin cushions and a green velour-covered ottoman. At the foot of the bed there was a settee upon which an assortment of men's clothing was haphazardly heaped. And in the canopied king-sized bed, clutching the bedcovers over him, thankfully up to his neck, lay a man.

He smiled sheepishly and waved to me.

"Hi, Dad," I said.

49

I spent the next day sitting on the couch with my laptop, suitably enough, on my lap. It was difficult to work, my mind still imprinted with the sight of my father in Mitzi's bed. It wasn't at all that I was shocked; rather, I was seeing U.G. in a new light. I would just have to deal with the fact that my father was a man, with sexual hungers and needs just like any other man.

Maybe one of the needs was to have someone share his life . . . and his bed. And if Mitzi was that someone, then awkward as it was, I would just have to accept it.

After a while, I settled down to the task at hand and went back and forth between Google and the Internet Movie Database, looking up Allegra Cort and her filmography. She had quite a lengthy and versatile list of starring vehicles, even playing a few historical figures such as Pocahontas and Amelia Earhart. I was even amused to learn Allegra had once portrayed a writer, the American novelist Louisa May Alcott.

From what I could tell, at least from the titles of her movies and what little information was given about the plots and other relevant data, none of the films had ever been shot in Alamogordo.

But that was far from proof beyond the shadow of a doubt whether Mitzi had been lying or not.

As I was checking out one of Allegra's credits, *It Happened in Sonora,* wondering whether that had been shot in old or New Mexico, there was a sudden banging on the front door and a deep, gruff voice called out, "Police! Open up!"

I froze, my hand still on the computer mouse. Was it really the police and was I about to be arrested? Or was someone claiming to be the police and I was about to be burglarized . . . or worse? Lionel wasn't home, so the ball was in my court.

"Just a minute," I said, trying to keep the tremor out of my voice. I went to the door, put on the chain, and opened it a very few inches. Immediately I closed it. It was Joe.

"Go away," I said, and went back to my laptop.

He said, "I come in peace."

"You come under false pretenses."

"Is that any way to talk to a guy with heads-up news for you?"

I thought about that. "You can tell me through the door."

"Nope. Can't."

"Then don't tell me at all." I moved the cursor around the screen, not really knowing or caring what I was doing.

Again came those loud blows on the door. "Police! Open up!"

Oh, God. Soon he would have the whole neighborhood roused up. Lionel would hear about it, and I'd be teased unmercifully.

I slid back the chain and opened the door. With my back to Joe, I returned to the sofa. He followed me closely, so close I could feel his breath warm on my neck.

Before I could sit down, his arms were around me and he turned me to face him. We stood like that, practically nose to nose, for immeasurable seconds. Then abruptly he let go and I fell backward onto the couch, right onto the laptop. I quickly moved over, determined not to let him get the better of the situation.

"Okay," I said. "Now what did you come to tell me?"

"You won't like it."

I picked up my laptop and stared at a blank screen. Great. My ass had deleted Google. Thoroughly frustrated, I closed the computer a little too vehemently.

I said, "I'm waiting."

"I'm hearing talk about convening the grand jury."

In a million years, I told myself, I would not ask him if that was pillow talk.

"You're right," I said neutrally. "I don't like it."

The function of a grand jury is to review the evidence presented by the prosecutor and decide whether there is probable cause to return an indictment. Despite its name, there is no jury; the prosecutor decides which witnesses to call, and the poor defendant—in this case most likely me—is not able to offer any conflicting evidence.

What is common knowledge is that the prosecutor could indict a ham sandwich if he so chose. If they did convene a grand jury and I were to be indicted, I would immediately be arrested.

Joe said, "You're not going to shoot the messenger, are you?"

"I can't. I'm not the one with the gun."

Moving the laptop to one side, he sat down next to me. His nearness was tantalizing. Now was the time to apologize for acting so ridiculous about Rita, I told myself. But the words wouldn't come.

Instead, I heard myself saying, "I hope you don't figure on staying. Kurt will be here soon."

"If you're talking about your bodyguard, there is no such animal. He's Lionel's boy toy."

"How'd you figure that out?"

"They don't call me a detective for nothing. But, no problem, I didn't enlighten U.G."

"Thanks for small favors."

"I can do you bigger favors. Let's go in the bedroom." He stood and extended his hand.

I wanted to. The familiar shiver down below told me how

219

much I wanted to. But should I give in this easily? What was it the guys in college used to say of women who were easy conquests? Oh yes. "She's a push-under. . . ."

But college was over. This was today and this was Joe. Once we were lying together in post-orgasmic rapture, I was sure the right words would come. . . .

I took Joe's hand and let him lead me toward the bedroom . . . just as a key turned in the front door and Lionel came in.

He took the situation in at a glance.

"Oh, hi," he said. "Am I interrupting something?"

"Yes," Joe and I said in unison.

"Well, please, don't mind me."

Neither of us said anything.

"I mean it. Ignore me completely. Just go about your little fun and games, and I'll be out here, quiet as a mouse, and hardly eavesdropping at all."

The issue might have been debated further, except for the fact that at that moment Joe's beeper went off. He looked at the number, then with an apologetic shrug in my direction took out his cell phone, made a call, and spoke briefly.

"There's a hostage situation," he said to me. "I've got to go."

I said, "Well . . . thanks for dropping by."

He nodded. "I'll call you. Bye, Lionel."

Lionel fluttered a wave and shut the door after him. He turned to me.

"Glad to see your here-today, gone-tomorrow love life is making the rounds again."

I grunted a no-comment.

"You can be thankful I came home when I did," he said. "Otherwise, a few minutes more and matters might have proceeded much farther along, and Joe's beeper would have gone off before he did."

"Oh, shut up."

I retreated to my room.

50

Sleep completely eluded me that night. If I were the kind who counted sheep, I'm sure all the sheep would have been swimming in the ocean behind a disappearing dinghy. So much for an insomniac's creativity.

Joe was one of the reasons for my restlessness. The other was the thought of the grand jury and what would happen to me if they issued an indictment and arrested me.

"They'll haul your ass to jail," Mercedes said.

Thanks for nothing.

Mercedes said, "I was in the joint once."

She certainly was. I remembered the scene I had written for my movie. It wasn't in the can as yet; I think it was on the production schedule for next week. Great. I wouldn't be there to watch over it and they'd probably make a mess of it. I wondered if they'd let Sheri say my scripted lines to whoever was playing the big black woman who shared Mercedes' cell, Dot:

". . . Right. My vibrator burned out. I've got this dickhead detective torn between trying to get in my pants and arresting me . . . I've got

PMS . . . and my best friend was just murdered . . . so if you want to jump me, now's not a good day!!!"

I sighed.

"Cheer up," said Mercedes. "Before long you'll be playing it for real."

Well, that was no consolation. If I was going to get my ass hauled to jail, then I had to do something pretty quickly. I just had to.

But what?

I closed my eyes and counted from a hundred backward to zero, by ones. Then from two hundred to zero by twos. . . . Then from three hundred and so on. . . . I was up to the sevens and on the very verge of being swallowed up by nothingness when suddenly a word surfaced to the summit of my subconscious. If I had been a cartoon character, it would have appeared in a balloon over my head.

"Alamogordo."

I blinked open my eyes and turned on my bedside lamp. Alamogordo? It kept bobbing up in my mind. There it was again. But what could it mean?

I knew that Holloman Air Force Base and the White Sands Missile Range were nearby. But I also knew that Allegra hadn't gone there to join the Military or to become an Astronaut. I also had learned that none of her films appeared to have been shot there. So why the mission to Alamogordo? She might have gone there on a publicity tour, but I couldn't be sure. I couldn't be sure of so many things. For example, had she made the trip before or after she had this baby?

And then it struck me. I propped my pillow at my back and sat bolt upright. Not before or after. During! Maybe that's where Allegra went to have her baby!

After that, I was awake for good.

51

I spent a good part of the following day at the Automobile Club getting flight information and making reservations. I also got a New Mexico road map and general information about Alamogordo.

It is located in southern New Mexico and is the county seat of Otero County. The name is Spanish, meaning "fat cottonwood." The first atomic bomb was detonated there in 1945, at what is known as the Trinity Site. Besides having the Air Force Base and the Missile Range, it is also the home of the International Space Hall of Fame, and if you were to go there you would see the grave of Ham, the first chimp in space.

So much for the travelogue. As far as Vital Records go, I learned that I could either have counter service in Santa Fe—impractical idea—or drop in at the Alamogordo Public Library for county data. On my list of things to do, I checked the latter.

True to his word, Joe did call me, but it was while I was conferring with the woman at the Travel desk. There were several obviously impatient would-be tourists, standing around, waiting for their turn at the desk, and I told him to call me back later.

He did, when I was at home that evening, throwing a few necessities into a small overnight bag. I just knew that if I spoke to Joe then, he would somehow tell from the tone of my voice that I was preparing to go away. He was that intuitive, and I was that paranoid. I didn't answer. I let him leave a message.

The fact that I picked up the message at Burbank Airport, at an ungodly hour in the morning, while I was waiting to depart for Alamogordo on a 6:45 A.M. America West flight could in no way be held against Joe. "I don't know where you are or what you're up to," he said. "You'd just better be behaving yourself."

You see? Typical of Joe. No "I miss you." No "I love you." Ha! Not even a "Call me back."

But right now I had other things on my mind. Yes, Jordan and Perez had asked me not to leave the jurisdiction, but I couldn't stick around doing nothing, keeping my hands outstretched for the cuffs they would put on me. Joe had told me there were rumors about convening the grand jury, but rumors were just that. I hadn't yet heard any definite news. If they were going to arrest me, I had to act fast, and the only possible clue I had, as speculative as it was, was Alamogordo.

Lionel had to be told where I was going, but I swore him to secrecy, no matter how hard Joe or U.G. or anyone else pressed him. He gave me a few admonitions, pronounced it "a fool's errand," and predicted all kinds of dire consequences, ranging from, "What will I tell the dicks when they show up with the bloodhounds?" to "I'll never be able to go to the post office again, because you'll be on a Wanted poster, and it will probably be a ghastly picture at that."

What I didn't let on to him was that Shep was accompanying me. In fact, he was driving me to the airport. It wouldn't have reassured Lionel knowing I wouldn't be alone. Instead, he would most likely have blabbed to U.G., and the two would have fallen over each other in their haste to tell Joe.

One thing in my favor was that at the moment Lionel was all

atwitter about going to see Kurt play in a local hockey game Saturday evening, and as long as I came back in time to go with him and do my beard act thing . . . well, then, okay. I knew he would be spending the interval tearing apart his closet for exactly the right outfit to wear. And knowing Lionel, by the time I came back he would undoubtedly have purchased a whole new wardrobe.

I needn't have said anything to Shep, of course. It was just that I had a lot of ground to cover in a very short time and the ground was purely *terra incognita*. I had no idea what exactly I was looking for, where to find it, or even how to recognize it when I saw it. Either Shep would be a big help or the two of us could fail miserably and I would return home to those waiting handcuffs. Right now he was my buddy and I desperately needed one.

The America West flight went to Phoenix. There was a forty-minute layover there, and then we would take off for El Paso. From El Paso to Alamogordo would be an eighty-mile drive by rented car. It was the best I could do. Alamogordo wasn't exactly a bustling travel hub.

Shep helped me pick out two paperback mysteries in the airport book shop for reading material at night. If Joe had been with me, I wouldn't have needed any. But if my aunt had whiskers, as they say . . . No, they don't say "whiskers"; they say "balls." But she still would be my uncle. . . .

We were scheduled to make one stop in Phoenix, and I actually fell asleep during the short hop of about an hour and a half. A first for me. No matter how long the flight, I usually stay awake in order to keep an eye on any problems the pilot may be overlooking. But two nights of wakefulness had taken their toll, and next thing I knew I was awakened by a sudden sense of lack of motion.

I said, "What happened? The plane stopped."

"It usually does when it's landed," Shep said. "We're in Phoenix."

I said, "I knew that," and got up to retrieve my bag from the overhead bin.

"Has anyone ever told you," Shep said, "that you're beautiful in repose?"

Repose? No one I know uses that word today.

On the segment from Phoenix to El Paso, I stayed fully awake.

52

It was around noon when we picked up our rental car at the El Paso International Airport, headed out on Airport Road, and eventually connected with US 54 East to Alamogordo. Shep said he would take the wheel and I would navigate. He got no argument from me. Actually, though, it would have been nice for me to drive an almost new four-door sedan instead of the leftovers I had been given at the studio. I decided to myself that I would do the drive back.

Conversation was minimal. I concentrated on the map and the scenery, and Shep told me about some of the articles he had done for *Vanity Fair*. It was an impressive detailing and I told him so. We agreed that the first thing we would do would be to check out those Vital Records, and whatever further searches that led to we could divvy up.

In Alamogordo we checked into an inn, one of a popular chain that featured a free breakfast bar, a fitness center, and an indoor pool and spa. The brochure also made mention of Internet Access, which, later, proved to be a single machine in the lobby area, adjacent to the gift shop.

Half an hour later, after dumping my bag in my room, which looked like countless other rooms in which I had stayed during my stint as an investigative reporter, making use of the bathroom facilities, and running a brush through my jet-lagged hair, I met Shep for lunch at the coffee shop next door.

"I've been making some calls," he said.

"Already? Good for you."

"You shouldn't have wasted your time peeing," Mercedes said.

"Not good for us, though. I've discovered that New Mexico birth and death certificates are restricted-access records and that only . . ." He pulled out his notebook and read from it: "'. . . that only upon written application and proven tangible direct interest may a certified copy of a vital record be issued. Immediate family is defined as the following . . .'"

"Never mind," I said. "I know what an immediate family is. So it looks as though we can't get into the birth records to see if Allegra had her baby here."

"Let's see . . . you're too young to pretend to be her mother. . . . How about her sister?"

"No thanks. I'm already a one-woman crime wave as it is."

The waitress appeared to take our orders.

When she moved away, Shep said, "Looks like we've come all this way for nothing."

"Don't be so negative," I said. I gave it a moment's thought. "What about the public library? I've had good luck with library research in the past."

"Sure. If you mean on Forty-second Street in New York."

"We'll give it a shot. Hurry up and eat."

"Whoa," he said. "She hasn't brought our food yet."

"Then let's not waste time."

I used my cell phone to make a call, ignoring the annoyed glances of the other diners. I made my inquiry, listened, and then said, "Great. We'll be right over."

228

Shep looked at me questioningly as I returned the phone to my bag.

"We're in business again," I said. "They have Internet access and, get this, local newspapers on microfilm dating back to 1899."

After lunch we drove to the library, which turned out to be only a scant half a dozen miles away. It was a low-lying building, a light terra-cotta in color, with a mild breeze rippling the American flag on a flagpole in front. We were immediately greeted and given the official introductory patter by a very plump, bespectacled librarian whose hair was done up in a coronet of braids and whose name badge proclaimed her to be Ms. Emily Birdwell.

In a suitably hushed voice, she gave us a laudatory account of their eighty-five thousand volumes, collections in German and Spanish, large type books and talking books, and children's programs. Her range of knowledge was an indication of the reason for her thick prescription glasses. She had probably read every one of those eighty-five thousand volumes.

Eventually, I had to interrupt. "Ms. Birdwell, I was told you had local newspapers on microfilm?"

"Yes, we do. If you'll just follow me."

We trailed her to a small corner room and, remembering what Manu had said about the date of his and Allegra's divorce, gave Ms. Birdwell the dates of the issues we wanted to research. Nineteen eighty-nine and nineteen ninety. Even as we told her, I had the uneasy feeling that it was all one big guessing game.

She nodded and got the reels for us. Then she demonstrated how to use the machine and left us, presumably to give her library sales pitch to any other tourists who might wander in.

53

Finally we were settled, Shep at the microfilm and me seated alongside to feed in each reel. We soon learned that the local newspaper, the *Alamogordo Daily News,* had begun continuous publication in 1898, the same year the city of Alamogordo was established. We also learned, unfortunately, after half an hour of steadfastly peering at the tiny print, that although the *News* covered the comings and goings of the city, for the time span in which we were interested—when Allegra might have been here—they printed the goings but not the comings. The obituaries but not the birth announcements.

Shep said, "Now can I be negative?"

"Nope. I have not yet begun to fight. Or investigate, as the case may be." If the truth were told, I was somewhat daunted. But I wasn't going to let on.

"I suppose," he said, "we could check out the local hospitals. Maybe they keep records."

I said, "Maybe they do. But they'll never let us have a look."

"Look who's calling the pot negative."

I had to smile at that, and we shared a moment of warm

camaraderie. Suddenly I became aware of a presence hovering at our backs. I turned around and there was Ms. Birdwell.

"How are we doing?" she said in a cheerful voice that was more like a series of chirps.

I said, "I'm afraid not too well. Your local newspaper is a wonderful source for telling us who checked out but not who checked in."

She stared at me blankly. "You mean at the motels?"

"She means birth announcements," Shep said, giving me a reproachful shake of his head.

Ms. Birdwell brightened. "Births . . . oh, you mean babies."

No, we mean puppies. I thought it but of course didn't say it. Not with Shep ready to ground me at any minute.

What I said was, "Yes, we're interested in the babies born in Alamogordo during those years."

"Well, no. The *News* doesn't report on that," Birdwell said, taking the reels from us. "It once did, but that would have been long ago. Before my time."

Shep said, "Thank you, Ms. Birdwell. You've been very helpful." Not really, of course, but a reporter learned always to be polite to sources.

We were practically at the door when Birdwell said, "Of course there's the *Gordo Gazette*."

We stopped. "The what?" I said, getting it out before Shep could.

"The *Gordo Gazette*. It was a small community publication, defunct for the last ten years. But it used to."

We waited, holding our breaths. Used to what?

"It did?" I said.

"Yes, it used to run all these columns about births and engagements and weddings and deaths. We called it the Hatch, Catch, Match, and Dispatch page."

"But . . . you said the *Gazette* is now . . ."

"Defunct." She nodded.

I ventured a chance. "Might you have it on microfilm?"

Another nod, bless her. "I keep it there for high school seniors to practice using the microfilm machine for their research papers. They get a kick out of seeing their parents' names, and, of course, their own."

She retrieved some more reels and fed the first one in. In a few moments, there it was on the screen: the front page of the *Gordo Gazette—Your Community Circular.*

"You'll find all this down-home stuff about local happenings," she said, "but you may also find what you're looking for in the birth announcements."

Shep said, "Where did the reports come from?"

"Our two major hospitals. You have your Gerald Champion Regional Medical Center and your Betty Dare Good Samaritan. All the girl babies were born at Betty Dare and the boys at Gerald Champion."

She said it with a perfectly straight face until the smile cracked through. "A little library humor."

I matched her smile and she went away with a parting flutter of her hand.

Shep took over the microfilm seat again and he and I went painstakingly through the "Hatch" columns. There was nothing with the mother's name being Allegra Cort. No Allegra anythings. No anything Corts. No de la Ruas or anything familiar. Not that I wholeheartedly believed there would be. If Allegra had been a patient in either hospital, she would have registered under a made-up name.

We scanned women with the same initials, but the fathers were also listed, along with their Alamogordo addresses, and they all seemed legitimate. Suddenly something jumped out at me.

"Shep—back up!"

"What? You see something?"

"Amy March."

"What about it? Who's Amy March?"

"One of Louisa May Alcott's little women. Allegra once played Alcott in the movie *Under the Lilacs,* remember?"

232

"No, but I'm glad you do. Think it's worth following up?"

"It's the closest we've come to confirming that Allegra had her baby here." I squinted at the screen. "At Gerald Champion Regional Medical Center."

Shep got up. "Think we should head over there? Maybe if I charm a few nurses, somebody will remember something."

"Let's split up and cover twice the ground," I said. "You go to the hospital and I'll do some more scrolling in case anything else looks promising."

"Fine. Keep in touch by cell and I'll be back to pick you up."

He left and I scanned through a few more of the *Gazettes*. Nothing. I turned off the machine, returned the reels to Ms. Birdwell, and regretted not having gone with Shep. Still, he would have a better chance of "charming the nurses" along with the administrative personnel of the hospital if I wasn't tagging along.

I wandered into the library's main room and took a copy of today's *Los Angeles Times* from the newspaper shelf. I pulled over a hard-backed chair, sat down at a reading table, and spread the paper out. Nope, there was nothing about the grand jury.

Finished with the *Times,* I put it back and exchanged it for today's *Alamogordo Daily News.* When in Alamogordo, do as the Alamogordians do . . . Or was it the Alamogordese? . . . In any case, there wasn't too much of interest, at least of what might interest Shep or me, and eventually, after digesting today's news items, I found myself idly scanning the announcements of social events scheduled for this afternoon and evening.

There was to be a meeting of the Adult Diabetes Support Group. Hey, I could go to that, I distractedly thought. The Fraternal Order of Eagles was getting together; so were the American Legion Auxiliary, the Women's Club, the Genealogy Society, the Loving Adoptive Parents group, the Golden Gears Car Club— Wait a minute. I went back to the Loving Adoptive Parents group, and for some reason I can't explain, I filed that away for future reference.

233

There was a posted sign in huge block letters about not using a cell phone in the library, so I went outside and called Lionel.

"It's about time," he said. "Everybody and his maiden aunt has been calling wanting to know where you were."

"Who's everybody?"

"Joe and U.G."

"I hope you didn't tell them."

"Of course not, darling. If nothing else, I am the very soul of discretion. Also of duplicity. I told Joe you were with U.G., and I told U.G. you were with Joe."

"Eventually they're going to talk to each other, you know."

"By then you'll be home, and I'll deny everything."

"Anyone else call?"

"Nobody—oh, wait, that lady dick."

"Rita Perez? What did she want?"

"Nothing. She just said to tell you she called. I told her you were with Joe."

I loved it. "And what did she say to that?"

"She said that was funny because *she* was with Joe."

MEMO TO MAGGIE: Never ask a leading question unless you already know the answer.

"Maggie, are you still there?" Lionel said.

"I'm here. Bloody but not bowed."

"Good. Remember—you promised to be back in time for Kurt's game."

We signed off. Somehow I got through the interval until Shep called and arranged to pick me up.

54

He hadn't made any headway at the hospital. He had been
relayed from one department to another, one staff member to another, and, finally, to a gorgon of a hospital administrator who
told him their records were inaccessible and that's all she wrote.

I thought about the little we had learned or at least imagined
that we had learned.

I said, "If Allegra really was this Amy March, and we don't
know that for sure, and if she had her baby here, and we don't know
that for sure, either, what we do know for a certainty is that she
didn't return to Los Angeles with it. Therefore . . ."

"The child is still here."

"Or somewhere else. . . ."

Shep said, "Are we a pair of crack investigators or what?"

We drove the rest of the way to our hotel in silence. But I was
thinking, trying to remember something. Something I had seen in
today's paper. Something that struck me in the Events column. . . .
Just as we pulled into the parking lot, it came to me. This afternoon there was to be a meeting of the Loving Adoptive Parents
group. LAP—a fitting acronym for Loving Parents.

I said, "Shep, what do you think are the chances that Allegra's baby was adopted by a couple or even by a single person right here in Alamogordo?"

He turned off the motor. "You're getting at something, aren't you?"

I told him about LAP.

"And there's a meeting today?" he said.

I looked at my watch. "Even as we speak. It's at the Community Center, wherever that is."

"I vote we find out." He started up the car again.

Inside LAP's meeting room at the Community Center, we were met by a small cluster of people sitting around in a semi-circle.

One of the women was saying, "I think we should do our Soft Landing picnic again this year. There are at least two new couples—"

She stopped, as we became the cynosure of all eyes.

"Uh-oh, that's her," Shep said, low in my ear.

I returned the whisper. "Her who?"

"The hospital gorgon."

I winced inwardly, but I wasn't to be deterred.

"Excuse us," I said. "We wonder if we might sit in on your meeting."

"Who are you?" said one man. He was in his early thirties, lean and rugged looking, and was holding the hand of the young red-headed woman seated next to him.

Shep said, "I'm a reporter from *Vanity Fair* and I'm doing a national article on adoptive parents."

You'd think he might have included me in on that.

"Who's she?" someone else asked.

"My wife," Shep said.

I tried not to glare at him, and, anyway, the gorgon was already up on her feet.

"Are you adoptive parents?"

236

I said, "No," quickly, before Shep could improvise again. "But we might be someday."

Shep said, "Look, Mrs. . . . ."

She ignored the cue for her name. "I remember you from the hospital, and you're not welcome here."

"A story in a big magazine like *Vanity Fair* could give you great exposure," I said. "The rate of people wanting to adopt would soar skyward."

Another man, older and heavyset, said, "That could have a positive aspect, couldn't it, Mrs. Hicker?"

Aha. The gorgon was identified, and she obviously wasn't too happy about it. She looked even less happy when a chorus of voices affirmatively echoed what the older gentleman had said.

Putting up a silencing hand, she said, "We'd have to ask Dr. Cruz. Dr. Cruz is our group psychiatric consultant."

"Fine," Shep said. "Let's ask him right now."

"Her," said Mrs. Hicker. "We'll speak to her tomorrow. Until then, don't call us—we'll call you."

How do you like that? Hicker could have a second career as a movie executive.

Shep and I both tried, but we couldn't budge the gorgon. There was nothing to do, in the face of her obstinacy, but to retreat.

First, however, I had to find the ladies' room. It was while I was at the sink, washing my hands, that the door opened and the young redheaded woman from the meeting came in.

"Hi," she said.

I nodded. "Hello."

"I hope your husband gets to do the article."

"I hope so, too," I said, once I remembered who my "husband" was supposed to be.

"We're new," the young woman said. "New adoptive parents, I mean. We have the darlingest little girl. Sophie Ann."

"Congratulations," I said, turning on the hand dryer. "I wish you all the best."

Okay, that was prosaic, but I did hope everything turned out well for the young couple.

She smiled back at me and entered one of the stalls. In another moment or two, the blower had finished its job drying my hands.

"Bye," I said through the closed door.

"Maybe I'll see you again," her voice came back. "I'm sure Dr. Cruz will give her approval. You'll like her. She's very generous with advice and she keeps all our records."

Bingo!

Back in the car with Shep, I told him what I had learned. "Let's call Dr. Cruz."

"Maggie, get with the program. She's a psychiatrist, for God's sake."

"But she keeps all the records. Maybe she knows if someone in Alamogordo adopted Allegra's baby."

"And you think she's going to tell us? She's bound by ethics. She's not going to breach the confidentiality of her patients."

"But we've come so far already."

"Right. And what have we learned? Nothing that could possibly tell us who the murderer is! It was a long shot to begin with."

I couldn't think of anything to say by way of rebuttal. He was right on all counts. Somehow getting at those adoptive records might have taken us one step farther. But one step farther to where? Time was running out and at any moment I could be apprehended as a fugitive from justice. . . .

Later, in my room, I had just finished my shower and was towel-drying my hair when Shep called.

"What are you wearing?"

"A towel."

"Perfect. Step into the hall and let me whisk you away. I've got a treat planned for you."

238

"If the treat requires me to wear just this towel," I said, "forget it."

"I really do have a surprise for you. Did you bring along jeans and boots?"

"I've been wearing my Durangos all day and jeans are my dress clothes."

"Good. I'll pick you up in ten."

Once more in jeans and old cowboy boots, I met Shep in the hall.

"What's up?"

"I thought you needed a break, so I'm taking you for a little trip."

"A trip?"

"Well, kind of," he said, "and you have to wear this." He produced a brand-new cowboy hat and plopped it on my head.

I couldn't believe it, but it fit. "How did you know my size?"

He said, "I think I have your sizes memorized."

I had no answer to that and, uncharacteristically, kept quiet.

55

We drove on Route 82, heading east toward the Sacramento Mountains, and, in about a half hour, came to the small town of Cloudcroft, whose welcoming signpost proudly announced it was "the pasture for the clouds."

A few miles farther on, we pulled up into a stable yard. A very old and dusty yard, with a spotless tack room and ten beautiful horses, each in its own stall.

"Horses?" I said.

"You ride, don't you?"

"Yes, but I'm a New Yorker. We ride English."

"You may have to learn to ride Western quickly."

Shep was right. The stable had no English saddles, just Western, so we saddled up and rode out, me in my new hat and Shep wearing an old battered one he'd clearly owned for years . . . just a couple of old cowhands from *Vanity Fair*.

It took me a little while to get used to the Western style, to the horn, and to my backside resting against the base of the cantle, the upward-projecting rear part, but soon enough I was riding as well as any dude on any dude ranch.

We were in the foothills of the mountains, just south of the Mescalero Apache Indian reservation. We rode for about an hour, through the cottonwoods and following a winding stream through the hills. The trees were whispering to one another in a slight breeze, and all my cares, all memories of Allegra and Lisa, seemed to drift away. I relaxed in the saddle, feeling the gentle rhythm of the horse beneath me.

Shep must have been feeling the same sense of serenity, because he matched my silence with his own. We rode, enjoying the freedom and each other's quiet company. I do so admire a man who knows when to keep his mouth shut.

Too soon, we turned around and rode back toward the stable yard, watching the sun set over the desert. Without a layer of smog to distort the colors, there were soft and subtle pinks and yellows and purples flooding the sky.

When we climbed back into the car, I felt refreshed and reinvented, mint new.

"That was wonderful," I said, my head resting on the back of the seat. "Where to now?"

"Aren't you hungry?"

"Ravenous."

"Before we left I asked the concierge to make a reservation for us at the finest restaurant in Alamogordo."

"The concierge?" I said, laughing.

"Okay, the desk clerk back at the motel."

I took a shower and changed into something more befitting "the finest restaurant in Alamogordo," which turned out to be the Blue Coyote, located in a small adobe building on a side street near the center of town.

Once inside the small entrance patio, we were led to a large outdoor terrace, surrounded by cottonwoods and high whitewashed adobe walls. Our table had a soft yellow cloth with matching napkins and three small yellow candles in the center. We faced a wall on which the movie *Red River* with John Wayne and Montgomery Clift was running, in all its black-and-white glory, silently, of course.

The trees had all those little white, twinkly lights that used to be for Christmas and are now up all year. Above, the authentic twinkling stars were bright in the clear night, and with the musky fragrance of the agave and the soft lilts from a strolling guitar player everything was conducive to a very favorable romantic evening.

Except, of course, that Shep wasn't Joe.

"When you're not near the man you love," Mercedes said, *"you love the man you're near."*

No! Not true! In spite of once being conflicted about both Henrik and Joe, I was never really the kind of woman who could be in love with two men at the same time. And I wasn't in love with Shep, I told myself. This was a time-out; that was all.

It might also be a time-out for Shep. I didn't really know anything about his personal life. Just for right now, we were both characters in some other writer's play.

56

You look especially great tonight," Shep said, holding out my chair for me.

"Thank you. I have hay in my hair, and my rear end is bruised beyond belief, thanks to your Western saddle. I'm grateful this chair has a deep cushion, or I would have to eat standing up."

"I thought you enjoyed the ride," he said. "Was I wrong?"

"Not at all. I loved the ride," I said, in all honesty. "I haven't ridden in years, and tonight was absolutely perfect. Thank you."

The waiter had delivered my iced tea and I saluted Shep with my glass.

"Cheers," I said.

He raised his glass of merlot in a return toast. "To us."

We ordered the specialty of the house, which was an appetizer of ceviche, then a fresh green salad followed by a plate of tamales with a *verde* sauce on the side.

Throughout dinner we told more stories about our investigative careers and traded anecdotes about Gracie, *Vanity Fair*'s Senior Articles Editor. Mentioning Gracie, of course, called for a few toasts in his honor, and I had even more iced tea while Shep filled his wineglass again.

For dessert, I assiduously avoided the flan Shep wanted to share with me and had a half cup of lemon sherbet instead, finishing up with *te de hiervas*, which sounds much more glamorous than "herbal tea."

It was a perfect ending to an almost perfect day, I thought. The exception to the perfection was, of course, our failure to learn anything about Allegra's child.

Shep said, "What happened? Your face just lost its light."

"I'm returning to reality. I can't believe we struck out as dismally as we did."

"It happens. Can't bat a thousand every game."

"Easy for you to say. You're not the one they're going to lock up. Do you think they'll make me wear orange coveralls? Orange is just not my color."

"No reason to panic. I'll come see you every week. Bake you a chocolate cake with a nail file in it."

"Now that cheers me up."

"I'll even sign up for a conjugal visit."

I knew better than to take him seriously, so I laughed. Obviously, he was trying to get my mind off my troubles.

"You know something," he said, "I like it here. Someday I may come back and do the whole tourist bit. Maybe even buy a little casita here when the writing dries up."

"You'd leave New York?"

"In a New Mexico minute."

That made me laugh again, and he joined in.

"You know, Maggie," Shep said, "I really enjoyed this."

"Me, too. But we should be getting back. . . ."

"It's not even ten yet. What's our rush? It's the shank of the evening. . . ." He frowned. "What the hell is the shank, anyway? Isn't it part of the foot?"

"I think it means the main part of the evening."

"How come you're so attractive *and* so smart?" He covered my hand with his on the table and I let it rest there.

I make no excuses for it. There are times in a woman's life when you can use the touch of a man's hand. This was one of those times. I wasn't being fickle. Or was I? Joe would have understood. . . . At least I think he would have understood. . . .

Why, oh why, then didn't I understand myself?

Shep took care of the check and we headed back to the hotel. The stars filled the sky along with a bright full moon. Shep let me drive. I was feeling happy, I decided, still a little dispirited from the day's lack of results, but all in all my frustration had subsided.

In the hallway outside my room, I retrieved my key card from my purse. "Good night, Shep. Thanks for being such good company."

"Hold it," he said. "My mother taught me that when seeing a lady to her door, a gentleman always takes her key and lets her in."

I held up my electronic card. "Be my guest."

He took my card and opened the door and I went in. I expected him to return my card and say good night. Instead, he closed the door behind him and followed me inside.

I switched on a light.

"How about a nightcap?" he said, putting the card down on the dresser top.

I gestured around the room. "There's no minibar."

"That wasn't the kind of nightcap I was talking about."

With that, he put his arms around me and pulled me close to him.

I don't know what kind of kiss I was expecting, but it wasn't the openmouthed, tongue-probing one he gave me. I struggled to free myself from his embrace, but his arms tightened around me as he forced me back onto the bed.

I lay there, curving into the soft mattress, with Shep on top of me, his hardness pressing against my pelvis, his mouth roughly seeking mine. Obviously an experienced lover, he was stroking me, fumbling with my jeans zipper, murmuring tender endearments, making me more and more and more weak and accepting—

I snapped to suddenly, as though recovering from a brief blackout. With every ounce of strength I could muster, I shoved him off me and managed to get up.

He rolled over and looked up at me from the bed with a puzzled look. "What's the matter?"

I kept my voice low, but my words were stony and their meaning unmistakable. "I'm so sorry," I said. "You'd better leave."

He got up slowly, straightening his clothes.

"You could have fooled me," he said. "I figured you were hot for it."

"You figured wrong. If I misled you . . ."

"If? If? Lady, this is the first time I've been screwed without ever being screwed!"

"Again . . . I'm sorry. Now please leave."

He went to the door. "Who would have thought it," he said. "The famous Maggie Mars a cock teaser. A regular goddamn little cock teaser!"

The door closed behind him and he was gone. I ran over to it, locked it, and put on the chain.

There was no point in going to bed and trying to sleep. After checking my blood and having to give myself an insulin injection, I took stock of my options. Tomorrow I would have to face Shep again, but by then perhaps we both would have cooled off.

57

His parting words had stung. Looking at it objectively, I guess I had led him on, but it wasn't consciously so. Wasn't that the purpose of the whole evening? To relax and enjoy ourselves? I just shouldn't have been so unprepared for how far Shep would want to take it. Perhaps tomorrow he wouldn't feel so suckered and would be willing to listen. We would talk things out; maybe I'd even tell him about Joe and not wanting to scramble my mind with another man. Meanwhile, I would concentrate on something else.

What I focused on was Dr. Cruz, the psychiatrist who kept the records of the Loving Adoptive Parents group. I checked my watch, expecting to see that it was after midnight, but it was only eleven. It was doubtful that Cruz would still be seeing patients this late. She probably had closed up shop around five, maybe six. However, since I knew she wasn't going to be forthcoming about her patients anyway, so much the better for me. . . .

I looked into the local telephone directory, and found a listing for Dr. Susan Larissa Cruz. Making sure I still had the keys to the rental car in my purse, I changed into sweats and tennis shoes. As

I walked past Shep's room, I paused outside his door and listened but heard nothing. Either he was already asleep or he was not there. Probably he was at some bar drinking it off.

Her office was in a modest medical building located in the middle of a small business complex. Fortunately, it was a one-story building, so in light of what I was planning to do, I didn't have to deal with elevators and security guards. There was only one car in the parking lot, and its plate bore the regular Land of Enchantment insignia.

There were lights on over each office door. I scanned the area hallway up high, looking for cameras, but I couldn't detect any. Thankfully, this neighborhood of Alamogordo was still relatively crime free and apparently low-tech.

I approached the entrance with noiseless footsteps and cautiously looked around. There was no one in sight. Putting my hand on the doorknob, I tested it, preparing to open it with my Slim Jim, credit-card look-alike lock opener. To my surprise, the knob turned in my grasp and the door opened.

I slipped inside and found myself in a waiting room, softly lit by one lamp. An assortment of southwestern prints hung on the walls. There were two chairs facing a couch that had a colorful Navajo blanket thrown over the back of it. The coffee table was a slice of irregular glass on a driftwood base. In one corner of the room stood a beautiful screen with hand-painted Palominos racing across its panels.

To my right, there was an archway, through which I could see an alcove with three metal filing cabinets lined up against the wall. Alongside the archway was what looked like a doorbell, and several framed certificates, attesting no doubt to Dr. Cruz's academic qualifications.

As I looked around, trying to gauge what my next move should be, the door to an inner office opened and a woman came out. She was in her fifties, of medium height, her graying hair cut into a stylish wedge, and she was wearing a very attractive short-skirted hunter green suit with a pale green satin blouse. If she was surprised to see me, she didn't show it.

She said, "May I help you?"

I was the surprised one. "Um. Yes. I mean maybe. Are you Dr. Cruz?"

"I am. Are you a patient?"

That confused me. Did I look like a psychiatric patient?

"No, no. I just didn't think you'd be here at this hour." I felt that an explanation was now needed as to why then I had come in. "Your door was open," I said lamely.

"I've been expecting a late patient. You're obviously not him."

"Not unless this is my night for cross-dressing."

She didn't smile. I was in trouble already and I hadn't even asked what I so desperately needed to find out.

"If you don't mind," she said, "I'm not going to wait for him any longer. I'll be closing up, so perhaps you can call the office tomorrow for an appointment."

I decided to plunge right in, even though I was fairly sure it would be hopeless. "Dr. Cruz, I came here hoping that you could give me some information about a birth mother—"

She stopped me with an upraised hand.

"It is eleven o'clock at night. You enter my office and don't bother to ring the bell announcing you . . ." I looked quickly at the "doorbell" . . . "and now you ask for privileged information. I'm sorry, but I can't help you. Even if I kept those records. Which I don't."

"Oh."

"I used to keep them, but that was some time ago. Nowadays there are different regulations having to do with confidentiality about the whole adoption process."

"Yes, of course." *She used to keep them,* she had said. "Well . . . thank you for your time."

249

I headed for the door, as she turned and went back inside. Almost immediately the lights in the filing cabinet alcove darkened. I went to the front door and closed it with a noticeable sound effect, but remained on the office side of it.

My glance traveled the room and lit on the decorative screen. In another moment I was hidden behind it, just as the doctor came out again and turned off the lamp in the waiting room. She exited, locking the door behind her. I waited, and before long I heard the sound of a car starting up. I waited some more.

When I felt reasonably safe, I emerged. In the darkness I unsteadily made my way through the waiting room to the front door, in the process barking a shin on the sharp edge of the coffee table. Once at the front door, I undid the lock. From past experience, I know that when you are engaged in dirty, rotten, sneaky tricks, as I seem to be so often, it is always prudent, if not always arrest-proof, to leave yourself an available escape hatch.

Back at the door leading to the inner office, I tried it and, to my relief, found it unlocked. I went in, taking only a few seconds to observe that there weren't any file cabinets in here. Figuring I could search her desk later if I struck out with the cabinets I had previously noticed, I went back to the waiting room and around through the archway.

There they were. The three metal file cabinets, four drawers apiece. They were locked, but for all I knew, inside one of them was the answer to all my problems. Don't ask me why I thought that. When you're running on empty, there always seems to be a filling station just around the next bend.

The problem I was confronted with now was how to get inside those locked cabinets. The Slim Jim wouldn't do it, and I hadn't thought to carry any other tools along with me, figuring I'd never get through Airport Security. Maybe I could look around in Cruz's office and find something.

I wasted five minutes looking around. There were no keys in

Dr. Cruz's desk drawer, but there was a sharp-pointed letter opener. I fingered it tentatively. Maybe it was worth a try.

I returned to the alcove and worked the point into one of the file cabinet locks. I turned it clockwise and counter-clockwise. Nothing. Exerting a little more pressure, I jimmied it deeper and said aloud: "Open sesame."

Sesame opened. It actually opened. I was incredulous. What was the matter with Susan Larissa Cruz, M.D.? She was the one who ought to have her head examined. Why didn't she have a more impenetrable lock? Didn't she know there were nefarious people around, people like me, who would risk anything to breach her precious confidentiality?

I settled down to work, now that access to the Promised Land was open to me.

The files were in chronological order, and I immediately went to the 1989 section, starting with January. There was nothing to be seen, and I say that quite literally, because the names of both the birth and the adoptive parents were in there and as long as it didn't concern Amy March, I really didn't want to pry into all that private knowledge. On to the next month, and then the next, and eventually June . . . and there it was.

Baby Boy March. Born to March, Amy. June 8. The adoptive parents were John and Kathleen Connell. The birth father was—blank.

I copied the information quickly into my investigation notebook and tucked it back into my bag. Then I closed the file, returned it to its drawer, and closed up. The lock didn't show any signs of having been violated, and it was while I was wondering if I should use a tissue to wipe off fingerprints that I heard it. The very slightest of noises, as if a car door outside had been opened and closed. . . .

I remained absolutely still. The moments went by. There was no further sound. No footsteps.

I made a decision to forget about prints, even though in the back of my mind was the knowledge that my prints were on file and could be easily matched. Right now, however, I had to get out of there as fast as possible. After looking around once more to be sure I hadn't left anything behind, I went back to Cruz's office and returned the letter opener to its place in her drawer.

Mission accomplished.

And then I heard it. The unmistakable sound of the "doorbell."

58

I opened the door leading back into the waiting room, and stopped short. Clearly silhouetted in the shaft of moonlight streaming through the window was the figure of a man.

I froze.

He didn't appear to be wearing any kind of uniform. This could be good or bad. If he wasn't a cop or a security guard, which was bad enough, what was worse was that he might be a burglar or a prowler.

I felt the situation called for me to go directly on the offensive.

"What are you doing here?" I said loudly.

He turned to face me. "You left the door open. You the shrink?"

"Huh?"

"The deficiency expert. The nut doctor. Whatever."

It dawned on me. He was asking if I was the psychiatrist.

"You mean Dr. Cruz? . . ."

"Yeah. You said I could come in tonight for our first session. Alex Humboldt, remember?"

Of course. He must be her late patient.

You know the expression about being impaled on the horns of

a dilemma? I was not only impaled; I was gored. If I denied being Dr. Cruz, he would wonder what I was doing in her office and that could lead to further complications. If I told him I was the psychiatrist, then he might unburden himself of some very personal information and ask for advice and I would be guilty of impersonating Dr. Phil.

Of course, that latter offense didn't loom very large compared to breaking and entering and especially to murder. My only recourse was to own up to the truth.

"I'm sorry," I said. "I am not Dr. Cruz. She has already left. You'll have to come back another time."

There. That was straightforward enough. So that was what being honest felt like. It felt strangely cleansing; it felt good. Maybe I would live the rest of my life without ever telling another lie.

"Then who are you?" he said.

"I'm her assistant."

So much for noble intentions.

"Then I suppose there's no way you can help me with the trouble I'm having with my partner . . ."

"No, no, I can't."

". . . and our kid."

"No way at all! Good night."

He was still grumbling. "You'd have thought she could have waited for me. I told her I have an issue to deal with. Next time I see her, if I do, I'll give *her* some issues to deal with."

Finally, he made it to the front door and let himself out, taking all his issues with him. I just hoped that in the half darkness of the room he hadn't gotten a good look at me.

I heard a car start up and take off. I waited a few minutes more, then opened the door and peered out. There were no other vehicles in the parking lot except mine. As quickly as I could, I locked up and hurried to my car. I was just about to get behind the wheel when suddenly a dazzling light shone through the window in my face!

254

The light came from a flashlight and the flashlight was in the hands of a burly uniformed security guard!

He motioned for me to get out of the car. I complied.

"You got a good reason to be here?" he said.

"You won't believe this, but I was about to ask you the same thing."

"Don't be funny."

"Sorry," I said. "I had a late appointment with Dr. Cruz, but she seems to have left."

"Oh yeah. She did tell me someone might be coming in." He checked a little notebook he had with him. "Name?"

I hesitated a moment before it leapt to my tongue. "Alex Humboldt."

He gave me a searching look. "I had the impression it was gonna be a guy."

"Everyone makes that mistake. The 'Alex' is short for 'Alexandra.' You know, the last empress of Russia?"

"Uh-huh." He absorbed this, then: "Listen, Alex, a word of warning. . . ."

My heart sank. "Yes?"

"Be careful driving home. This time of night, there are a lot of crazies on the roads."

I thanked him and took off.

59

Back in my motel hallway, I stopped to listen at Shep's door. Still silent. Once in my room, I did a phone book search for John and Kathleen Connell, the adoptive parents of the Amy March baby, and found an address. I wrote it down, then undressed, washed up, and crawled into bed.

The incident with Shep still bothered me. He had taken our togetherness, our being comfortable with each other, our laughter, all the wrong way, and surely I had contributed to that misdirection. I fervently hoped that we could mend things tomorrow. Perhaps, if only to relieve the guilt I felt, it wouldn't hurt to give him a token of my good faith.

I picked up the phone and called the hotel operator. I told him I didn't want to disturb the guest in Room 211, but was there a way I could just leave a message for him without actually ringing his room? Yes, I could leave it on his voice mail. I did. I gave Shep the name and address of the adoptive parents and suggested we meet at the hotel breakfast bar around nine. That would give us a chance to get over there and interview them before we left for the airport and our flight home.

My voice was normal and friendly, as if nothing had happened. I hoped he would accept the message in the same manner. That done, I closed my eyes and fell into a heavy sleep.

Shep was a no-show at the breakfast bar. I waited till nine thirty, and then rang his room. No answer. The very helpful clerk at the front desk told me that Mr. Scott had checked out at 7:20 A.M. He had called for a taxi. I groaned inwardly. There was now no doubt that Shep was pissed off at me and wasn't interested in a cease-fire. I'd probably run into him at the airport, but first I was going to pursue the lead I had on the Connells.

It dawned on me, but only with hindsight, that Shep had the same lead. He had it because I had given it to him. Shit!

The Connells lived in a simple single-level adobe home, badly in need of a new paint job, with a formal living room, wood-paneled den, and eat-in kitchen area. I knew all this because the information was carried in the plastic pocket under the FOR SALE sign that was implanted on the front lawn.

A tall, pleasant-looking woman with ash-blond hair and a tired look answered my buzz at the door.

I said, "Mrs. Connell?"

"That's right," she said. "But if you're here to see the house, you'll have to go through our real estate agent."

"No, no, it's not about the house. I'm a reporter from *Vanity Fair*, and I'm doing an article on—"

She interrupted me before I could spin one of my fairy tales.

"You're the second one."

"Second what?" I said, with a sinking heart. I knew what the answer would be.

"Second *Vanity Fair* reporter. He was here a little while ago.

257

Sheppard Scott was his name. He gave me his card and everything. You know him?"

I said, "I thought I did."

"So, you might want to talk to him. I'm waiting for my real estate agent to show."

I was running out of time and desperate. "I'm so parched. Might I trouble you for a glass of water?"

Southwestern hospitality prevailed.

"Sure thing. Come on in."

I walked into the "formal" living room, done in blue and white, and I do mean done. This room was straight out of an article in *Home Decorating Magazine* on How to Do It Yourself on High Hopes and a Low Budget. The curtains were blue and the couch was trimmed in the same blue, and remnants of the curtain fabric were used to cover four pillows on the couch, two on each side. They had been plumped up, and I knew whatever I did, I dare not sit down there and mess up the arrangement.

The furniture was white wood, and the single adornment on the white coffee table was a large blue vase filled with fake blue flowers.

Mrs. Connell returned with a glass of water. I took it and began to drink, slowly, while considering my options.

"What a lovely room," I said, winging it. "So refreshingly clean and pure."

"Yes, thank you. We wish we didn't have to move to an apartment, but, you know, what with taxes going up every year and the upkeep . . ."

She didn't elaborate and I didn't encourage her. Instead, I said, "How nice that the room's not cluttered up with all sorts of, you know, collector's items."

She looked a little doubtful at this, and I hastened to amend, if not downright contradict, my previous opinion.

"Unless, of course, I mean, it's family memorabilia, pictures and stuff. I love that."

"That's exactly what you'll find in here," she said, and gestured to a room off the far end of the living room.

I kept sipping my water and walked to the back, and found myself in the wood-paneled den. Looking round, I saw an array of family photos covering the fireplace mantel, the tabletops, and the bookshelves.

"The other reporter was interested in these photos, also," she said. "Especially the ones of our son."

"Your son?" I walked around looking at the pictures, still nursing my drink.

"Yes, I told him all about Kevin. That's our son's name. We adopted him when he was two days old. Here . . ."

She showed me some small prints that were taken from a distance and overexposed. I picked them up to stare more closely, but I couldn't make out the features of anyone.

"I know. They're not very good. I'm not much of a photographer."

"I see." Rather than succumb to despair, I took one more chance. "I'd like to meet Kevin. Is he home?"

"No, he drives a truck, making deliveries for one of the local supermarket chains. He's on the road right now."

That was it. There went that fragment of hope.

"He would have liked to have gone to college," Mrs. Connell said, "but you know . . ."

Again, she didn't elaborate, but she didn't have to. It was painfully clear that the Connells were not in the best of economic straits.

"Arizona State in Tempe maybe," she was saying. "Kevin always wanted to study computer engineering."

I said, "Mrs. Connell, are you positive you don't have another picture of Kevin?"

She shook her head. "The only good one I gave to your associate. It was a picture of Kevin in his letterman sweater. He played football in high school. I made Mr. Scott promise to return it. Do you think he will?"

"Oh, I'm sure he will," I said.

Which was another scurrilous lie. When it came to Sheppard Scott, I couldn't be sure of anything.

60

There was no sign of Shep at the airport. My guess was that either he was going to stay in Alamogordo and investigate some more or else he had already taken another flight. Obviously, his intent was to avoid me, and I really couldn't blame him.

I didn't catch sight of him in El Paso, either, when we made our stopover. Since I had to kill time waiting in the terminal anyway, I called him on his cell phone.

There was the usual not-available message. I left a message of my own.

"Listen, I know you're sore, but get over it. This may be a byline to you, but it's my ass at stake here! So call me back!"

My voice had reached such a shrill level that people in the terminal were stopping to look at me and I saw a uniformed Texas Ranger glance in my direction. I smiled sweetly at all concerned, and added a "please" to the "call me back." Then I turned off my phone and stashed it away.

My flight the rest of the way was uneventful, except for the descent into Burbank, when I was overwhelmed by a sudden anxiety that I would be met at the airport by an armed posse waiting to arrest me for unlawful flight to avoid prosecution.

It was worse than an armed posse. It was U.G. and Mitzi. I couldn't believe my eyes, but as I came out of the terminal building there they were.

"Let me take that," U.G. said, indicating my overnight bag.

"No!" I held on to it tightly. "What are you doing here?"

"We're your ride home," U.G. said. "You don't have a car here, do you?"

"She doesn't," Mitzi said, quite matter-of-factly.

I couldn't quite process this turn of events. How did Mitzi even know I was on this flight?

"Wait right here," U.G. said. "I'll get the car."

He left us there. Mitzi was the first to break the uncomfortably extended silence.

"I know you don't believe in my powers," she said. "But I knew you were in Alamogordo."

I wasn't to be cornered. "That could have been because I asked about it at the séance," I said. "Or Lionel might have told you. . . ."

She shook her head. "Maggie, you must accept that I am deeply attuned to your energy field. You are presently in a very vulnerable state."

"Not that aura stuff again."

"Colors and intensity of the aura, especially around and above the head, have very special meanings. Watching someone's aura, you can actually see the other person's thoughts."

"You couldn't have read my thoughts. I wasn't anywhere near you."

She smiled. "Have you ever heard of psychometry?"

I had seen something about it in a movie once. "The psychic or whoever holds an object in his hand or against his forehead," I said, "and then he can tell the whole history of the object's owner. I don't believe in that drivel, either."

"What if I were to tell you that your father gave me a book you had lent him? It was charged with your emotions. When I touched it I had sensory impressions of where you were and even what you were doing there."

She couldn't have, I thought. It wasn't possible. It just wasn't.

"I also felt a distinct chill, a negative imprint of that man who was with you. Sheppard Scott."

That gave me pause. No one, not even Lionel, knew that Shep was accompanying me. Was it possible, just possible, there was something to her "gift," after all? Something explainable, of course, only so far I had been unable to come up with an explanation? Perhaps I should test her by asking where Shep was right now and why he wasn't answering my phone calls.

It was at that moment that U.G. pulled up. He was driving the Hummer. I was actually going to ride in that High-Mobility Multipurpose Wheeled Vehicle, the symbol of so much material excess and environmental inefficiency.

Letting Mitzi get in front with U.G., I climbed in the back. Actually, the interior was quite comfortable, with leather-trimmed cloth seats in tasteful shades of ebony and pewter. When U.G. started off and blended into the departing airport lines, I had a pleasant ringside position overlooking the rest of the traffic.

"To think that my ass might now be in the same hollow that Schwarzenegger's ass once indented," Mercedes said.

We rode in what might even be termed companionable silence for a while, with me making sure that U.G. was indeed on the route heading to my place.

"You ought to see how this baby handles uneven terrain," U.G. said.

"Yes, Dad, but please let's stay on the paved roads."

"This is true cutting-edge big-engine technology," he said. "And wait till you see the newer models. They've got advanced tail-fin designs, dent-resistant bumpers, and seven-inch halogen headlamps."

"And how many miles do they get to the gallon?" Mitzi said.

I silently applauded her for that.

"They're working on that," U.G. said, refusing to be cowed.

He raved on some more about the car, and I only half tuned him in. My mind was seesawing between Mitzi and Shep. Was it at all likely there was a bit more to Mitzi's "gift" than met my first skeptical appraisal? As for Shep, I continued to wonder what he was up to with Kevin Connell's photo in his possession and why I hadn't heard from him. There was a good chance those two puzzlements were connected, but the link, if any, was beyond my comprehension.

Suddenly I became aware that we had stopped. Deep in introspection, I hadn't noticed that we were no longer on the road on which we had been traveling and were now on a side street parked at the curb.

"What's the matter? Why did we stop?"

U.G. said, "We need to talk."

"Why can't we talk while we're moving? I'm going to be late."

"You mean for the hockey game. Mitzi told me."

All right, now how in the world did she know about that? Was there a puck in my aura? Obviously, Lionel must have said something. It was the only reasonable answer.

"Please, Dad, I need to get home."

He said, "We don't think you should go to the hockey game."

"We?"

"Well, Mitzi says . . ." He let it trail off and looked to her for support.

"There is danger," Mitzi said. "Great danger."

I knew better than to make any jokes about the obvious aggressive nature of the sport. Her voice was too grave.

I chose my words carefully. "Look, Mitzi," I said. "I'm sure you are sincere, and possibly you sense something—"

"No possibly about it," U.G. said.

I continued as though there had been no interruption. "But I have to be there. I promised Lionel."

264

"What about Shep?" Mitzi said.

My insides clenched. "Shep?"

Mitzi said, "He mustn't go, either."

I felt relief. "Well, that's a no-brainer. There's no reason whatsoever for Shep to go to the hockey game."

"Danger and death," Mitzi said again.

"Maggie, you must listen to her," U.G. said. "Please. . . ."

I shook my head. I said, "Dad, if you don't start this glorified armored tank this very minute, I am getting out and calling a taxi."

I put my hand on the door to open it. Immediately U.G. touched the switch that locked all the doors and windows.

"I'm going to scream," I said. "At the top of my lungs. I've had a lot of practice at it lately. And when someone stops to see why I'm screaming, I'll tell them I'm being kidnapped."

"No one will hear you. We're soundproofed," U.G. said.

"Then I'll call nine-one-one on my cell phone."

"And wouldn't the cops love to hear that you've spent a few days in New Mexico out of their jurisdiction?"

"You'd rat on your own daughter?"

U.G. sighed. "No. It's no use," he said to Mitzi. "She's very headstrong. Always has been."

Mitzi said, "I can only impart what I sense. The rest is up to her, Ulysses."

Ulysses! She had called my father by his given name. For some reason it spoke of an intimacy far closer than if she had called him U.G. as everyone else does.

With another sigh, he put the Hummer in motion, and we were on our way again.

No more was said about Mitzi's foreboding. But I couldn't help asking myself why I was so stubborn about having to go to this game. Yes, I had promised Lionel I'd be there to carry on with my duties as a beard and I didn't want to let him down. But in the light of Mitzi's demonstrated knowledge about the future, was I being foolish at great risk to myself? Or was it because I was

265

headstrong, just as U.G. had said, and still not willing to put any stock in her powers?

When we stopped in front of the condo and U.G. had gotten out to help me retrieve my bag, I hung back to hug him.

"Dad, please don't worry. I'll be with Lionel and Kurt. I'll be fine."

"You're my little girl and I love you," he said. "Worry comes with the territory. If anything should ever happen to you . . ."

He was too emotional to go on. I kissed him. "It won't," I said.

Lionel wasn't home, but he had left a note under a refrigerator magnet: "Welcome back. I bet you've forgotten we're going to the hockey game tonight."

Very obviously I hadn't. I just wished Mitzi's ominous words weren't still buzzing in my ears.

I checked the machine and there were no messages from Shep. I tried calling him again. No luck. Wearily I took off my shoes and stretched out on the couch, with Harpo and Groucho curled up at my feet. For the hundredth time my thoughts strayed to the Connells and that picture of their son, Kevin, and why Shep had taken it with him . . . and what he could be planning to do with it.

Hello. . . ."

"Hi, there. This is an old friend, Sheppard Scott."

"What do you want?"

"Now is that any way to talk to me? Especially when I bring you tidings of great comfort and joy."

"Look, I've got someone on the other line. Either cut to the chase or you'll be listening to a dial tone."

"Okay. What would you say if I told you that I happen to know that Allegra Cort had a child? A child who is now eighteen years old?"

Silence.

"Are you there?"

"I'm here. Go on."

"That's it. She had an affair, wasn't too careful about taking precautions, and in due course a baby boy was born and was given up for adoption."

"I thought your specialty was fact. Not fiction."

"Oh, this is fact, all right. Right now as I talk to you, I'm looking at a picture of the kid, and guess what. He looks like someone we both know."

"So we're talking blackmail, is that it?"

"Blackmail? Come on. You insult my professional integrity."

"Yeah, like you had some. Okay, what is it you want?"

"I want you to let me interview you for the article I'll be writing."

"The hell I will."

"If you don't talk to me, then I'll write the story anyway, and you won't be able to put your own spin on it."

Silence.

"Well . . . I'm waiting. . . ."

"Anybody else know about this?"

"Of course. You think I wouldn't have backup?"

"Maggie Mars?"

"I'm not telling."

"Look, I really have to get off now. Suppose we meet somewhere and discuss this?"

"I don't know what there is to discuss, but okay. Tonight?"

"I'm going to the hockey game."

"Fine, I'll meet you there."

"The front entrance of the arena—say, at six thirty."

"I'll be there."

"And bring that damned picture."

61

The phone rang, jarring me from a semi-doze. I reached for it, thereby dislodging the cats, who hissed disapprovingly.

"Hello?"

"Where the hell have you been!"

I might have known. "Thanks, Joe. I've missed you, too."

His tone softened. "I'm serious, Maggie. The grand jury could come in with an indictment on Monday."

"Well, if they want me, they know where to find me. Want to go to a hockey game with me tonight?"

"Can't. I'm on a case."

"A case of Rita Perez? Okay, that was rotten of me. I'm sorry."

He was quiet for a moment. Then: "Maggie, if the game goes overtime, and if I can make it, I'll be there. If not, we'll talk to-morrow. You and I are going to get all this crap out of our system."

I couldn't ask for anything more than that. Well, I could ask, but there was no guarantee I would get it. We said our good-byes and hung up.

Once more I tried to reach Shep, and again there was no answer.

Just that maddening voice counseling me to wait for the beep. Well, beep him!

I drove to the hockey arena with Lionel. Troy wasn't with us. It turned out he disliked any kind of violent sports and solemnly declared that he would accompany us only if we were going to a chess match or a Sudoku tournament.

As for me, I didn't know what I was doing going to a hockey game, either. I knew very little about the sport, other than unlike baseball players, the hockey guys didn't stand around shifting and scratching their privates in public. That was probably because with all the heavy protective garb they wore, they couldn't find their privates.

I had occasionally gone ice skating when I was a little girl, but my ankles were so weak that my mother made me wear ankle braces, which didn't do much good, either, and I didn't cut quite the fashionable figure I envisioned for myself. It was plain to see I wasn't going to be another Dorothy Hamill.

Besides, what was I doing acting as a beard for Lionel when an indictment for murder still loomed in my future? When Shep hadn't answered my calls and right now could be resorting to any manner of duplicity? When Joe and I still needed to talk things out in a large way? What I needed more than anything else right now was a "Get Out of Jail Free" card. . . .

"Lionel," I said, sighing. "I must love you very much."

"Of course you do," he said. "All the world loves a lover."

Kurt had arranged for Lionel and me to be given Guest Passes for after the game when we went to the Locker Room area. We picked them up at Will Call just inside the front entrance, along with our tickets, and, of course, as was S.O.P. in this post-9/11 era, had to submit to searches. Lionel had a small cologne dispenser in the purse he carried, and the uniformed security guard made him spray himself with it, I guess to make sure it wasn't a poisonous gas.

There are times that Lionel uses so much of the floral-scented stuff that I've often had doubts myself.

Our seats were on the main level, just behind the team benches—the home team and Kurt's visiting team. Lionel and I arrived early enough to watch the fifteen-minute practice of the two teams, and Lionel was beside himself waving excitedly to Kurt. Then, having second thoughts about his perhaps imprudent behavior, Lionel lifted my hand and made me wave excitedly to Kurt. For my taste, several of the other players were much sexier looking, but I wisely refrained from saying so.

Just before the game started, the Zamboni came out to clean and smooth the surface of the ice. There is something hard to describe about the Zamboni and the fascination it elicits. It's a large, unwieldy trucklike vehicle with a large blade in front. This one had a Gardening Supplies ad on one side that said FERTILIZER HAPPENS and on the other side an ad that read MAUI WOWEY. I couldn't tell if it was promoting travel or a trip.

I watched as the Zamboni lumbered across the ice at a blistering speed of 9 miles an hour, laying down a thin layer of heated water, which instantly froze to form a surface devoid of pits and ridges. I knew all this not because I suddenly became a hockey maven but because, between bites of his hot dog, Lionel provided me with a running commentary.

Then there was the National Anthem, sung by a young woman wearing what was described in the program as an Ice Maiden costume, although to me she appeared to look more like Hans Christian Andersen's nasty Snow Queen. She did, however, hit most of the high notes and she remembered all but a few of the words.

Finally, the game started. I sat there for over two hours, not having the slightest idea of what was going on, but trying to keep track of the fast-moving puck and at the same time absorb terms such as "face-offs," "icing," "offsides," "slap shots," "power plays."

Lionel was an adept instructor, but he was also caught up in cheering for Kurt and his team, and when, at the end, they were at the losing end of a 3–1 score, he was inconsolable.

"Cheer up," I said. "I thought that Kurt played really well, except maybe for the time he slammed that other guy into the boards."

Lionel gave me a look of utter contempt. "He didn't slam him—he bodychecked him."

"Whatever."

"And he was only sent to the Penalty Box for two minutes."

How nice, I thought. Only two minutes. And here I was, on the verge of being sent to San Quentin's Penalty Box for who knew how many years. Or worse.

Even as I sat there, Mitzi's warning of death and danger sounded in my ears. Not to mention that the grand jury could be convening and issuing an indictment with my name prominently featured. How I could be so calm I didn't know. Maybe it was the memory of my mother, who always said that everything would always work out in the end. And if it didn't—then it wasn't the end.

62

We showed our Guest Passes and took the elevator down from the main level to the service level in order to wait for Kurt outside the visiting players' locker room. The sign on the door read NO UNAUTHORIZED PERSONNEL, and there was a small gathering of friends and family hovering nearby.

I had to remember that Kurt was supposed to be my heartthrob, not Lionel's, so I smiled in companionable fashion at the other women there and made suitable comments deploring the team's loss.

After a while, however, when most of the waiting people had dispersed, but Kurt and a few other players still hadn't emerged, I whispered to Lionel, "I've got to go."

"You can't go! You have to be here for Kurt!"

"I mean I have to find a restroom. I'll be right back."

A question of one of the other women solicited the information that I should "go to the kegs of beer and make a left."

I moved down the hall, passing several dressing rooms that I gathered were used for concerts and other star events. I seemed to be in a backstage area, which was littered with packing boxes, lighting gear, and crates of supplies and cleaning equipment. At last I saw the stack of empty beer kegs and I took my left. But the restrooms weren't there. Surely, if people had imbibed all that beer, there would have to be restrooms nearby. Obviously I had taken a wrong turn somewhere. Maybe I should have taken a right.

I wandered in the deserted area for a few minutes, absolutely lost, despairing more and more that I would ever find the ladies', when suddenly I was stopped by a familiar voice calling my name. I turned to see who it was, and there, coming toward me, was Lew Packard.

He came up beside me. "Amazing how many friends you can meet where you least expect to."

"Friends with small bladders," I said. "I didn't know you were a hockey buff."

"Oh, I come occasionally. But tonight I'm here with Krystal Moore. She's one of our studio's rising stars."

I made the connection. "She sang 'The Star-Spangled Banner.'" I refrained from any comment on her rendition.

"Right. I figured this would get her some publicity. She's got talent, this girl. Maybe you could write a part for her in your next movie."

"Uh-huh. By any chance, would you happen to know where the restrooms are?"

"You've asked the right person. I've just come from there. I'll show you. . . ."

He took my arm and led me down an intersecting corridor. It, too, was deserted, piled with empty shipping cartons that had once been filled with items for the concession stands.

"This is a stroke of luck, running into you, Maggie," he said. "We need to talk."

"If it's about the studio car, you can have it back tomorrow."

"No. We'd like it back, but this is about something else."

"Some other time, please, Lew. People are waiting for me, and I really, really have to *go*."

273

"I'll only take a minute." He gripped my arm. "Let's just stop right here where we won't be overheard."

We stopped a little ways off down the isolated corridor. From somewhere I heard a machine start up, probably one of the heavy-duty cleaners.

"What is it?" I said, impatient to get to the restroom, doing everything I could to refrain from hopping on one foot and then the other.

He said, "It's about Allegra's baby. I'd like you to tell me what you found out about him."

"Well, I really know very little, except that—" I stopped there and stared at him. "Lew, you said *him*. How did you know she had a boy? And how did you know I found out anything about him?"

He shrugged. "Shep told me. I guess your colleague doesn't keep secrets as well as you do."

An alarm bell clanged in my mind. My thoughts raced, helter-skelter, chasing one another to the inevitable unwelcome conclusion.

Shep had told him? When had Shep spoken to him and why had he needed to? Shep had taken that photograph away with him. Had he shown it to Lew? Why? What did that photograph show?

The alarm bell was still going off, and my skin was crawling. Did Lew recognize that photo? Something had him spooked. Had he seen a resemblance to someone?

And then I knew! Just like that! The resemblance was to himself! The picture pinpointed him as the father!

But so what if Lew was the father? That didn't mean he was a killer. A man who had a wife and children, who was a devoted family man. A man who was admired and celebrated throughout the movie industry. A man like that couldn't have anything to do with murder, could he?

I was inching away from Lew, trying to do so as unnoticeably

274

as I could. But I had the feeling he was noticing. And all the while, my suspicions were growing and taking form and shape.

Supposing Allegra had threatened to reveal her secret and expose Lew. He wouldn't have murdered her—and framed me for the crime—simply because Lewis John Packard, the outstanding community leader, the devoted family man, the movie mogul, the gubernatorial aspirant, could not afford to let it be public knowledge that Allegra Cort had borne him an illegitimate child whom he had never officially acknowledged or supported.

"Fuckin' A," said Mercedes.

"There is a time for departure," Tennessee Williams wrote, "even when there's no certain place to go."

I took off running.

63

Off to the side ahead of me was a stack of pallets, precariously balanced. As I ran past them, I reached out and pushed them. They came crashing down, effectively blocking Lew's way. But it was only a momentary obstacle. From the sound of his footsteps, I could tell he was skirting his way around the wooden boards and was still coming after me.

I screamed. And kept on screaming. The sounds bounced against the walls of the deserted corridor and reverberated in shrill echoes, but they were no match for the drowning-out noise of the heavy-duty cleaner.

I didn't hear the shot he fired at me, but I saw the dimpled indentation it made in a large garbage sack, as I tore past a jumbled heap of them. Ahead of me there was a set of massive double doors, wide open, and I headed straight for them. Lew was somewhere behind me. I could hear him, his footsteps now rapid and steady, closing in. Another shot whizzed past my ear, barely missing the left side of my head.

Oh, God! I was really in trouble! Jail would have been like a Riviera resort compared to the situation in which I was now embroiled.

Through the wide doors I ran—and straight out onto the ice! The ice was so unexpected I lost my footing. For a moment I teetered there and then I fell hard on my rear end, just as another shot chipped the frozen surface ahead of me.

I managed to regain my balance, cold bottom and all, and stand upright, but I couldn't make much progress. My rubber-soled tennis shoes were absolutely the wrong thing to be wearing for this. I was slipping and sliding all over the place.

I could hear behind me that Lew, wearing his customary Armani loafers, was slipping and sliding, too. But the big difference between us, besides designer shoes, was that he had a gun and he was firing at me. Because he was slipping around, the shots were going wild, but eventually, even if by accident, one could hit the target—namely, me!

I grimly wished that I had worked out more often and slimmed down so as to give him less of a bull's-eye. I had no breath for screaming; I was too busy keeping out of Lew's gunshot range. Maybe Mitzi and her doom-and-gloom prognostications were for real, but this wasn't the time to think about that.

Lew must have fired several more shots, because I heard them *ping* on the surface of the ice. I hadn't kept count. How much longer did I have before either he ran out of ammunition or one of his bullets found its mark and I wasn't just cold—I was cold stone dead!

The answer came all too soon. I felt the sting on my left shoulder and saw the blood almost at the same time. Doggedly, I tried to remain upright, but I couldn't help myself. I fell sprawling on the ice again.

As I struggled to get up and keep going, I stole a look back at Lew. He wasn't far behind me, but now he was standing unsteadily on the ice, doing something with the gun. I suddenly realized he was reloading.

By now I had reached one of the team benches. The Zamboni was parked alongside, looking even more hugely monstrous now that it was up close. Then I noticed something else. There on the bench lay a partly filled Gatorade bottle. Ignoring the searing pain in my shoulder, I reached over the dasher board and picked it up. With great effort, I flung the bottle at him, at the same time offering a silent tribute of thanks to U.G. for having taught me to throw overhand when I was a little girl.

The missile flew at Lew and hit him square in the nose. Blood and splashed Gatorade streamed down his face. The gun fell from his hand and slid across the ice toward me.

We both made a grab for it. The next moment Lew and I were a jumble of arms and legs spread awkwardly on the ice, as we grappled with each other. I had heard, of course, of the rowdy fights that broke out at hockey games. And here I was in the middle of one. A deadly one.

The gun lay nearby, and by stretching I could almost reach it. At that moment Lew dug his fingers into my wounded shoulder. I screamed in agonizing pain and then, by turning my head, managed to sink my teeth into his wrist, hard enough to draw blood.

"Bitch!" His messy face, only a few feet from mine, was contorted with pure hatred and anger.

Meanwhile, the damn gun skittered even farther away.

Lew made a great physical effort to rise. Somehow I was able to grab at one of his legs. He managed to pull away and stand up, but in the process his shoe came off. I scrambled to my feet as well, but Lew was already going for the gun and he had a head start. I had to get away as fast as I could.

Like a signpost to safety, there was the Zamboni, dead ahead of me. Clutching my shoulder, I half-ran, half-dragged myself to it, and agonizingly hoisted myself aboard the idling machine.

Lew, still slipping in one fancy loafer and one silk sock, wobbled toward the gun, which had come to rest almost directly in front of the goalie net. He reached it, picked it up, and turned as though to come back toward me. Then he must have thought better of it, because he stopped, stood still in one place, and took steady, two-handed police-posture aim.

I crouched down behind the Zamboni steering wheel as two shots in succession struck the side of the machine just in front of where I was sitting. Now that Lew was standing still and not moving, he was steadier on his feet and he was firing at me with increasing accuracy. I had to do something fast.

What I did was step on the accelerator and then push or pull every lever I could see. Unbelievably, the Zamboni started to move. There was no windshield to give me cover, but I rose from my crouch long enough to steal a glance around me and determine Lew's position. To his rear I could see the goalie net. With one useless arm I turned the steering wheel toward him, crouched as low as possible, and kept going. I was barely conscious that all the while the machine was shaving the ice ahead of me.

Becoming aware of the behemoth approaching, Lew started to back up. But he couldn't move. He had forgotten that the net was behind him. He had nowhere to back up to.

He could, however, still shoot. Another shot missed, going off to the side.

I couldn't see in front of me but I kept plowing ahead, slowly and inexorably, until I felt the front end of the Zamboni run into something and heard a loud, terrorized scream.

Me and my Zamboni. We had run into Lew.

I looked up quickly and then back down again. The blade was driving Lew into the goalie net, but he was still firing his gun at me. Another shot bounced off the vehicle and I kept coming, pushing Lew and the net into the back dasher board.

I peeked again at the front of the machine. Lew was staring straight at me over the machine's front end. Then he raised his weapon once more with me directly in its sights. He was grinning. A death skull grin. I was looking into the face of death.

Frantically I searched for a gearshift or something that would

279

put the machine into reverse. I spotted a lever I hadn't tried before and pulled on it. The next second, I stared, totally astounded, as the Zamboni top raised up, opened, and dumped its load of ice shavings all over Lew.

The guy was a Sno-Kone!

They came running out on the ice, of course, the Zamboni driver and security personnel and Lionel and Kurt and several late-staying hockey fans. I'd been so busy saving my own life that I hadn't noticed all of them, yelling and screaming, slipping and sliding toward me.

They asked a barrage of questions, all at the same time: What in the world happened? Was I all right? Who was that under all the ice? Where was all that blood coming from? Had I actually driven the Zamboni? Was I all right?

I put up a hand to silence them.

"Listen, guys," I said. "I'll tell you all about it. But right now I really have to go to the ladies' room."

"Too little, too late," said Mercedes.

64

Never had I been so happy to wake up in my own bed, in my own room, in my own—well, okay, in Lionel's house—as I was the following morning.

Lionel had insisted that I go to the hospital last night, and Kurt drove us to the emergency room. The verdict was a flesh wound, a little more than a graze, barely missing my shoulder blade. Hospital records showed that I had been there once before, with a bullet in my right shoulder, so now I was balanced.

"Physically, but not mentally," Lionel said.

That was the good news.

The bad news was what Joe delivered when he showed up at the hospital. Holding my good hand, he told me that Shep was dead. His body had been found partially hidden in the brush behind the arena's parking lot. A guy walking his dog discovered the body.

I was having a hard time processing the information. "How did he die? Was it an accident? What happened?"

"It was no accident," Joe said. "Someone took him out. We won't know until Ballistics compares the bullets, but we think he was shot by the same guy shooting at you."

I said, "Lewis John Packard."

I realized now that Lew would have done anything, even resort to murder, to keep his sparkling reputation free from scandal and to gain the governor's seat in Sacramento. He may even have harbored dreams of reaching all the way to the White House. The revelation of an illegitimate child, who had been adopted and raised by others in less than affluent circumstances, would kill those dreams.

It wouldn't have been the disclosure that his son was born out of wedlock that would have ruined Lew's political ambitions—it would have been the fact that he had never acknowledged his own flesh and blood. Hard to see Lew as a man big enough to run the state when he couldn't even reach out a hand to help his own son financially, to make sure he had what he needed, went to college, and became whatever he wanted to become.

Joe's voice broke into my thoughts. "Shep's right hand bore the arena's stamp, so we're surmising he must have met Lew inside and then gone out to the parking lot with him. Once Packard thaws out from his ice bath, he'll be in for some heavy questioning."

I looked away as Joe went on. "A reporter's notebook and pencil were found alongside the body. Our conjecture is that Shep might have gone there to interview Lew for a story. Know anything about that?"

I turned back to Joe and shook my head. Later, maybe, I would tell him everything. But not now. It was too soon and too much mine, too personal.

Lying on the examining room table, thinking about Shep, I felt the tears well up, even though I tried to tell myself not to cry because it's over but, rather, to smile because it happened.

Joe, looking as though he wanted to hold me close but couldn't because they were treating my wound, just kept patting my hand, over and over. I cried even more, remembering Shep's words: *"We're a good team, you and I."*

"This doesn't hurt that much, does it?" the E.R. doctor said.

282

"It hurts like hell," I said, sobbing.

After a while, they let me go home, with antibiotics to prevent infection and a blue canvas sling to prevent overexertion.

I pushed my bedcovers back and swung my legs over the side.

"Don't move!" said Lionel. He was standing in the doorway, holding a breakfast tray.

"I have to," I said.

"No, you don't. I'm going to feed you."

"I have to go to the bathroom," I said. "Can you help me out there?"

After a few seconds, he said, "Okay. Go. But pee as fast as you can."

I did. But I cheated, taking my cell phone in with me and calling Gracie in New York.

"Fuck!" he said when I told him about Shep, and I knew he wasn't thinking about his article. We chatted some more about Shep, without my telling Gracie how the two of us had parted—I swore to myself I would never reveal that to anyone—and before signing off, Gracie gave me the go-ahead to take over and write the story for *Vanity Fair*.

Then I came back to bed and endured Lionel's ministrations. I was sure I could have fed myself, but why look a gift helping hand in the mouth?

"Kurt will be on the road for a while," he said. "But we'll e-mail and visit each other. I'll have to do a lot of wardrobe shopping, especially for the out-of-town games." Almost as an afterthought, he said, "So will you."

"What!?"

"Sorry, but your days as a beard aren't yet over."

I said, "Okay, but I am not doing the out-of-town bit."

"Then I'll just have to borrow some of your clothes."

283

I almost choked on the oatmeal he was feeding me. "You mean you'd cross-dress?"

"You know what necessity is the mother of," he said. "I'll be my own beard."

"Probably more of a goatee," said Mercedes.

After breakfast, he adjusted my sling, draped one of his own creamy satin robes over my shoulders, and accompanied me out to the living room, where he gently eased me down onto the couch.

I said, "Lionel, this is ridiculous. I'm perfectly capable of taking care of myself."

"No, you're not," he said. "Or you wouldn't go around all the time almost getting yourself killed."

I had no answer for that. Instead, I said, "Lionel, be a good caregiver and bring me my laptop."

"You can't type with one hand."

"Of course I can. I practically do anyway."

He threw up his hands in frustration, but he brought me the case and opened it for me, then headed for the kitchen. "I'll be keeping an eye on you. Don't try to go out."

"Only if you can get me out of these pj's and into a bra and panties and T-shirt and jeans."

"I could, but I won't. And don't beg." He disappeared inside.

I looked at the keyboard in front of me and, after a moment, slowly began to type one-handedly: "*'Close-up on Murder.'*"

The doorbell rang.

"I'll get it!" came the shout from the kitchen. Lionel came bounding out, a frilly white apron tied around his middle.

I glanced up, quite incuriously, to see who was there. It was U.G.

"Nice pinafore, Alice," he said to Lionel.

"Like it?" Lionel said. "I can get you one in the short, squat size."

"That's enough," I said. "Go back to your corners."

Lionel retreated to the kitchen. U.G. gave me an affectionate kiss. "How are you feeling?"

"Pretty good," I said.

"What I don't understand is where your bodyguard was when all that craziness was happening."

I thought fast. "Um . . . that's just it. He was nowhere to be found. So I fired him."

U.G. said, "He really wasn't your bodyguard, was he?"

I shook my head no.

"That's what I thought. I finally figured it out. He's Lionel's new hunk, right?"

"Dad," I said, anxious, "you're not going to out him, are you?"

"Are you kidding?" U.G. said. "Kurt may be a little light in the loafers, but he looks like he's heavy in the fists."

I decided it was time to change the subject. "Dad, tell me, how is Mitzi?"

"Wonderful," he said, his face lighting up. "Hey, she's predicted that someone will soon be making me an offer for my Hummer. So I might sell it and buy us a pair of His and Her Harleys."

I said, "If you're trying to make me feel better, that's not going to do it."

"Well, anyway, Mitzi's good company and we enjoy being with each other. That counts for something, doesn't it?"

"It counts for a lot," I said, and meant it.

After a while he left, and I went back to my laptop and typed a little more: "'Close-up on Murder,' Written by."

The doorbell rang again.

"Don't move! I'll get it." Again, Lionel came rushing out. This time he had a spatula in one hand.

It was Joe. "Hey," he said.

"Hey yourself."

Lionel said, "Now don't get her all excited. I mean any more excited than usual."

Joe nodded. "I'll behave."

"Why do I doubt that," said Lionel. "If you hang around, I've got banana walnut pancakes coming up." He retreated back to the kitchen.

Joe sat down alongside me, kissed the top of my head.

"You feeling better?"

"Much," I said. I indicated my laptop. "I'm writing the article for *Vanity Fair.*"

"Could you use the latest news?"

"Always."

"Lew broke down and confessed to the three murders. Allegra, Lisa, and Shep. Also to pushing you overboard. So you're not as loony as we all thought."

I shook my head, trying to absorb the enormity of Lew's crimes.

"He'd had a long-ago affair with Allegra, and claims that it was only recently that she told him about the pregnancy, so he never had the chance to make things right. But with him in the political limelight, she saw her chance and resorted to blackmail."

"So he killed her to keep her quiet?"

"He claims it was an accident. They had a fight about it."

"And Lisa? Was she an accident, too?"

He shook his head. "Seems she knew he was in the trailer bedroom and must have killed Allegra. She wanted to leverage that for big money and a better job."

I sighed. "And Shep—please tell me that wasn't blackmail."

"Don't think so. Lew admits to Shep showing him a picture of his son—we found it in his car and it looks just like him, except for the broken nose—but he says the reporter wanted to interview him for a story."

"Unbelievable."

"Speaking of unbelievable, guess who's going to defend Lew?"

"No. . . ."

"Yep. None other than Heinrich."

"*Big whoop,*" said Mercedes.

"Henrik," I said automatically. "He's making a good living out of defending people who've tried to kill me."

"Well, how about you don't throw any more business his way." Joe rose. "Well, I'd better get going."

"You won't stay for banana walnut pancakes?"

"Can't. I'm on duty. Tell Lionel I'll take a rain check." He bent down to kiss me lightly. "By the way," he said, "now that you're no longer a person of interest, I may be asking you to move in with me again. I'm just not sure yet."

"If you do ask me," I said, "I may accept. I'm just not sure yet, either."

"Okay." He nodded. "How about in a few days, when you're fully recovered, I pick you up, you spend the night at my place, and we talk it over."

I thought about that. "Okay, but why wait a few days? I'm only slightly incapacitated, and when it comes to making love, you've always been able to improvise."

He sat down again and pulled me close, taking care to be gentle with my arm.

He said, "Maggie, no more improv. This time around I want you and me to get it right—and keep it that way."

I kissed him, and not at all lightly.

"You're on," I said.

I waited till the door shut behind him, and then returned to my laptop and the last words I had typed: *Written by.*

I finished it off: *Written by Sheppard Scott and Maggie Mars.*